I0664286

The Last Revelations:

The Beginning of the End

A Vicky Donahue Novel

Steve Dwight Nichols

This book is a work of fiction and the product of the author's imagination. Names, characters, places, events, incidents, business entities, religious entities, and organizations are used fictitiously. Any resemblance to actual places, organizations, business entities, religious entities, incidents or persons is entirely coincidental.

ISBN: 978-1-7365728-2-5

Steve Dwight Nichols

Books

1. Murder and the Preacher's Wife

2. The Sinner's Reckoning

3. The Good Samaritans

4. The Last Revelations: The Beginning of the End

5. The Inception War

Prologue

She quickly ran to his position and pulled his security key card, which was attached to a nylon strap from around his neck and then unlocked the door. She rushed into the foyer and aimed her gun at Burnside, and without hesitating pulled the trigger twice. She had turned toward the escape route and started to run back out the door when she noticed he had not moved but actually smiled at her. He was sitting behind a large table. The bullets ricocheted and must have hit the wall to the left. His smile grew and then he said, "I have been waiting on you." He raised his hands, "Well, me and my men have been waiting on you. Please come in."

Vicky noticed movement to her left and looked over. Out walked two men with machine gun pistols with extended magazines pointed at her. She heard someone clear their throat behind her from the hallway and glanced in that direction, and there was another man standing behind her near the dead guard with the same type of pistol. A fourth man walked out from the door to the right with a gun. She was surrounded. She had just walked into a trap.

Chapter 1

The man bent and looked down into the valley at the small huts built in the open field. He was hidden at a perch overlooking the frozen village scanning with his binoculars. His eyes were focused like a bird of prey. His anticipation was magnified, to see if his supply of humans could be met at the first group of huts. He knew his comrades did not like being in North Korea. At first, they told him no. He had pulled his pistol and shot the middle-aged man in the head to make certain the rest knew they really did not have a choice. With the dead man lying on the boat dock in the Philippines, he announced this was not a committee, but an order. He told two of the men to place the dead man in the boat and cover him with the tarp. He had said, "We will drop him over the side of the boat once we are a few miles from shore. Your cut of the money just increased with you two getting a portion of his share." They had smiled at the dead man bleeding from his head wound lying on his side on the dock. The two men were from Mongolia, and they had resented working with the now dead Chinese man.

Beyond, he could see the fields and the dirt road leading further inland. He saw one maybe two young girls picking up firewood. From this distance he could not be certain. He felt a sudden concern, and he could not place what was bothering him. He thought the feeling was like the one when you know you are forgetting something. His sixth sense was magnified. He hesitated and then looked back at his guide, pointed to the two possible targets, and motioned for him to lead the way. He looked a second time to make certain there were no government patrols in the valley. His team was a group of ex-drug smugglers who had survived when others in their groups had not. The drug business in Asia was layered with perils, and men who ran the business were absolute killers with no mercy. Unlike the human slavery business, the authorities hunting down the drug smugglers were just as violent. He knew his men would cut throats without hesitation, and the one female in the group was crueler than any of the men. She often seemed to take pleasure in beating the children and probing them with her flexible fiberglass rod below deck while en route to the staging area for the upcoming sale. The fiberglass rod hurt but left no marks. She provided the female touch in the negotiation and was very persuasive in front of the families in providing the opportunity for the kids with explanations how the child would be better cared for, and they could provide the family with money. If the negotiation seemed to stall, she would suggest the child could work and return to the village in two to three years with additional money for the family. This method of paying the small fee was better than stealing the kids and having to evade the authorities in the future. This way there were no authorities involved, and they could return in a few weeks for another purchase. The man knew the small amount of money spent on the purchase was money well invested.

His team felt safer doing this line of work dealing with kids and women than dealing with drug dealers and hiding from the authorities. The group never had any questions about what happened to the kids and women once they had been sold. They only had one obstacle. They had to close the deal with the man of the household.

The man had learned over the years in dealing with poor families an additional mouth was hard to provide for over a long cold winter. He also had learned to talk only to the alpha male of the household. Sometimes this would be the father and sometimes it would be the oldest son if the father was absent. Either way the custom in Asia was the oldest male would make the decision. Experience had taught him to try to make the deal with the alpha male with the mother not present. Often times the mother could present an extra hurdle in the negotiation. But either way the alpha male would make the decision.

The guide approached the first hut and asked about the two girls, and who they would need to talk with about the purchase. The elderly man listened without ever making eye contact and then pointed to a man in the frozen field. The guide led the way down the path to the field and introduced the man. The man could be very convincing and always carried money. He had a very caring smile when he wanted to be persuasive. The farmer walked out of the field when the guide mentioned thirty-five dollars. The farmer called his daughter over for the man to inspect. The farmer would not sell his son. He inquired about her age and tried to determine if she had bled or not. The man did not want to ask her to remove her warm clothes to know for certain if she was ready for the trip. This time of year, it was just too cold to tell with the package covered in several layers of clothing if she would be of a priced value.

The young girls just maturing would bring more money than a boy or a young adult female. He would find out soon enough if his first purchase was indeed a prized package. The farmer took the money and explained to his daughter she needed to leave with the group.

There was no hugging or saying goodbye. Her mother watched from the door of the hut as the daughter was pulled by her hand by the assistant. She started crying, but knew she had no choice. She looked at the men and the one woman with guns and knew this group were not nice people. She had always hidden in her family hut with her younger brothers and sisters when the mean-looking army patrols came through the areas. They were always in trucks and the community could hear them coming. This group had shown up on foot and walked from the shoreline to the small village without any warning. She had heard what groups of people like this did to kids. Her mother had insisted that the kids were hidden during the North Korea Army Patrols. The soldiers, she was told by her mother, would do bad things to kids and young women.

The man told an associate in the group to take her to the extraction point and wait for the boat. The man pointed to the guide to lead the way on up the road to the next village. He knew what the contract party had desired. He also knew the perfect package could render him close to five thousand with the seller making as much as twenty thousand and maybe as high as twenty-five thousand dollars depending on the timeliness of the auction. For that much money, he knew he would push on deeper inland and further away from his boat and his route of escape.

He had never been caught or questioned by one of the Asian country's police forces. This was the type of activity that went unnoticed and not reported. However, he had never been to the fertile grounds of North Korea. He knew if the North Korean Army caught him and his men, they would be whipped and forced to live out their lives in a labor camp. No one was allowed to enter North Korea. They had planned to stay away from the larger populated areas and try to blend in with the farming families. They had planned to split up and act like they were part of the community if they were cut off. The plan would be to blend in with the peasant families and then head for the shoreline in the cover of darkness. They all dressed in apparel similar to the peasant families. He hoped to spend up to two hundred dollars and make twenty-five thousand after expenses. He only needed ten packages. He did not want to flood the market. He wanted his price to stay at two thousand or more per package. The male packages sometimes did not bring as much as the female packages. The market was not as competitive for the male packages. He just did not feel good about being in North Korea. The North Korean Army, unlike the other Asian countries, watched their borders and shorelines with live patrols daily. He knew they needed to hurry. The winter was a blessing because the number of patrols was down compared to the warmer months. Also, the ground was frozen, and they left no tracks.

Chapter 2

Vicky's cell phone vibrated. Mia said, "We got a lead in the Yellow Sea with the help of Mr. Ho's computer." Mr. Ho was the physics professor from China educated in the United States, who had been shot in the back of the head from a quarter of a mile away while being held by his ankles as he dangled over the railing on the 7th floor of the motel in the Philippines while being questioned. Mia had finally been able to break through the fire walls and at least pick up the location of the incoming signal pinpointing the location of the slave trader's position from Mr. Ho's computer. Mia had been able to cross link the signal on the dark web from that region and had been monitoring the computer that sent the email. "We have located the computer on the boat. It looks like the cargo boat called 'The Delian' is picking up humans for trade. The boat is registered as a commercial transportation company with the home of origin as the Philippines. We also have a good satellite feed. The trace has been verified. This is a one-time shot. I will not be able to duplicate locating the signal on the dark web. I had to leave a link and a footprint in the software that will be obvious. The link will be shut down."

Vicky called Max and updated him on the new information. Max said, "No. We need to concentrate on the primary mission." He knew as soon as he made that statement, Vicky was going to balk.

She kept stressing this is the head of the snake that is taking the Asian kids. "My team will be up and running in one hour. We will be leaving the Nashville International Airport and headed well into the Pacific region in four hours. This could set the slave traders back a year if we take out this part of their network. Max, this is my unfinished business. All the analysts and support staff in the CIA working on this project could not locate the breadcrumbs, and Mia has somehow acquired this information. We know where they are in the China Sea, and they are in the open. We may never have this opportunity again. I must do this." She finished the statement to herself, "Or God won't forgive me of my sins."

Max tried to explain that the President's orders were to locate the missing National Security Agency (NSA)Director, and this diversion to the China Sea was not part of his mandate. Vicky countered and said, "This is why I signed up to work for the CIA to hunt down and take out the slave network. This is why the United Nations wanted the United States involved to eradicate the entire world in trading humans into slavery." She could feel Max getting upset as she kept telling him this was the first opportunity to actually catch the people in the network that were taking the kids and delivering them to be auctioned and then raped and killed. Vicky gritted her teeth and finally said, "The children need to be protected. They are never provided mercy. I have seen these kids held in crates and butchered when they are used up. This, Max, is about doing what is right. The other unit set up by the State Department will not be able to handle this in the manner it needs to be handled. You know this to be true. They spend their time investigating but hardly ever stop the problem at the source. I will call you when we return." She abruptly hung up.

Max considered what President Grant had discussed in the brief meeting. He wanted Burnside dead. He wanted to issue a standing kill order for Burnside, but he also knew there were moles hidden in the CIA who were loyal to Burnside. He knew Vicky and her team should be focused on the former NSA Director Burnside, but he also knew Vicky was not going to listen. She was too invested in stopping the slave runners. He thought about the pros and cons of hiring personnel from the private sector. They needed to locate the real threat before Burnside turned and wanted asylum in one of the foreign countries adverse to the United States. He sat in his chair and rubbed his face. The American people were frustrated with the United States Government. The old Senators in both parties kept making the same mistakes. The American people had voted for a President who was a billionaire outsider independent as a protest to the traditional nominees. The rumors were this President had a very low tolerance for not following orders. He was known to fire people in the private sector daily. Max thought, "He fired my boss the first day he took office." Max asked himself, "Am I going to get fired for allowing the unit assigned to the case refusing to do as they were being told?" He was hoping Vicky's mission would be over fast so her team would move onto the mission locating the former NSA director and then the science behind the Zipline Vortex. The world as he knew it was in grave danger.

***

During the flight, Mia Zbar, the computer CIA expert born in Pakistan and graduated from MIT at the age of nineteen was reviewing the intel. As a teenager in Pakistan, she had been taught the art of hacking computer systems around the world, and she had self-taught herself a few tricks along the way. She now was a world class hacker. The CIA had by chance discovered her trying to hack into the Iranian Government's monetary system. Instead of having the Pakistani Government arrest her, the CIA monitored her activities and were impressed with her desire to expose human rights violations in certain third world countries while stealing from the wealthy Iranian Government officials and giving the stolen proceeds to the poor. The CIA worked out an agreement with her father for Mia to attend school in America. After graduation, her first assignment was to assist Vicky's unit. She was the fourth member of the team, and she was telling Vicky and Wayne they had solid satellite coverage for the next six hours. Wayne Tipton and Vicky had met when Wayne was the sheriff in Butler, Tennessee. Wayne was the second member of the team and now worked for the State Department and was assigned to Vicky's unit. Max and former President Truman had formed the unit with both the CIA and State Department being involved.

The CIA needed to have the cover of the State Department working inside the United States and also the State Department could provide a liaison position in working with the United Nation representatives outside the boundaries of the United States. Very few countries would knowingly allow the CIA to operate inside their country, but the United Nations had been able to forge the path to allow the representatives from the State Department to work to stop the slave trade industry. The foreign countries and the United Nations were not aware of the CIA's involvement.

Mia had further communicated there was at least two other smaller boats involved. They had traced their movements to the ports in Inchon located in South Korea and Shanghai, China. The unit would be landing on the Naval ship in the area located in the Philippine Sea and transported to a fishing vessel owned by the CIA where they could enter the East China Sea undetected by the Chinese and North Korean governments.

Vicky said, "Max and I did not agree on us taking this mission, but he finally called, and there are some issues in Asia. Max indicated this is a restricted territory, and we will have limited support. He reiterated under no circumstance can we enter the North Korean territory."

Vicky then announced the plan was simple, and with that Wayne placed his hands over his face. Wayne said, "This plan was simple, but so far, all our plans have been simple, and there were dead bodies left behind all over the globe. I have the scars to prove that simple plans are lethal." Vicky, Little Jimmy, and Billy Ray smiled.

She indicated this mission is going to be cold. "The high this time of year is below freezing in some of the Asian countries. The combatants are not expecting us. We should be able to surprise them and hope to be in and out before we get frostbite. No one has policed this issue in Asia."

***

They pulled alongside the small fishing boat. The Vietnamese captain was adamant they could not come aboard. The sea was calm with small waves, little wind but the wind chill factor was still below zero. The crew on board started yelling. Billy Ray was hidden on the top of the wood crates which were secured with straps to the deck. He had a visual straight out from between the crates and the hanging tarp. He was lying in the shadow between the tarp and the larger crate. He kept switching from looking at each of the four men through his scope.

He also was trying to adjust for the waves and rocking of both boats and the tarp flapping beside him. He was using the tarp to conceal his position. He finally said into his mic, "These men are experienced fighters. They are drawing us in close and then they are going to shoot us. I can see the stock of one AK-47 rifle and the barrel of another they have hidden. They are spread out on the deck, and I can take the one on the east end. I cannot rotate fast enough to the other two before one of them levels their guns on us. You will need to take out the guard nearest the captain. The captain is driving the boat. He will not be an immediate threat.

Billy Ray was from south Texas and joined the Army when he was eighteen years old. He was the fifth member of Vicky's unit. He was on loan from the special forces.

Vicky said, "Roger that." She looked at Little Jimmy and said, "You need to provide cover fire with the shotgun."

The other boat had cut power and was floating on the waves. The four men had not changed positions. Billy Ray kept the scope dialed in on the furthest man to the stern. He looked wild and high. The boats were now ten feet apart and getting closer by the second. The man reached behind the deck rail with his left hand. Billy Ray could see the gun stock move as he touched the barrel sitting on the deck partially hidden by the rail. He pulled his gun from behind the rail, and Billy Ray shot him dead as he started to raise his AK rifle in a threatening manner. Little Jimmy leveled his shotgun, and he shot the second guard in the chest and spread several shots across the surface of the ship.

Vicky shot the third guard at the same time Wayne shot him with his M4 rifle. Little Jimmy had shot at the captain and hit the glass windshield cracking the glass from side to side. Seven seconds later the captain held his hands up.

Little Jimmy had met Vicky in Butler, Tennessee and had assisted Vicky and Wayne with saving a young girl. The three had become friends. Little Jimmy was hired by the CIA as an independent contractor to provide extra security to the unit. Little Jimmy was the third member of the unit.

The three guards fell back on the front of the boat in a bloody mess with the bullets and shotgun blast ripping through their bodies. The captain stood still with his hands up. There were four men on the deck, three were dead, and the captain, who looked scared.

Once the extra two crew members tied off their larger boat to the smaller fishing boat, Little Jimmy jumped onto the smaller fishing boat and pushed the dead men over the side of the boat. The boat looked to be forty years old and not maintained. The fishing nets were rolled up in piles in the back of the boat. The captain spoke a little English and kept saying something about choices. Wayne jumped over to the deck while Billy Ray covered him. Vicky jumped over to the deck and immediately opened the door to the lower cabin. She aimed her 9mm Beretta down the stairs as she entered the narrow passage. She inched down the stairs and found the three kids sitting on a bench with three inches of water under their feet. The chains running from the welded brackets connected to the ceiling of the dark storage room were fastened to their wrists. She felt relieved once the chains were released. She secured photos of the kids as proof of the crime. The girls were taken aboard the CIA boat and provided food and their statements were secured by the local CIA translator. The parents had been told the girls would be well cared for and provided better opportunities.

After approximately fifteen minutes of forcible questioning with his shoulder being pulled out of place and then a couple minutes later shoved back in place by Little Jimmy, the captain provided the details of the mission and the name of his partners. He swore he was forced to take the job. They were going to kill him if he did not use his boat to transport the people.

Vicky knew with the shoulder being pulled out of joint and then forced back in joint, that the pain was overwhelming. The person would almost pass out from the acute pain. She also was aware there would be no scar and no sign of torture from the interrogation, which was against the law set forth by the United Nations and most countries around the world. The United States would arrest any government official who was caught applying physical or emotional pain to a held suspect. She also knew torture produced results, and these men were selling kids to people who would rape the kids and then pass them on to additional people to rape them until finally they were used up and killed. The unit had very little patience with the slave traders. They had all seen how the children were treated.

Vicky looked at him and asked, "Why the assault rifles, and why shoot at us?"

He knew the Americans standing in front of him did not believe him. He also knew he could not endure the pain of his shoulder being ripped out of the socket again and the huge black man was capable of pulling his shoulder in and out of socket several times. The captain said, "Some of the associates are from Bangkok, two are from Vietnam and the leader was from the Philippines." He was not certain where the others were from. The group entered North Korea and were purchasing the kids and then sending them to his boat to be taxied to the larger boat named Delian. Vicky wanted to keep him alive for further questioning.

Vicky had told Wayne to give him a shot of morphine and cuff him. "We need to sink his boat." Billy Ray placed the two sticks of dynamite on the bottom interior side of the boat a few inches above the floor. He left all the doorways open and lit the fuse. He knew all he needed was a twelve-inch hole and the boat would fill and sink within a few minutes.

Vicky had remembered Max saying they could not enter the territory of North Korea. She had not considered someone going into North Korea to purchase women and kids. She was not going to allow these slave traders to escape. This might be their only opportunity to apprehend them and with the intel from the captain, they had them trapped. She wanted to cut the head off the snake, and these men were ground zero with the ones taking the children. She remembered meeting Wan Yibin, the President of North Korea a few months prior in the lower level of the White House. President Truman was meeting in secret with President Wan Yibin, and he had seemed sincere about stopping the human trafficking. President Truman wanted to be remembered as a human rights advocate. He was pushing his agenda with fighting against worldwide slavery. His presidential campaign had mimicked Jimmy Carter's 1976 presidential campaign fighting for morality worldwide. Wan Yibin and President Truman had not been able to agree on other issues, but they did agree to curtail the slavery problem worldwide. President Wan Yibin had requested to meet Vicky since she was the one who had saved the child taken from North Korea. The two had exchanged cards with phone numbers.

She pulled out her cell phone and called the personal number he had provided her to reach him directly. Vicky was surprised he answered. She explained the details and the need for help. She reminded him he agreed to assist the cause when she met him in the White House. She sent him photos of the kids and the captain of the boat and her location. He said he would provide additional help in the form of the North Korean Army. He seemed outraged and surprised with the slave traders entering his country without his daily patrol's knowledge. They agreed to meet the General at the point of entry near the China and North Korean border.

They approached the restricted area and noticed the boat was headed away from shore in a hurry. They turned to intercept the small boat and with the intent to board it. This vessel had a small sail that was not in use. The motor was an old rebuilt car motor which was billowing smoke. The boat would not slow until Billy Ray fired a rifle shot four inches from the captain's head hitting the pole supporting the main sail. The captain realized he had no choice; he could not outrun the bigger boat and was an easy target in the open. He was either going to be shot or comply. Once they pulled next to the boat, Vicky's translator indicated the captain was going to report their activities to the authorities. The captain kept yelling at them in an Asian dialog. Her translator kept relaying the message. They had no right to board his boat. Little Jimmy jumped from the rail onto the smaller boat and pulled his heavy coat off and pushed the captain down which quietened him. Wayne followed and located one child under a tarp tied up and announced only the one man who was driving the boat appeared to be on board. Vicky stepped over to the boat with the interpreter.

The captain would not answer any questions but kept saying the kid was his nephew. They had no right to be on his boat. He was a skinny medium height man with scars on his arms and left cheek. His teeth were either missing or brown. He finally responded when Little Jimmy broke his ankle by stomping on his leg. His partners had emerged from the jungle and realized the boat with the captain had already pulled away from the bank, and they had nowhere to run and no way to escape the North Korean Army Patrol. The captain had heard the gunshots between the North Korean Army and his partners. He was trying to make it to open water before he got cut off. The partners were running down the shore while being chased by elements of the North Korean Army. No one wanted to be taken by the North Koreans. The best they could hope for was a fast death and the worst was a long prison sentence in a work camp. The captain understood he wanted to leave with the Americans and once he started talking, he would not stop. He explained he was transporting the kids and young women to the freighter. The child was the only one on board, but the men had gone inland in hopes of buying several people. Once they purchased one person, that person was escorted to his boat. Once he had two or three passengers, he would taxi them to the bigger boat waiting and another smaller boat would rotate to this position and wait. He emphasized they were helping the kids and the families. Nothing was illegal.

They tied the captain to the deck and lowered the inflatable boat in the water from the CIA boat using the winch with the intent to meet the General of the Army. Vicky could tell the interpreter was very nervous being asked to talk to the North Korean Army. He kept saying no. Billy Ray pushed the smaller man toward the boat. He was shaking he was so nervous. He told Vicky he never agreed to meet the North Koreans. She could tell he was very scared, but she knew she needed him and his ability to translate. She said, "This will be over soon. I need you to translate."

Vicky had introduced herself to the North Korean General once they got to shore with the help of the interpreter.

The man looked at his female partner and yelled, "We cannot be taken alive. We are surrounded." He turned facing the fast-approaching helicopter and pulled his pistol. She did the same as both started shooting into the sky at the chopper. They stood in the open on the beach as the bullets from the thirty-caliber machine gun first ripped a path in the sand until several bullets hit the mark. The man and woman running on the shore had been shot into pieces by a North Korean helicopter which had flown down the shoreline and caught the fleeing two in the open beach.

The North Korean General understood these were the American contacts. Vicky had explained they were guests of the North Korean President. There was a standoff with several guns aimed at her and Little Jimmy. Vicky called President Wan Yibin in front of the General and thanked him for allowing her and her team the opportunity to catch these men in the act of kidnapping the kids. The General was more hospitable once he realized Vicky was face timing with his President, and he did not have that number. President Wan Yibin was yelling at his general while on Vicky's phone telling him he was going to have to answer how he had allowed these men to come ashore and steal the kids under his watch. Vicky had Billy Ray and Little Jimmy bring the child and the captain to the shore and presented the child to the General and explained the child was being held under a tarp by the captain.

The North Koreans hated the countries around them except for China, and Vicky knew there would be no mercy provided these men who were selling kids into human slavery.

She now was worried about the people, which had already been moved to the Delian freighter in the China Sea. Once word got out these men had been captured, the slaves were a liability and proof of the crime. She feared they would be killed and thrown overboard. The Navy had intended to cut the ship off once it crossed into international waters. Now the North Korean Army had sent a naval ship and China had done likewise. Vicky had no contact with China. Max had alerted the Embassy in China and played this as a joint operation with the Chinese, North Korea and the CIA. Vicky knew the freighter would want to be taken by the Americans. The North Koreans and Chinese government would provide fast lethal punishment for the captain and employees of the freighter. The captain of the Delian had not counted on the Koreans being so fast to deploy their ship and block the passage into international waters. At that point, the freighter was cut off and surrendered.

Vicky told her team they were finished. "We will step back and allow the North Koreans to handle the mop up of the slave runners. They will take the freighter, the Delian, and rescue the passengers." Vicky knew sometimes the foreign countries could better handle criminals in a more economical and faster method. There would be no court, no jury, and no attorneys. As far as Vicky was concerned dealing with kidnappers and slave runners the lethal fast and cheap method provided by North Korea and China was satisfactory with her. On the boat ride back, Vicky remembered the Asian girls in the crates, the hidden graves with the skeletons of the young Asian bodies, the maid who had been killed and left in the open. She dropped on her knees and prayed to God, "Thank you Heavenly Father for providing me the fortitude to do your will."

Vicky's cell phone vibrated while on board the American Navy Ship. Wan Yibin had thanked her and wanted to update her. There were fifteen people being held on board the Delian freighter. Seven were kids and all were Asian from different countries. They were going to provide the fifteen safe passage back to their homeland, keep the freighter, and provide fast fair judgement to the kidnappers. He was gracious. Vicky agreed to call him on the next mission and before they each said bye she added, "President Yibin, we did this working together."

Vicky checked her watch and smiled. The mission was completed in less than six hours once they left the United States navy ship. She looked at Wayne and said, "We got their asses. Sometimes missions are simple." He smiled. They walked out to the helicopter landing pad for the flight to the airbase in Hawaii, where the unit would fly to Nashville on the CIA plane, listed under some insignificant transportation company.

Vicky looked forward as she and Wayne walked to the helicopter, "Max does not have the same focus as I do. I am trying to save lives and especially kids. He saw the request from NATO to intervene in the human slavery industry as an opportunity for the CIA to meet the underworld characters and build a rapport in foreign counties. We have successfully built a relationship with the Catholic Church in South America, and with one of the largest cartels in that continent. We have a substantial contact now in Russia in the underworld. He did not know I had the phone number to President Wan Yibin. He was not in the room at the White House when I met the North Korean President."

Wayne looked at Vicky, "What we have been able to accomplish is extraordinary. The contact with the Russian underworld through Von Chevron and the contact in South America with the cartel is priceless."

Once aboard the flight, Vicky looked at Wayne and noticed the other unit members were out of hearing range and wearing their headphones listening to music. She had known him for close to nine months, and they had become friends and partners. They seemed to have become as close as a man and woman could come without being intimately involved. Their relationship was similar to a brother and a sister. She knew something was eating at his soul. She had understood his wife had passed away years ago, and he never seemed to move forward with another relationship. She had understood except for an occasional visit, he had stopped going to church about five years prior. She said, "You know I love you. I trust you. You are a great partner." Wayne looked up and smiled slightly.

"You know my husband might be able to help you. He is very good at understanding people and helping them with life choices. I know there is something eating at you. You seemed to fear relationships."

Wayne hesitated and rubbed his face. He said, "My wife died of cancer in a room by herself. She deserved to be treated better. She would try to talk to me, and I was just so consumed with my homicide cases when I worked in Memphis. I tuned her out and was selfish. She was a strong person and felt trapped. She wanted out. If I won a lottery, I would have given her a million dollars even after we were separated or divorced. That was the guy I wanted to be. She never told me she had cancer until she was two weeks from dying."

"Will you meet with my husband and at least talk with him? We all live with guilt and our Lord is an understanding Lord. I pray every day for my soul, and what I need to do in the form of reckoning. I hope I can be forgiven. My sins are of greater magnitude than yours."

Wayne looked at Vicky with a questioning expression but knew not to ask what her personal sins were. He said, "This is the most rewarding and exciting thing I have ever done. I love traveling around the world with you and these guys. I believe little by little we are making a difference. There is no doubt we saved those kids and no telling how many more from being treated like cattle after being raped. I will consider calling Preacher Donahue."

Vicky's phone buzzed. She looked at the caller ID and knew she should not have hung up on Max. He was her boss and the Operational Manager for the CIA under stress running the agency until a new director would be named. "Hello, this is Vicky."

Max said, "You and I must report to a meeting in the White House at 8 a.m. in the morning. I hope you can appreciate the gravity of this meeting. This a mandatory meeting with his entire security council. This President is not like other presidents who have all been very skilled in the arena of politics. He wants to be hands on and push the envelope of what we can legally do to the limits. He has specifically asked for your presence."

"Who is on the council?"

He hesitated to wonder why she asked the question. "I don't know. I am not certain what to expect. I am the Operational Manager for the CIA. The CIA director has yet to be announced. I have never been to a meeting with the entire security council." He paused and said, "I hope you can make the meeting. I signed off on your present mission, so I could provide you and your team cover if the mission went sideways."

Vicky knew the urgent nature of locating the rogue former National Security Director. She had not told Max;

Mia had discovered a way to reverse the computer signal which could pin down his location. She had hoped to hear from Mia. She also was concerned with Delores who worked for the FBI and was the sixth member of her team. Her training was to investigate and arrest, which had become part of an FBI agent's DNA. Delores believed everyone deserved their day in court. Max had told Vicky the former NSA Director needed to be taken out. "He was a traitor, and he knows too many secrets about the defense of the government. The United States government cannot afford for him to seek asylum in another country like China or Russia. He needs to be killed as soon as possible." Max knew these other countries would be looking for him to try to work out a deal.

Vicky told Max the mission in Asia was completed and had gone better than expected. She knew he had already been updated as he was monitoring the mission on a live feed. She just wanted to mention it, so Max would understand how she felt about stopping the slave movement. She said she would land in Nashville in a few hours and could fly to D.C. at seven a.m. in the morning. Max seemed relieved and mentioned they needed to meet about fifteen minutes prior to the meeting to discuss the possible topics.

Chapter 3

Vicky drove into the church parking lot. She knew her husband was meeting with the thirty to fifty age church men's group. She had not seen him in a few days. He had been busy with his job and working toward his doctorate in physics. He considered physics a hobby. His full-time career and passion was being the head preacher at Middlebrook United Methodist Church in the small town of Butler, Tennessee. Matt enjoyed conducting the men's group and liked the camaraderie with the adult men. He and Galon Hipshire, the assistant preacher and youth director, took turns working with the different committees.

She opened the door to the church and listened in the front foyer to the meeting in the conference room. She knew the meeting was winding down. She truly loved Matt and wanted to surprise him. She heard him saying, "I truly believe the special time a couple can spend together is the most important time in a relationship. With life ever-changing and kids being introduced into the equation, extended work hours, the special time couples try to set aside often are forgotten. The sandwich generation is the new generation being named by sociologists. The sandwich generation is caught between elderly parents and kids coming of age. The additional work hours with employers demanding more work with less employees has extended the work week. This generation has more stress placed on them than any generation studied. You have a difficult time adapting to the demands. What studies have indicated is that sex is about fifteen percent of a healthy marriage with kids. The other eighty-five percent is income, security, emotional support, and love for the kids and each other. The divorce rate is above sixty percent all because of the fifteen percent failure with sex." Vicky knew Matt tried to study this generation, so he could provide support for the families. The men's group at church seemed to be growing with this generation trying to help one another. She reached for the doorknob as she heard a new member mention the difficulty of raising young kids.

Vicky loved her husband, and she knew he was wanting to have children. She was not certain when she would be ready. She wanted to hear her husband's response. Matt said, "I will give you the short answer because we are running over. I have not had the privilege or challenges with raising kids. I have read a truckload of material on the subject, and I have concluded that a parent needs to connect with the child in every year of the child's life, even through adulthood. The research now is indicating that the human brain does not stop growing until age twenty-six." He looked at the group. "I have read some journals from experts suggesting parents need to be parents and not try to be friends with their kids. Instead, I believe a parent needs to either create hobbies or discover the kids' hobbies and spend good quality time with the kids in these hobbies working with them as friends. During the hobbies is the best time to emphasize to the kids morals, the golden rule, how to financially plan, how to be creative, how to love, and most of all to know our Lord will love them as they are. You may have to play with dolls, and you might get involved with sports, remodeling a home, or other activities you are not interested in. Remember, for every single one verbal correction there needs to be four verbal compliments. But most of all this is true for all parents to understand, God created the perfect place on earth which was called the Garden of Eden and yet there was still sin present. Remember the serpent? My point is as a parent, the parent needs to understand past sin, present sin, and possible future sin to be able to live with guilt, to cope, to avoid present temptation and assist the child with sin in the future. Sin is normal that is why we pray daily." They ended with a prayer.

Vicky removed her hand from the doorknob as she thought about Brian, the young man she had seduced, and the guilt she felt for his death. She asked God to forgive her. She reached for the doorknob and smiled as she said hi to the group and announced she needed to see her husband and have some special time with him. They all laughed.

Chapter 4

Vicky was leaning back in the taxi trying to relax. She was headed to the White House. Her phone buzzed with a new text from Mia. Vicky read the text, "I know where the former NSA Director Burnside is hiding. He is in a second Viatect office location in Annapolis."

Vicky texted back, "Tell only Wayne and keep it a secret. I will be home later today. We need a plan of action, and we need to respond fast."

Meeting with the president, security council and chief of staff was not what Vicky wanted to be doing. She knew Mia had located the signal and the rogue National Security Director, and she needed to be part of the planning.

Vicky was ushered to a hall where Max was waiting. The people in the hall all noticed Vicky's beautiful appearance standing in her heels and navy suit with her long permed dark hair with the ends highlighted light brown. Vicky sensed Max seemed a little uptight. He took her to the area in the corridor and the open doorway to the exterior for privacy. He said, "All the armed services divisions, CIA, State Department and NSA have submitted their reports to the new administration. I have updated President Grant in a verbal report when I first met him with the new information on the Syndicate, the threat assessment and the Vortex. I told him you are point for the mission and by the way, President Grant asked that you attend this meeting. The normal protocol is the Chief of Staff would be hosting the meeting and then report to the President."

Vicky looked at Max in the eyes and now understood why she was asked to attend this meeting. Max said, "Vicky, whatever you do, do not say anything. This is a room full of sharks fighting for control. He wants to meet us after the meeting."

"Is there anything else you need to tell me?"

"He also understands the importance of locating Burnside." Max looked around making certain no one could hear him. "Burnside must be dealt with. He has contacts within all our agencies and that is making this mission tricky and that is another reason you and your unit are on point."

Max then said, "The rumors are that the Chief of Staff, Stewart Andrews had an old business partner who might be nominated for the vacant CIA Director's job." He rolled his eyes when he said it. Vicky glanced around the hall area where they were standing. She could see people in groups of two to four talking, waiting for the meeting to start. She noticed there was only one other female. There were no friendly smiles, and everyone had a look of concern on their faces.

Max looked toward the large office and saw the four aides opening the double doors sliding the door stops under the doors. "Here we go."

The aides ushered the audience to the meeting room and showed them to their seats. There were name plates on display for the individuals sitting around the large oval table. Max took his seat across from the Army General. Vicky was ushered to the corner seat along the wall next to the double doors furthest away with some other low-ranking aides and support personnel. She sat down, and next to her was an Army colonel who she had seen talking to the Army General in the hall. Vicky had not met any of the twenty-five attendees in the meeting except Max and the FBI director, Alexander Bass.

The President and chief of staff, Stewart Andrews, had been on the news every day for six months during the Presidential campaign. Vicky had understood that President Grant and the chief of staff had been in the same fraternity while at the University of Texas. They both had made millions in the gas industry and had diversified into the medical supply industry while building and buying a string of hospitals nationwide. The two had tried to corner the hospital market and capture seventy nine percent of ownership of the private sector hospitals nationwide. In order not to be classified as owning a monopoly in the industry, they kept the ownership at less than eighty percent. The revenue in their owned hospitals had doubled and the expense had remained the same. President Grant had been able to turn the negative publicity on how he had taken advantage of the high medical cost and made billions and told the American people during his campaign that this showed he knew how to run the country.

The President and chief of staff, Stewart Andrews, walked into the room with Stewart telling the President he needed not to listen to the liberal media and the liberal members of Congress. Everyone stood. They both took their seats across from one another in the middle of the table. Everyone sat. Vicky was surprised Stewart started the meeting by ramming his index finger into the table surface while looking at the Army Chief of Staff and saying, "We need to bomb the maniac in North Korea." He then looked at Max and said, "We need to assassinate him. We need to show the world we have a backbone."

Vicky looked at Max. She then brushed her hair back with her hand and blew out air. The Army colonial next to her glanced at her from his peripheral vision. Max was sitting in his chair not saying a word. The Army General finally spoke up and suggested no one in the world doubts the United States' ability to wage war. He suggested diplomacy. Stewart said, "The hell with diplomacy. Diplomacy is for cowards." The general's face turned red as he looked at Stewart.

The President finally asked "Does anyone have a better plan? This is an open forum with North Korea being one of the hot topics."

Vicky looked at Max, and he looked straight ahead. She remembered Max had told her under no circumstance should she say anything. He had explained that Stewart was a loudmouth, cussed every other word, and acted like he won the election. The President was passive and allowed his friend to do most of the talking.

Stewart looked at the general and asked, "They just started missile testing last week with them firing off intercontinental rockets. How close is the maniac to getting a nuke and being able to send it into our heart?" The General held his ground. He replied "You have our report. Our intel is a fair assessment. The North Korean government is not a threat to our country."

Stewart said, "That is not what I understand. Do you remember Pearl Harbor? Prior to WW II, the United States was not prepared for the war. There were at least ten countries with larger standing armies than we had in 1938. Once North Korea obtains the nukes, we will be living in constant fear. We need to hit them first and then not worry about them ever again."

Vicky was getting upset. She needed to be working the case locating the rogue NSA director. That was the biggest threat this country faced and here they were talking about North Korea. "Why don't we invite Wan Yibin to a summit and talk face-to-face with him? We do not need to assassinate the president of a foreign country. Besides, North Korea already has nuclear weapons. They are crude compared to ours." Vicky had made the statement before she realized the words were out of her mouth.

Stewart's head spun around and looked in her direction. "What in the hell do you know about any of this? Who are you anyway?"

No one said a word. Vicky did not answer, and the Army colonial tried to lean back in his chair to take the glaring focus off him. She looked straight ahead. "We all would appreciate it if you little lady would stay out of this conversation and let the men handle this."

President Grant abruptly pushed his chair back and walked over and stood in front of Vicky. "Please tell me what you suggest. Now is the time to talk if you have something to say."

"I would suggest we contact president Wan Yibin and meet him in a summit."

Stewart said, "What do you know about Wan Yibin?"

"I know when I talk to him, he is very nice, polite and seems to want what is best for his people. He is a smart man and knows he needs friends."

Stewart asked, "Who are you? How did you get in this meeting? I do not remember your name being on the list of invitees. But since you are here, how the hell did you get in touch with Wan Yibin? No one is allowed to talk to him without the consent of my office. North Korea is banned from any American visiting and that certainly means you are not allowed to talk to their government officials without consent from me."

President Grant stood in front of Vicky. He turned and looked at Stewart and the others at the table. "I invited Mrs. Donahue."

Vicky had decided her patience was extended to her limit. She had more important tasks at hand. She stared into President Grant's eyes and said, "I am Vicky Donahue. I work for Max Doran at the CIA. I believe the American people would want you to try to reach an amicable agreement with North Korea's leader in a diplomatic manner. I believe this would increase your national approval ratings to be able to accomplish this so quickly after taking office last week. Besides, I just got back from North Korea talking with President Yibin. We had a mission in play, and President Yibin assisted us. We have common grounds to agree on. I would suggest a summit, so we can move on to more important issues."

Stewart said, "You can't just call Wan Yibin. I find that very difficult to believe."

President Grant had been briefed by the CIA on the unit nicknamed the Good Samaritans. He had seen Vicky's picture on the first page of the report. The photo was taken when she first joined the CIA. No one else had been provided the written reports or the more in-depth verbal reports from the prior administration. He knew who Vicky Donahue was and what she had been able to accomplish.

"I have his personal cell phone number on my cell phone. Here I will call him Mr. President and if he answers, you can talk with him. There is a thirteen-hour difference." Everyone in the room stared at Vicky as she stood up and placed her phone in front of her. The voice came online with an Asian accent and said, "Hi Mrs. CIA." Vicky smiled and explained she was in a meeting in the White House with the newly elected President Grant and others. She announced they were discussing setting up a summit with North Korea and would like to know if he was interested. "My new president would like to say hello."

She handed him the phone. President Grant said, "Yes. President Yibin, we would like to see if you are interested in talking with us and working out possible financial assistance and lifting the embargo set up by the prior administration. We would like to be friends, but we do have concerns we hope to discuss."

"Yes. I would very much like to meet you, Mr. President."

"Then it is settled. I will have my aide set this up for next month."

"I look forward to it. I want to congratulate you on winning the election with fifty-two percent of the votes.

Everyone in North Korea voted for me." Some of the people in the room laughed.

The men said goodbye, and the President gave Vicky her phone. He went and sat down. "Now, I am glad we have that issue moving forward and that phone call just saved us weeks of discussing our next move." He looked at one of the aides and said, "Prepare a news release on the summit with North Korea. Does anyone else have any questions or suggestions?"

Vicky said, "Yes."

Everyone turned to look at her. The President asked, "Yes, Mrs. Donahue?"

"I would suggest you promote Max Doran to the position of Director of the CIA. He has worked in the CIA for over thirty years and has a great deal of experience. He is well respected. We at the CIA need a strong leader, and I believe Max could provide the leadership we need."

The President looked at his aide and said, "Draw up the paperwork, and we will submit it to the Senate for approval."

Max looked like he was indifferent. He showed no emotion.

President Grant glanced at his watch. "I need to have a word in private with Mr. Doran and Mrs. Donahue."

The President looked around and stated, "I have all the reports and if I have questions, I will contact you. Now, everyone else please clear the room."

Stewart did not move as everyone else was leaving. President Grant looked across the table and said, "Everyone needs to leave."

Stewart said, "You appointed me your Chief of Staff. This is the security meeting with the security counselors. We all have been cleared for the intel."

The President looked firm, "Everyone needs to leave except me, Max Doran and Mrs. Donohue." Stewart stared at Vicky as he walked out the door. He was obviously upset.

The aides closed the doors. "I need you to update me on the Vortex and this Syndicate and the threat they pose."

Vicky waited for the President to sit. She looked at the two men and said, "Mr. President, the information we have on the Vortex is very thin. We understand the theory behind the Vortex. I will provide you with an elementary briefing. The earth is spinning a thousand miles per hour and the solar system is traveling thousands of miles per hour and the Milky Way Galaxy is traveling thousands of miles per hour. Everything is moving in space. I have read reports which indicate our Galaxy was located on the other side of space bumping up against other galaxies sixty million years ago. We know our Galaxy is moving. The theory of the Vortex is basically holding something still in space or in this case on earth and letting the earth spin or space spin around the item. More specifically, the molecules of the item are held still inside the Vortex. We know molecules are constantly traveling through time, space and great distance through dense materials such as rocks, trees and planets in our galaxy. Other than that, we have very little understanding of how molecules can accomplish this. What if someone has figured this out? The item would enter a zipper or a doorway into a Vortex which could be a ship, a bomb or anything. Then the item would appear when the zipper opens on the other side of our planet or galaxy. The item is the only thing not moving inside the Vortex. The Vortex holds the items still in space or on the earth free from gravity influence." She looked at the two men. "Now that we understand the data, we also understand our planet may have been visited from a faraway place." She looked at both men. "The Bible has references to space travel and the Vortex helps explain the missing data and our existence. We now are discovering that the average intelligence level, the IQ, in humanity has not increased. Knowledge and the number of people on earth have increased. With more people and more knowledge, we have advanced from one generation to the next with more knowledge. Our IQ level worldwide over the past ten million years has remained the same. The Vortex and space travel explains how humanity jumped ahead of the other animals on earth. The Gods came down from space and had intercourse with the human women and the result was a noticeable increase in the IQ level with the offspring. This seems more likely than not, and this explains the how part of the equation, and how humanity moved forward. Once a zipper is open and then closed, a void or a tunnel in space may be created. If the Syndicate obtains this information and is able to create these tunnels on earth, they could in time control our world. Bombs could be sent from almost any location and delivered to another location without warning. No one would be safe."

President Grant listened. "How did you have dictator Wan Yibin's personal cell number?"

"I met him here in the White House with President Truman. He was in Washington to pick up a North

Korean child that had been sold into human slavery. We exchanged numbers, and he pledged to assist us with the fight against human slavery. I just got back from the China Sea where several slave traders were captured or killed. He helped."

Max said, "Sir it was an operation we did not report. We need to keep the CIA out of the news if we are going to have any chance with future operations."

President Grant watched the two as they spoke. He then looked at Vicky. "I want you on point to take out Burnside. He is a threat against our national interest."

Max said, "Sir, if I understand you, you are giving us a kill order on an American citizen."

He frowned, "You know I cannot give you an order to kill an American citizen, but you two need to do your job. This meeting is over." President Grant immediately stood and walked out the door.

Max and Vicky walked to the security detail exit door and then into the parking lot. Max thought about characteristics of CIA agents. Some agents were good at desk jobs and had insight and were motivated into studying threats and people. Some agents were good at surveillance and could go unnoticed and blend into different environments. In the spy world, Max knew he needed people who could also kill. Finding someone who would pull the trigger and then live with the results was a challenge. He also knew of agents who enjoyed killing too much. Collateral damage of an innocent person was not acceptable. Finding the agent with the perfect balance was the challenge. He did not know Vicky personally. He had recruited her after his analyst had discovered she had killed two international hit men and appeared to be fearless and intelligent. She made quick decisions. They had completed a full background check into her, and Max liked what he saw. He looked squarely at Vicky. "Do you understand what you are being asked to do?"

Vicky thought back to her parents arguing when she was eight years old. They were driving on the back country road leading to an uncle's home in Texas and watched as the oncoming vehicle hit a dog and then drove off. Her father had stopped the car and pulled his handgun from under the seat. Her mother had cried and suggested they take the injured dog to the veterinarian in town. Over the years, she never understood how they had come together and fallen in love and married. They were truly opposites. Her mother loved books and taught college English. Her father was a pilot in the United States Airforce. He grew up hunting, fishing and farming.

Her father had pulled his gun and walked toward the injured dog which was yelping and lying on the shoulder of the road. She had jumped out of the backseat of the vehicle and ran to her father and asked her father not to shoot the dog. He had bent down on his knee next to her and said, "A good man must make tough decisions in life. I am not going to allow this dog to suffer. The dog, sweetie, has two broken legs, and maybe a broken back, with internal organ damage. I am a good man. I love you." He walked closer to the dog and pulled his gun and shot the dog in the head. Vicky looked at Max and shook her head yes and opened her car door.

They both snapped their seatbelts. "I do not believe he understands the Vortex and the threat."

Max said, "I do not believe he is buying your theory with regards to space travel and some of the females becoming pregnant by men from outer space. Does the Bible really say that?"

Vicky thought back to her conversation with her husband about Professor Ray Baine, and how he had described how the human DNA could be enhanced with a certain modified protein and inserted into the female egg. The offspring could have an elevated IQ level which could be doubled or even tripled the norm with other enhanced traits. She then thought about his death. "Genesis chapter six verse one through four clearly states the Gods came down from space and had intercourse with human women. The newer versions of the bible have been altered by mankind in the translation. Read the original Holy Bible written before the fourteen century. The message is clear. There is a movement with scientists which are starting to recognize that our IQ level has not increased in ten thousand years. The only explanation the IQ level can increase in a species is through genetic breeding. That is why the other animals on planet earth are not helping us build spaceships. There are more smarter people on planet earth now because there are more people. Overall, humanity has not increased the IQ level since the space travelers. We have been able to record our thoughts and our history which helped us advance one generation at a time, but our IQ has not increased."

Chapter 5

Billy Ray thought as he was driving his Harley on the interstate heading toward Nashville, "What am I going to do? I need to keep her occupied for four hours at most. This should provide Vicky time to return from Washington, gather the team, and leave without Delores and the FBI knowing anything about the mission." He glanced down at the side of his bike and could see the white tennis shoe with the top of Delores's foot and ankle. He could not believe Mia and Eric talked her into a motorcycle ride. Wayne had mentioned a diversion, so Delores and the FBI would not be involved. Delores was the seventh member of the unit, but she still worked for the FBI as a liaison between the unit and the Special Case Division of the FBI.

Billy Ray rode the bike into the parking lot of the Lonesome Bar and Grill off Locust Street in Nashville and asked Delores if she needed to use the bathroom or was she thirsty? He glanced at his watch. He needed to kill three more hours.

Delores said, "Both." She had never ridden on a motorcycle, and she loved the feeling of freedom and the

59

excitement of doing something new. Wayne and Mia explained to the unit that they had run into a block wall looking for Burnside. The two had suggested everyone needed a break. Eric of Newport had mentioned to Delores the fun of riding a motorcycle. Delores had always suspected Billy Ray had been the one who had pulled the trigger and killed three men with one shot a few months prior saving her life. She also could tell the look in Billy Ray's eyes as he looked at her and always complimented her on her attire and looks. He had a crush on her. As he got off the Harley, he turned his phone off and slid the phone into the saddlebag and locked the bag. He did not want Delores asking him about the unit and any follow up meeting and without his phone, he could deny knowledge of the unit leaving.

When Delores walked out of the bathroom in the newly purchased white leggings and pink tight workout shirt, all eyes were on her. She was the only black female in the honky-tonk bar with the sound system playing country music. Billy Ray had joked with Delores about introducing her to country music. He was fairly certain she had never been in a country western bar. He explained he wanted to broaden her horizons. She walked into the bar hearing the music by Hank Williams, Jr.

singing about all his rowdy friends coming over. They sat down at the bar, and Billy Ray said, "I will buy the first round." They laughed and after three rounds, they ordered steaks. Dolores could not resist asking Billy Ray about the tattoo on his neck that said Redneck. Billy Ray said, "That is a long story, but the story has to do with why the communities across the country should support laws not allowing underage drinking."

She busted out laughing. He said, "I woke up with the tattoo and three days later my ass was in the Army." She laughed again.

After the steaks and a couple of beers, Billy Ray noticed a couple of people were dancing to the country music. "Maybe I can broaden your horizons more with some dancing. It is called the Texas Twostep." He glanced at his watch. He needed two more hours.

To his surprise Delores hopped up with an eager smile and said, "Heck yes. Let's go. I thought you would never ask."

Billy Ray was taken back by Dolores' ability to pick up the dancing and was a natural. She watched other couples and was soon loving the audience watching her. The bar had started getting crowded by 9 p.m., and after thirty minutes of dancing, Billy Ray suggested another drink.

Chapter 6

Wayne had briefed the unit, "This is going to be a CIA hit on American soil. Viatect is a large corporation making high tech ammunition and guns for the Pentagon. They have several offices located in different states and foreign countries. Viatect also has a myriad of retired military personnel hired to work for the United States Government as private contractors. The company's contracts were in the billions. We know where Burnside is located. If we miss him, we might not locate him again. We must strike now."

Eric looked at the satellite pictures and asked Mia to enlarge the front right corner. Eric was the sixth member of the team. He was the hired help who had just been released from the Tennessee penitentiary to assist with certain aspects of the missions for the CIA unit. He had a certain skill set that could not be taught, which he acquired growing up in a family of crime. He had been Little Jimmy's cellmate for two years, and they had become friends. Everyone called him Eric of Newport in prison and the nickname had stuck. His parents and one uncle had been arrested for running a chop shop for stolen automobiles, and Eric was arrested two years later for stealing vehicles when a girlfriend turned him in to authorities for cheating on her with her mother.

Wayne looked at his watch and then said, "I asked you here to come up with a plan to breach the security system and reach Burnside before Vicky returns." He then looked at Mia and asked to view the guard house and note how often the guards made the rounds and when they had breaks and shift changes. Mia was going back and forth between screens. Wayne finally said, "We're going to need more time. That place is well guarded. We won't be able to get past the guards, and we do not have time to watch the building and wait for him to leave."

Little Jimmy said, "She is not going to like that. She will want a plan to take him out while Billy Ray has Delores entertained. The two went toward Nashville on his Harley."

Mia said, "I could hardly work on locating Burnside with her coming over and standing behind me watching my scenes. I would pull up his history and act like I was looking for clues into his military background."

Eric in a surprised voice said, "Look at the elevator shaft and the brick wall sticking out. The distance between the main wall and the elevator wall is about three, maybe four feet. Count the brick. I can scale that wall to the fifth floor and drop a rope."

Wayne looked with a surprised expression at Eric, and Mia turned her head from the computer and said, "The hell you can."

Little Jimmy walked over and said, "The former NSA director will be on the top floor. That looks like a living area with balconies. The bottom five floors are offices and production areas for the engineers. If Eric says he can climb that wall, then that is good enough for me."

Mia said, "I have been checking further into Viatect, and they make some very dangerous high-tech toys with an army of covert operatives. They're not just a high-tech arms dealer, but they have operatives stationed all over the globe. They make bombs to burn through buildings and have some labs which are not even mentioned in the reports to Congress. They may be into germ warfare. I bet Congress has no clue what they are doing for the Pentagon. They have satellite offices in Africa, Japan, and Germany just to name a few locations. The contracts are with the Pentagon, and they work with the Army Intelligence Division."

"I can scale the wall by placing one foot against one wall and the other against the other wall and hop up the wall. It really is easy. The pressure from my legs will hold me in place. I can tie a rope off to the flagpole and use a pulley to assist Vicky up to the fifth level. I can then climb the flagpole by using my legs to push back against my hands, which will be wrapped around the pole. I can walk right up the pole. I saw men in a show on TV do this in Hawaii to retrieve coconuts from the top of the palm trees. After watching the show, I went outside when I was thirteen and climbed several limbless pine trees. That is not hard either. I can then jump over to the balcony and drop her a second rope. I can get Vicky inside the building. We can cut through the outer fence, but we need to be able to cut through the inner electric fence and reach the wall without being seen. The group looked at the picture from the satellite on Mia's computer screen.

Eric looked at Wayne and pointed to the elevator shift and the nook area in the outside wall, "That is how we can obtain access."

Wayne sipped his coffee and then said, "The guards will not be expecting a break in from the top floor. The security cameras and guards will be set up for the bottom floors. The security guards will be relaxed. They most likely have been watching for something for years and would not be expecting a break-in. The boredom will be their weakness. This might work."

Mia asked, "Are you certain Eric of Newport, you can climb that wall without a rope and tie-off from the top?"

"Yes. I can show you how easy it is. All I need is to be able to stand between two walls that are about three feet apart. I can zoom right up the walls with one foot on each wall hopping up one foot at a time. The pulley system will lift Vicky up to the fifth-floor ledge, and then I can climb the flagpole to the top floor and jump to the balcony. Once there, I will tie off and drop another rope for Vicky to climb up. I can cut the glass in the window and in she goes."

***

Once Vicky arrived in Butler, she stopped by the loft. Wayne presented the plan, and Vicky liked the fact it could be executed within the next few hours. It was also simple. The satellite imagery showed the entire complex. Mia had been able to retrieve electronic copies of the architectural plans for the interior. Wayne had estimated the time to be within thirty minutes once they arrived at the north fence at Viatect's perimeter. They would be back home before the morning sunrise. She knew she needed to inform Max of the plan, but she still wondered about him. She reached up and started rubbing the cross hanging around her neck. She thought about the old saying, "Keep your friends close and your enemies closer". How could someone at his level in the CIA not know more about the syndicate? Trust only went so far, and a few hours earlier, she had recommended him to be the Director of the largest spy ring in the world, the CIA.

Chapter 7

Delores had never had so much fun. Other guys were asking her to dance, and surprising to her, Billy Ray was happy she was having so much fun as he glanced at his watch and noted his estimated four-hour time period had elapsed.

Her dance partner obviously had been dancing to country music for years. He was very good. Finally, Dolores said she needed to rest and headed to the bar. Billy Ray said as she approached, "You lied to me."

Delores thought here it comes. Every man she had ever been out with had always tried to either show her how tough they were and wanted to fight other men or accused her of flirting. She looked at Billy Ray. He leaned over, and said, "You told me you never danced to country music. Yet, you are the best female dancer in this place and some of these women have been dancing for years."

Billy Ray turned to the good-looking guy she had been dancing with and said, "I told you she could dance."

For the first time in her life, she was surprised a man was happily watching her have fun without being jealous.

The man said, "Not only can she dance, but she is the prettiest girl in the place."

Billy Ray said, "Hell yes, she is, and you won't have any problems finding a dance partner after dancing with her. The other girls will think you are special." The two men smiled and drank from the bottled beer.

The man looked at Delores and let his eyes roam from her feet in the white tennis shoes, to the tight white leggings and up to her tight pink workout shirt. He could not help but like the curves in her body. He smiled.

Billy Ray heard a slow country song and said, "I believe I can dance to this speed. Let us try a slow song." They walked out onto the dance floor, and Billy Ray pulled her tight against his body. She could instantly feel his body become alive below his belt and push against her. She felt the pressure in her body and his big strong hands holding her tight. She looked up into his eyes and smiled. He knew he was told to keep Delores preoccupied for a few hours, but now he realized he did not want to let her go. He finally tilted her head up and kissed her, and to his surprise and delight she kissed him back. The next song was another slow song, and they kissed during the entire song. They walked off the dance floor, and Billy Ray asked if she would like a drink for the ride home?

"Yes. Make mine a double."

They got their jackets and helmets from the bar area. Billy Ray said, "It may rain and without you having a rainsuit, a ride in the rain is a no go." He looked at Delores and explained, "Going about sixty, the raindrops feel like being shot constantly by a BB from a BB gun."

Delores looked up with a matter of fact look and said, "Maybe we should get a room at the motel."

Billy Ray said, "Yes. There are a few near the interstate."

"I saw a twenty-four-hour drug store down the block. Let me run in and then we can go get a room." Billy Ray waited on the bike as Dolores ran into the store. She came out about five minutes later carrying a bag. The motel was two blocks away. Billy Ray knew Delores was drunk, and this was going to be a one-night stand. There was just no way a lady with a law degree from Harvard who was as pretty as she would ever consider dating him. She was just wanting a good time and would regret this night in the morning. He also had been surprised with her kissing him while on the dance floor. Her smile and her joyful personality were all perfect. He thought about how pretty she was with her perfect body, high cheekbones and beautiful smile. His anticipation had spiked and was hard for him to control.

Once in the room, he was surprised to see the baby oil and lotion when she set them on the nightstand. He pulled her to him and started kissing her. He turned her around and started kissing her while standing behind her. He pulled her shirt over her head and then pulled her leggings down with her thong panties. He said, "I believe I can help you with this oil and lotion."

He pulled his clothes off and laid her on her stomach placing a pillow under her midsection on the mattress. He recalled watching Delores a few months ago through the window from across the street in Washington D.C. when he was asked to protect her. He remembered how much time she took with washing herself in the tub and then rubbing the body lotion on herself while standing in front of the window. He had thought about the scene every single day since, and he wanted her to enjoy this night.

Chapter 8

Little Jimmy was certain the device would block the deadly current in the electric fence around the perimeter in the three-by-three-foot square. He just had to convince Eric of Newport. "The device will be grounded in the soil twelve inches. Just stay on the rubber mat while touching the fence." Little Jimmy looked at Eric of Newport, "Just connect these specialized clamps to the ground rod and the fence, and the current will be neutralized. If you stay on the rubber pad you will be okay. It is like a man with a wooden leg can stand on his wooden leg and lift his other leg off the ground and not be shocked by an electric fence when he touches the fence, but if he touches another person while holding onto the fence with his other hand, the current will transfer through the one person to the other person, and the second person will be shocked from the current."

"Hell, can't we try this out first and test it? A show and tell session would work fine with me. The warning sign says 2000 volts. That much voltage would melt a wooden leg." Eric looked worried. "I have always respected electricity. I had a neighbor growing up who was a state-licensed electrician. He died in a flooded basement where an old electrical cord was plugged into the ceiling area with an extension cord extending below the waterline of the basement. The breaker box was located on the two wooden poles in the basement about ten feet from the bottom step. The breaker had not flipped off. His first step in the water was his last."

Little Jimmy said, "We are running out of time. It will work. I have studied the procedure. You must trust me."

***

During the quiet drive on the country curvy road, Eric, who was driving the car, had noticed there was nothing but darkness. They were approaching from a side road, so they could reach the west side of Viatect after crossing vacant woods and fields. There would be no way to approach without being seen on the main dead-end road leading to Viatect. He had finally built up the nerve to ask Vicky what it felt like to kill another person.

Vicky noticed Eric was quiet and she could sense he had reservations about something. She glanced at him after he asked the question and said, "Listen Eric, you won't need to kill anyone doing your job. I understand your concern. I won't put you in a position to ever have to pull the trigger. I really hope you never have to find out what it feels like, but some people need to be protected and some need to be killed. People who sell kids and women into slavery need to be killed. Burnside used the slave network to promote his agenda with the Syndicate. He needs to be killed." They rode in silence for a short distance.

Vicky knew her commitment to God. She went on and said, "In the Bible, the Jewish tribes united to wipe out the sinners in the cities of Sodom and Gomorrah as told in the book of Genesis. Lot was the only man who was spared. I have accepted my fate. The Jewish tribes loved our Lord, and they killed the sinners for our Lord. Eric, I also work for our Lord. I pray my actions will provide atonement for my past sins."

They had driven in silence the rest of the way to the pullover location approximately two miles from Viatect Headquarters with Eric thinking that Vicky never answered his question. He was concerned about living with the guilt of killing someone. He had pulled into the turn off and the isolated driveway where the phone company had a fenced in area for the phone line relay junction box. He opened the trunk and got his gear. He looked at Vicky who was standing to the side of the trunk and looked to be at total ease with herself. He knew this was going to be dangerous, and her job was to kill a man. His job was to get her inside the building, but she showed no sign of any reservations. He thought she was truly fearless and confident. Eric looked at his compass and said, "We need to head that direction." He pointed northeast. They had the plan mapped out. Wayne had devised the plan and estimated the time it would take them to reach the two perimeter fences. They were cutting through a cow pasture and then woods to come into the side of the fenced area on the west side of Viatect near the front entrance. The contour map of the area had them crossing a field and two barbed wire fences and proceeding along a small, wooded valley with a creek and then over a hill which overlooked Viatect's main office all in the dark of night. The main office was located in the rural area about ten miles from Annapolis off Highway 214 near Birdsville. The building could not be seen from the highway and was a solitary building at the dead-end of a short country road. The local community had hardly noticed the building. With the dead-end road leading from Viatect to the main highway and then the short distance to the ramp to the interstate, the company was well hidden in plain sight. No one in the community had an idea what the company did for the Defense Department.

Both Vicky and Eric of Newport were dressed in black with their faces covered with black hoods with eye holes. They had changed clothes on the CIA jet. At 11 p.m. they both set their stop watches. The night sky was full of clouds where it had rained for two hours. The building was well illuminated with lights in close to the eight-story building. Eric and Vicky had made it to the first fence through the woods. Mia had watched the guard from Viatect's computer security system. She had hacked into the private security company hired to provide the perimeter and exterior security. Viatect security provided their own security team for the interior. She indicated the best she could calculate; they had thirty minutes based on the guard's walking speed before he would be back around to the front. The other guard would remain in the gate house watching the front driveway facing away from the building. "You are clear."

The building was two stories below grade. The nook was in the shadows where the elevator shaft protruded out eight feet, and Eric knew not to hesitate. He figured he would trust Little Jimmy and breach the fence, scale the five-story brick wall, then climb the flagpole, jump to the small balcony, and cut the glass on the sixth story window, which would provide Vicky the access. He would then leave and wait for Vicky to meet him at the hidden car two miles away. His part should be over in less than fifteen minutes.

Wayne and Little Jimmy had talked in the briefing about the security inside the building and knew it would be top rated and deadly. The guards would be ordered to apprehend or even kill on sight anyone inside the building without a badge. Vicky had said, "We've got no choice. We need to get this done tonight. The target will be on the move soon. We must take our chances."

Wayne had suggested maybe allowing the FBI to storm the building with a warrant. Vicky said, "No. There will be no court for Burnside, and there will be no jury unless we are caught. Then, we will be the ones who need a team of attorneys to defend us. This mission is not on the books. The President and the CIA will both claim full plausible deniability. We are on our own on this mission."

Once they made it to the first six-foot-high chain link fence with three strands of razor wire on top, Eric cut through the fence and proceeded to the second fence. He set up the equipment and pushed the grounding rod as deep as it would go. He glanced at the white sign with large red letters attached to the fence, "WARNING HIGH VOLTAGE." In small print the sign said 2000 volts, do not touch. He poured water around the rod and forced the rod another four inches into the ground. The rod was black, small in diameter, and very sharp on one end. They had to go unnoticed and making a sound using a rubber hammer to drive the rod was not an option. They had chosen to approach the fence in the area which was partly in the shadows. The ground had washed, and they could use a small ditch and a tree in the tall grass to stay hidden. Eric laid out the rubber mat and bent down on his knees on the mat. He connected the clamps on each side of the area he was going to cut. He then inspected the connected rod and the six clamps located around the three-by-three section of the steel fence. The wires connected to his clamps were attached to the top clamp and kept the circuit connected. The upper part of the fence and the wires would allow the 2000 volt current to keep flowing, which also kept the alarm from being activated. Once in place, he hesitated about a second, looked at the fence and the warning sign, reached up, and made the first cut in the metal wire fence with the hand-held cutters. He whispered, "I am still alive. Damn this might really work."

Vicky smiled and noticed Eric hesitated and inhaled a breath. She softly said, "I wondered. I stepped back a couple feet. I thought you might look crisp after you cut into the wire. I can't believe you actually were brave enough to do that. There is no way I would have cut that fence. Did you not read that warning sign?"

He smiled knowing Vicky was joking. They both had a crash virtual course on electrical current provided by an electrical engineer working as a subcontractor for the CIA. He had taken the time to not only explain what they needed to do but also why it would work. Eric quickly made the rest of the cuts and pulled the cut wire out of the way. He made certain Vicky stayed on the rubber mat and did not touch the wire fence as she crossed through the cut-out area onto the grass-covered ground on the other side. They ran bent over to the nook in the brick area where the elevator shaft protruded out of the building. Eric immediately started climbing up the wall as planned. Vicky kept a watch out for the guards. She would glance up at Eric every few seconds as she was on one knee at the edge of the nook wall watching for the guards. Eric reached the top of the wall where the building had a ledge. He had to jump upward and held his position with his grip. He then swung his legs over the concrete wall. He crossed the roof wall. He tied off the rope and dropped it to Vicky. She used the pulley system on her harness to lift her up. Eric helped her across the wall at the top of the fifth floor. Eric did not hesitate. He climbed the flagpole by using his hands and arms to pull back against his legs as he walked up the pole. Vicky kept a watch and made certain the hanging rope was in the shadow of the wall. She knew this was their path to exit if everything went perfect. Eric jumped over to the balcony and dropped his second rope to Vicky. She duplicated the use of the pulley while Eric cut the glass with the circular glass cutter. He very delicately pulled the glass out with the black suction pad and looked at Vicky standing next to him. He placed his finger on his mic and said, "Good hunting. I will see you at the rendezvous spot." He spoke into his mic, "She is going in."

Mia came on the line as she glanced at the stopwatch sitting on her desk, "Roger that. You have twenty-two minutes. You are forty-two seconds ahead of schedule."

Eric was relieved. He had four tasks on this mission with the last one being completed with Vicky entering through the glass window. He wanted to retrieve to safety and make his trip back to the car and wait.

Vicky pulled her Kimber Micro 9MM pistol with suppressor and stepped through the opening. She immediately headed for the apartment. She wanted to enter the apartment, take the shot, and exit back through the window, down the two ropes and exit through the two fences all in forty seconds. Wayne had figured she could be back through the second fence before the security detail could secure the facility. She approached the closed door and pulled her pick, the new model City Rake lock pick. Mia had been able to locate on her review of the architect and contractor computer data the smallest of details. Through the contractor's invoices, she noted not only the manufacture of the lock but the model. Wayne had hurriedly purchased the same model of the Yale lock and set it up on a display for Vicky to practice. Vicky had practiced on picking the lock and perfected the procedure down to three seconds. She eased the pick inside the Yale lock and twisted her right hand. She felt the door lock shift and gently turned the knob. She entered the second hallway and walked to the end of the hall and knew the entrance to the living space doorway and hall were around the corner. She looked at the exterior window and could see the reflection of a guard standing at the interior French doors at the end of the hall. She held her position and waited for the guard to move. She figured any guard protecting Burnside was considered collateral damage. She had no reservations about killing this guard. He should have known better. She took a deep breath and noticed he looked at his watch. She walked out from the hallway and squared her body for the forty-foot shot. The guard looked up from his watch and had no time to react to the danger. The hollow point bullet hit his center forehead as he fell backward against the wall and slid down onto the floor. She quickly ran to his position and pulled his security key card, which was attached to a nylon strap from around his neck and then unlocked the door. She rushed into the foyer and aimed her gun at Burnside and without hesitating pulled the trigger twice. She had turned toward the escape route and started to run back out the door when she noticed he had not moved but actually smiled at her. He was sitting behind a large table. The bullets ricocheted and must have hit the wall to the left. His smile grew and then he said, "I have been waiting on you." He raised his hands, "Well, me and my men have been waiting on you. Please come in."

Vicky noticed movement to her left and looked over. Out walked two men with machine gun pistols with extended magazines pointed at her. She heard someone clear their throat behind her from the hallway and glanced in that direction, and there was another man standing behind her near the dead guard with the same type of pistol. A fourth man walked out from the door to the right with a gun. She was surrounded. She had just walked into a trap.

"Please lower your weapon and place it on the floor. Otherwise, my men will shoot you dead." He hesitated and noticed Vicky was considering her options. He then added, "I assure you my men have been trained and are very skilled with guns. They won't miss."

Vicky thought about her choices. She had no way to win this battle. Matter of fact, she did not see how she could kill any of these men before being shot. She now realized there was a glass between her and Nathanial Burnside which no doubt was bullet proof. She laid her pistol down.

The man behind her quickly walked up and pushed her hard forward and pulled her hood off. He then kicked the gun away from her and placed his gun in his holster pushing her again hard into a chair. He tied her wrists while the other three men stayed in their position with their guns aimed at her.

Nathanial Burnside stood with his diabolic smile and walked out from behind the glass and said, "Pull her shoes off and submerge them in the fish tank just in case she has a hidden transmitter which she can activate with pressure from her foot. Check her for weapons and a radio signal." The man pulled her shoes off and placed them in the tank. The man from the right doorway came over and tied her ankles to the chair with zip ties leaving her bare feet dangling toward the floor. The man ran a signal device around her. He announced she was clean. The man then searched her by rubbing his hands all over Vicky. He looked at her in the eyes with a wide smile as he felt her breasts. He then reached up and held her chin tight as he licked the side of her face and across her ear. She squirmed in disgust as he stepped backward and smiled.

Nathanial stepped closer and said, "You have caused me a lot of problems. You have caused our country a lot of problems. You have killed my men and forced me into hiding. How does it feel to be betrayed? You walked right into my arms." He smiled.

"You are a disgrace and a coward. You use kids who were raped and killed to forward your agenda. You and your men will burn in hell. You did not provide the kids any mercy and whoever betrayed me will have to answer to our Lord."

He smiled and raised his hands, "So, that is what this is all about? You are here because of the kids? Well. Hell, lady, I am sorry." He chuckled. "You have killed my friend Senator Davis. You killed Judge David Larkin. You killed several others who were in line with our idealism. You killed my employee, Travis Borne, all over kids from foreign countries. I had no idea what motivated you. Hell, the Russian nuclear warhead you intercepted set me and my plans back years. We will have to find another." He paused and stared at Vicky. He then smiled. "However, if you would come to work for me, I can make all this better. I need someone with your skill set and passion for the job. Max somehow kept you under the radar. My contacts inside the FBI could not find out about you."

Vicky thought he reminded her of John Wayne, the old actor. She did not want to be manipulated. She accepted her death. "I will never work for you. Go ahead and kill me."

He chuckled again. "You leave me no choice. However, I am not going to kill you. I am going to fly to another hidden location with two of my men. The other two men will deal with you as they see fit. After all, the man you shot in the doorway was their friend, so, I can't say I blame them for wanting to kill you after making the last few hours of your life hell."

"Why?"

He turned in a half circle looking at the surroundings, "Because I can. The Vortex is real, and I will have more power than God. I am so close. You have no way to know what you have done. When you killed Senator Davis, you killed the muscle. Everyone in the Syndicate feared Senator Davis with his proven assassins. There was no one safe from him. He kept everyone in line with fear. When he died, the balance for control shifted, and I had to intervene."

"Your country does not deserve to be double crossed and sold out. You were a general in the United States Army. You used all those kids to promote your psychotic attempt to promote your agenda. Do you really believe the world is going to allow you to take over?"

He turned and looked at Vicky sitting restrained in the chair. "No, I do not believe the world is going to allow any of this. There won't be a world as you know it. My focus is to gain the access and understanding to the Vortex and then I will have the power of God. You have no clue how much control and power that I will be able to command once I have the ability to use the Vortex. We believe once we open the zipper with the uranium from a nuclear bomb, the tunnels in space will be established. There are others who have a plan to deal with the billions of people who have caused over-population. This is all part of the plan. They even have plans to change our genetic code to enhance humanity. As far as the kids, they were a necessary cog in the wheel."

He turned and said, "Get the chopper ready. We need to leave. She works alone. There is no one else with her." The man spoke into his mic telling the pilot. She could hear the chopper engine start. Nathanial Burnside turned and walked out the back door to a stairway with two men following.

The one guard walked in front of Vicky and said, "We can make this easy on you or extremely painful, but either way, it is going to happen. It is what it is." He stared into her eyes with a slight smile.

Vicky looked up into his eyes and realized there was nothing she could do to prevent her death. She felt a warm calm come over her body knowing she was going to die. She immediately had a flashback, to both her parents during her childhood and then when she met her husband and all the fun they had while dating. She remembered him buying her the yellow thong two piece and carrying her to the condo pool while she displayed it. Matt would rub suntan oil on her while over fifty condo guests watched as he would tell them how sweet and innocent she was. She remembered the rush in her body knowing all eyes were on her as Matt rubbed the oil on her back side three times. She remembered looking up and seeing the men standing watching with absolute hunger and animal desires in their eyes. She had a flash of all the men who Matt had set her up with while he watched. He would coach her on how not to be good in bed but how to be great in bed. How to quench a man's desires. How different women around the world had specialized in doing certain things to enhance the experience for the male. What an exquisite and quintessential time period that experience had been in her life. She now loved Matt more than ever and realized he truly loved his God. He had been the perfect husband for her. She also had a flash of Brian Foster, and the guilt she felt for his death. He was the eighteen-year-old who lived in Butler, Tennessee and was starting his freshman year to play baseball for UCLA with his entire adult life in front of him. She had seduced him and then Brian was killed trying to do the right thing after the two witnessed a murder while in hiding. Her entire life had flashed in front of her. She knew her time was about to come to an end. She not only blamed herself for Brian's death but blamed herself for living the self-absorbed lifestyle, and her not spending that time working as a shepherd for the Lord. "May our Lord forgive me of my selfish lifestyle and falling short of my reckoning. Please, Lord forgive me of my many sins. I ask the Lord the following: may the Lord send an avenger to kill these men who stopped me in my task, so they can burn in hell. Amen." She opened her eyes and looked at both men.

The other guard looked hungry for her. He was a big man and said, "Let's tie her face down on top of the table. We can take turns with her ass." He walked over and grabbed her ponytail and held her head back while he tied a rag around her head gagging her. He whispered in her ear, "Honey, you certainly are a pretty thing." He carried her by holding the chair with one hand and her ponytail with the other. Her hands and ankles were still tied to the chair, and he lifted her onto the large table setting her on her knees face down. He was not gentle. He cut her left wrist free, and Vicky tried to fight. He was too strong. He immediately tied her one wrist to the leg of the table and cut the right wrist free and tied her right wrist to the other leg of the table. She was on her knees with the chair still tied to her angles with her head turned and her right side of her face pushed flush with the table while the other man held her in place. The man jumped on the table and cut her feet free while pushing the chair to the floor and then sat on her. The other man pulled her right foot tight and tied it to the leg of the table. The man started pulling her cargo pants down and getting ready to cut her clothes off with his knife.

He said, "I am going to fuck you through this table. Then my friend is going to do the same. We are going to take several rounds on you. Then, I am going to cut you up in small pieces and flush you down the toilet."

Vicky kept kicking and fighting when she felt him release his grip on her cargo pants and heard him fall off the table. She felt her foot being released and heard the other man fall. She thought she heard the unmistakable puff sound of a gun with a depressor attached. She rotated her head forward and glanced toward the door and saw Eric of Newport standing in the doorway with his gun aimed at the two dead men. She moaned through the gag for Eric to hurry and untie her. The target was getting away.

Eric made certain the two men were dead by shooting both in the head and then cut the plastic ties off Vicky. He watched her pull her pants up and reached for her gun sitting on the floor. She had told him to get her shoes from the fish tank, and she immediately ran to the back door and up the stairs. Eric could hear the chopper flying off, and he knew Burnside had gotten away. Vicky had run back down the stairs and yelled, "Let's go."

As she was preparing to rappel down the rope to the fifth floor, she looked at Eric of Newport and said, "Thanks for coming back for me."

They made it through the two fences and ran the two miles to the car. Eric sat down out of breath and started to drive away and asked, "What went wrong?"

Vicky looked over at Eric and said, "You said you were leaving. Why did you not leave?"

Eric was looking forward as he was driving the car double the speed limit. He was concentrating on the curvy road. "I thought you might need some help, so I waited. When you did not return, I entered and saw the guard on the floor in the hall and the double doors ajar. I followed the noise. I am glad I was there for you. You would have done the same for me."

She looked straight ahead with a determined look on her face, and said, "It was a trap. Someone told Burnside I was coming alone for him. He was sitting behind bullet proof glass. He knew when and how. Do not repeat this part to anyone on the team, but I am going to find out who betrayed me. Those men you shot were full of Satan, full of hate, and would have killed again if you had not ended them. Burnside had said they were going to kill me for shooting their friend in the hall. I do not believe that for a second. Those types of people have no true friends. They do the devil's work, because that is who they chose to be. You ask me how it feels to kill someone. Well now you know. For me, killing a person full of evil and stopping them from spreading death is being provided the privilege to act like an angel or an archangel. The Bible says in 2 Kings 19:35, the angel of the Lord put to death over 185,000 Assyrians. I have no regrets with pulling the trigger, and I hope you don't either. It is the other stuff I have done that I regret and ask for forgiveness."

Eric did not say anything. He kept driving, looking straight ahead.

Chapter 9

Delores woke up feeling very satisfied. She opened her eyes and saw Billy Ray with his face within inches of her watching her sleep. She smiled. He said, "Don't worry; I won't ever tell anyone about this. Thank you for allowing me to kiss every inch of your perfect body. Men like me are never so blessed as to be with a high-class intelligent beautiful woman like you. I have truly been blessed."

She smiled and pushed Billy Ray over on his back and started kissing his chest and moving down his body. She looked up and said, "I never had me a redneck before until now. I want to enjoy myself."

***

About 3 p.m. Billy Ray and Delores pulled into the back parking area behind Prestige Clothing Store. He did not see any vehicles in the parking lot except for Little Jimmy's pickup. He walked up the stairs, and Delores followed him to the loft. Billy Ray held the door open. No one was in the loft located above Prestige Clothing. He looked around and immediately started worrying about the mission. He had intentionally left his phone off, and he confirmed he had no missed calls. He had wanted to be part of the mission at first, but he was told to take Delores on the bike ride.

He said, "Little Jimmy might be downstairs working. I will go see him and find out what's up."

Delores took her shoes off and said, "Please give the shoes back to Tiffany and tell her thanks for allowing me to borrow them."

Billy Ray looked at Delores's pretty bare feet and the shiny pink polish and took the shoes and walked out. He went in the back door to Prestige Clothing Store. Little Jimmy was working with a customer. He seemed busy. Little Jimmy walked over and said in a whisper, "The target got away, and we about lost Mrs. Vicky."

Bill Ray said, "Shit. I knew I should have been with her. What is the next move?"

"Mia seems to believe we got a solid lead on the missing science behind the Vortex. The CIA is pushing to locate another angle. The target is well hidden. We are not certain we can locate him fast enough. Max is meeting with the President. It all went to shit. We had a great plan, and Vicky won't talk about what happened except to say the target got away." He turned and walked back to the customer.

Chapter 10

Vicky woke up and pulled her tee shirt on. She had slept in the nude and had shown Matt how much she had missed him. Her body had been peaked with stress, and she used her husband for the release. He enjoyed Vicky being on top and riding him until both were satisfied and tired. She was drinking her second cup of coffee and noticed Matt was in his office reading the Bible. He had been studying since 5 a.m. He had hardly slept. She was thinking about the mission, and what went wrong. She knew it was a high-risk mission, and they could not wait. Now Max was trying to explain to the President what happened. The State Department and the FBI were starting to point fingers. She had failed. She walked into his office. He looked up. "How is your research going?"

"I stopped and started reading the Bible. I was reading about Paul and how hard he kept trying and not giving up even when he was in jail. He knew his time was short, and the Romans would execute him at some point. The Jewish Pharisees had sent a request all the way to Rome and were requesting the Roman leader Caesar Augustus to execute Paul while he was in prison, and yet he still worked endlessly as a Christian. Paul is credited with writing about sixty percent of the New Testament with most being while he was sitting in a jail cell. His writings always help me stay focused. He was a true believer like I strive to be."

"Are you frustrated with your thesis on the Vortex, or you frustrated with me?"

He looked at her and said, "I am never frustrated with you. I love you very much. I fell in love with you when I first met you in the doorway of the library in college. I loved being with you last night." He smiled, "You seemed to have more energy last night. You acted like a wild tiger between the sheets. Come over here."

She walked over and sat down on his lap. They kissed. She pulled away and asked, "What's bothering you? It is not like you to be frustrated with school."

"I picked a subject I thought no one knew about and the next day it was in the Washington Post about being a possible new energy source. So much for being a surprise."

Vicky knew Max had leaked the story to a contact at the paper. With the news breaking, Max felt that was the best way to protect Matt. He would be just another person researching the topic with people all over the world now looking into it. Matt had said every time a new source of energy is mentioned, several hundred institutions around the world start researching the possibilities. The return on investment would be billions.

Vicky asked, "Are you still sad after hearing Professor Ray Baine died right after providing you information about the Vortex? You described him as such a smart and upbeat person."

"Yes. Suicide is a sin. I wished I could have counseled him. Mental illness sometimes can be well hidden by a person. We can sometimes sense depression or bipolar traits but recognizing a borderline personality disorder can be well disguised in the personality." He shakes his head in disbelief. "I was surprised he committed suicide. It has been over four months ago. He was a neat person. He seemed so enthusiastic talking about genetic engineering, and how they could fine-tune the human DNA before the birth of a baby to produce a baby that could never have cancer and about fifty other genetic diseases. They had also learned how to spike the intelligence and physical abilities as well as sharpening other characteristics such as leadership, empathy, and memory capabilities. He must not have had God in his life. I wish I could have been there for him."

Vicky knew he was killed because someone had traced the research on the Vortex to him, but there was no proof. She had hoped the killer had not known the research was sent to Matt. "He was from India and graduated from Princeton undergraduate and received a doctorate degree in biology from Stanford. He was teaching biology at Tennessee Tech located in Cookeville, Tennessee. He still had an open portal at Princeton and located some hidden letters between Albert Einstein and a Jewish professor from Germany dated 1928."

"Did you say he located some old research into the Vortex through the records at Princeton completed by a German prior to World War II?"

Matt nodded his head yes. "The German's name was Epstein. He wrote some letters to Einstein. Professor Baine and others thought the letters were encrypted, but he pulled the letters up on his monitor, and I noticed they were written in a very old dialogue used two thousand years ago. They were written in an old Hebrew Language. I recognized the symbols and letters from my study into Jesus and his pre-training which occurred prior to his teaching. We know Einstein wrote him some letters, but they were not copied and not preserved. According to the letters the two men had met in Germany at the university in Berlin in the late twenties. Einstein had referred to Dr. Epstein as the smartest man to ever live. One of the letters thanked Einstein for the compliment. The letters from Epstein to Einstein suggest an undiscovered electron force that could neutralize gravity on earth and in space by holding molecules steady. Einstein wanted to concentrate on nuclear power and never believed in the Vortex. Epstein was asking for a peer review from Einstein and evidently Einstein declined. He indicated he did not have time. Without Einstein's endorsement to provide credibility to the theory into the Vortex, no one else studied the theory leading to the understanding of the Vortex. Epstein claimed in the last letter, he had completed the research and needed to experiment with the data and then he just disappeared. In the old days between the 1300's and 1950, a researcher had to have a second party to provide a peer review in order to have the study validated for a scientific study. Without Einstein's review, the research never got substantiated. I spent three days translating these letters, and then I knew what I wanted to research. I believe Einstein was just too busy working in the nuclear engineer field to spend time on these. The letters went unnoticed in the archives in Princeton library, and no one ever translated them."

Vicky reached over and kissed her husband. She then got up and said, "Don't give up. I believe in you. I will go on a jog and to the store to get us something to eat."

Vicky called Mia and asked her if she was able to get some sleep. Mia replied she got two hours asleep and now she was on her third energy drink. She could not sleep being puzzled over locating Burnside. Vicky said, "I need to meet with you. I have a long shot, but I need all the information on a professor in Germany by the name Epstein in the 1920's and maybe 1930's. He seems to have disappeared. He might have been Jewish. I will see you in the bonus room."

***

Vicky walked into the bonus room and noticed Little Jimmy sitting at the table eating out of a large box of food from a local Chinese restaurant. Wayne had just walked in and sat down. He looked to be angry. Eric stood up and started throwing darts. Billy Ray walked in from the balcony. He looked tired. Mia walked in while drinking a bottle of water. She also looked tired. Vicky said, "We can't win them all. It is after 5 p.m. You guys will need to get some rest."

Wayne looked up and started to say something when the door opened, and Delores walked in wearing the same clothing she had on the prior day when she had met part of the unit in the bonus room before she changed clothes for the motorcycle ride. She looked around at everyone and asked, "What happened?" No one said anything for the moment and Billy Ray ducked his head.

Vicky said, "After you left yesterday, Mia located the intel that placed Burnside in the Viatect Corporate office outside of Annapolis. We did not have time to plan. We hit him, and he escaped. Three of his guards were killed."

Delores was obviously upset. She blurted out, "You didn't wait on me and my team of FBI agents. We could have gotten a warrant and captured him. We need him. The FBI has fast response teams set up for that type of mission. I should have been in the loop" She looked at Mia and said, "Please tell me you can locate him again." Mia shook her head no. She looked at Vicky, "What were you thinking?"

She stepped backward and looked at the faces of everyone while Eric kept throwing darts. "Damn you.

You waited until I left and then went for the target." She looked harshly at Billy Ray.

"I have another lead. It is a long shot, but worth taking. Burnside said he is close to understanding the Vortex. What if we can beat him to the science? At some point, we will locate him, but in the meantime, what if we were able to acquire the science before him?"

Delores said, "Burnside may jump the fence. He may realize his only chance to live is to change teams." She looked at Vicky knowing Vicky was very much already aware of the problem. Delores then asked, "What is your plan?"

Mia listened and said, "I will see what I can locate."

No one else said anything. Vicky looked at everyone and said, "You all need to get some rest. I am going home to eat." She walked out.

Chapter 11

She had told her boss at The Children Around the World organization she needed a couple days off. It had been two days since the mission had failed. Her job working to raise money for the group The Children Around the World was her official job. Her CIA job was always in stealth. Vicky was surprised when Ethan Howard had called her. He announced the school they had funded through the contributions in Bolivia, South America was getting ready to open.

Ethan Howard said, "I wanted you to see the grand opening in two days. I will send you the details. The mayor of the small community wants to meet you and personally thank you. You did a great job. The hospital for the kids will also open soon. It is behind schedule but moving forward. The opening will be in the news and covered around the world. This is a big deal for us."

Vicky thought how nice. "I might be able to fly down for the day, maybe two."

She knew she would love to see the school, and she needed a break. She knew Matt was upset with her traveling so much. He got frustrated when she missed church on Sundays. She knew it did not look good for the wife of the preacher to miss church. She felt guilty. She wanted to support her husband.

***

Vicky told Matt about the school and showed him the articles on the internet about how The Children Around the World had made all this possible. She acted excited to be part of this group, which made the school and hospital conceivable. Matt could see the excitement in her eyes. He said he understood, and she agreed to fly back home the next day. She went into her closet to retrieve an outfit. She smiled picking out her heels, the backless dress that buttoned up the front. She placed the items in her overnight bag. She opened her chest drawer and pulled out her white lace thong panties. She smiled as she looked at her panties before she placed them in her overnight bag. She wondered about Michael, the man she had met in Argentina on a prior mission. As she stood in her closet, she hesitated while rubbing her finger across her thong feeling the material and wondering if she would ever see Michael again. She knew she would never forget the sexual excitement while in his bed. He was the son of Vance Canteno, the leader of the Canteno Cartel. She still remembered that night and the special time they had spent in each other's arms. She had cried when she told her husband. Matt had been understanding, and he knew of her struggles. She knew he loved her.

***

The small private jet landed, and the taxi was waiting. She checked into the motel, changed clothes, and walked out of her second-floor room headed for the elevator. She noticed the cleaning cart on wheels sitting in the hall unattended. She turned the corner to walk down the hall toward the elevator as she walked into the needle. She looked up into the man's eyes as he pushed her down on the floor and covered her mouth with a rag. She immediately recognized the smell of chloroform. He pulled the needle out of her stomach and placed a gag in her mouth as she rolled her head to the side, and noticed another man appear with a knife and cut the carpet on the floor in a square. She could see but was paralyzed. The men rolled her up inside the carpet. She tried to yell for help but could not speak. She realized she was going to pass out as the rag was held compressed against her mouth and nose. When she awoke, she was still paralyzed and disoriented.

She was carried down the hall and the emergency stairs, out the back door, and placed in a waiting van. The chloroform effects had dissipated, but the shot effects had not. She could not move her extremities or talk. The van immediately accelerated and drove away. She was trying to wake and keep track of the curves in the road and listening for sounds. The van suddenly stopped, and she was carried to a helicopter. Vicky thought they would throw her out the helicopter door while flying over the mountains or ocean. She knew there were only two groups of people in this area of the world who had access to helicopters: one being the government and the other being the cartels. She also knew the government would not roll her in cut carpet after drugging her. She kept trying to move. Her arms were starting to have feeling, although she could not move them. Her legs were bound by the carpet she was rolled up in. The tightness of the carpet prevented her arms and legs from moving. She could hardly breathe. She had to tilt her head upward to breathe through the opening at the end of the carpet. She finally was able to spit the gag out of her mouth.

She felt with her wrist. She realized she still had her pistol in her dress pocket. She knew if she could get her hand on her pistol, she would shoot the next person she saw. The chopper was in the air for close to an hour when it finally landed. She was carried to a waiting vehicle and placed in the rear hatch. The road was very rough with potholes as the vehicle sped around curves. The vehicle would brake hard from time to time and then speed up.

When the vehicle finally stopped, she was carried and placed down on the floor. She heard a voice, "Mrs. Cruz. I am Pedro Guints. This was all done for your protection. Mr. Juan Canteen wanted to meet you. I am going to cut the ties holding the carpet and let you out."

Vicky gritted her teeth and said, "Pedro, I am going to kill you for this."

"Then, I will untie you and leave. You can unroll yourself. Please don't be mad at me. I was just following orders."

She felt the tightness of the carpet give where the straps were cut and heard footsteps hurry away and a door open and shut. She immediately rolled over and felt the gun pushing in on her hip each time she rolled. She rolled over three times and struggled to sit up. Her hair was a mess, and she brushed it out of her eyes. She looked around and recognized the great room. She said to herself, "I am going to kill that bastard."

She jumped up and figured Juan would either come through the front door or down the hall. She sat down on the large kitchen table. She took one heel off and set it next to her and loosen the strap on the other heel. She wanted to be ready to fight. She had remembered on an earlier mission being at the Catholic Church and the priest describing how Juan was the cartel's enforcer. He had people killed daily. She figured she could shoot Juan and then hide behind the table and shoot as many cartel men as she could before they killed her. She heard the doorknob to the large exterior door turn and in walked Juan. He closed the door behind himself. He had a stern look on his face as he walked toward Vicky. She held her left hand up for him to stop. He held his hands out to his side gesturing and said, "My queen. I am truly sorry about this, but this was the only way to protect you."

Vicky aimed her pistol at Juan's chest through her pocket in her dress. He gestured, "I am truly sorry my queen but this."

She cut him off in mid-sentence. She knew Juan would never take orders from her or anyone, and she wanted a better reason to kill him. She demanded, "Take off all your clothes and throw them in a pile."

Juan hesitated. Vicky knew he would have heard the story of her having to stand in front of his father, his brother Michael and two other men naked a few months ago during a prior mission. She also knew she would not miss at this range. The pistol was still well concealed in her baggy dress pocket. To her surprise Juan took his tie off, and then his shirt. She was surprised to notice how hairy he was. Most men tried to have excessive body hair removed. He had thick hair on his shoulders, back and his chest which looked like a rug. He was a big strong-looking man. He took his shoes and socks off and then his pants. He looked at her as he removed his underwear. Vicky stared at him and was surprised he had complied.

Her long hair was all out of place, and she tried to use her left hand to push it out of her face. There was an awkward couple of seconds. Her other shoe accidently fell from her foot. Juan looked at it and asked, "May I pick it up for you?"

Vicky shook her head no. She harshly said, "Why do you call me your queen? The last time I met you, you resisted even giving me a glass of orange juice. You acted like you wanted to kill me."

Juan remembered that morning seeing Vicky sitting in his father's chair at the dining room table in nothing but his brother's dress shirt. "I need your help."

"Where is your father and brother?"

"They were both killed. They were gunned down in a very orchestrated hit."

Vicky was surprised. She looked at Juan very angrily, "I am sorry to hear of your loss. What does this have to do with me?"

"My wife was also killed."

"You know I have a gun aimed at you."

He did not show any indifference. He shrugged his shoulders and raised his hands without a concern.

"When did this happen? What is this all about?"

Vicky could tell Juan was becoming more relaxed, and his body was becoming aroused as he looked at her. She glanced at her lap and realized the split in her dress was exposing her upper most thigh. Juan said, "This happened eight days ago. I am going to find out who did this, and I will have my revenge. We captured one of the men. It is just a matter of time until he talks. I have no one I trust. Michael said I could trust you."

"What else did Michael say?"

"You were the bravest person he had ever met, and I could trust you to do the right thing."

"What else did Michael say?"

"You were the best lover he ever had." Vicky stared at him. He said, "I need your help. Money won't be an issue. Just name your price. I need you to locate a safe home in America for my two kids. They are not safe here in South America. The federal police and local police are all dirty. They know my business has been wounded and the outside cartels are like vultures. The police will sell out to the highest bidder. They will come after my kids to get to me. My kids will not be allowed to live." He made a pleading gesture with his arms and hands. "My kids need your help. I cannot stand to think about them being tortured."

Vicky realized he was trying to protect his children. She knew too well what would happen to the kids if the other cartels could get their hands on them. He wanted them out of the way and protected, so he could start his war. Vicky knew he was going to kill the people behind this attack. She felt angry with herself that she made this proud man take off all his clothes and submit to her, a man who loved his kids so much, and he wanted to protect them. Vicky could not help but notice the naked man in front of her. He looked like a werewolf with big shoulders, strong arms and all the body hair. She knew this was an opportunity. She thought about the Apostles and their sacrifices and the need for contacts in this part of the world. She stood up on the table, "Bring that rubber door mat over and lay it on the table."

She watched as he bent down and grabbed the mat and laid it on the table next to her feet. She reached behind her neck and released the one button holding up her dress as she stared into Juan's eyes. She did not break eye contact with Juan as she removed her thong. She used her thong to remove the hot light bulb from the nearest chandelier hanging over that end of the table. She looked at him as she dropped the bulb and panty on the floor. She stepped on the rubber mat and stuck three of her fingers into the light socket. "You may service your queen."

Juan had watch men being tortured with car batteries hooked up to them. He knew how much the electric shock could hurt. He also noted the men applying the torture always stood on the rubber mats. He walked over next to the table and placed one of his hands on the rubber mat and the other around Vicky's waist and pulled her toward him. When he was about one inch away, he saw the blue spark shoot out toward his tongue and felt the tingle as the spark hit the end of his tongue. He felt her reach with her other hand and placed it to the back of his head pushing his face into her lap. He could hear her moaning and feel her squirming with every touch of his tongue. He struggled to hold her mid-section still as she kept rotating her hips.

***

On the plane ride, she thought she might know the perfect parents. Their son had been killed by a rogue Tennessee Highway Patrolman. They would be super foster parents. Having two beautiful kids would help them move on in life. She would mention it to Matt, and they could meet with Brian Foster's parents. Juan had left over a million dollars in her name in a bank to use to raise the kids which could be used for nice clothing, food, automobiles, and private Catholic schools. Juan no doubt wanted the best for his kids and trusted her with their lives. Vicky thought Juan might be so full of hate and high on his drug product; he might be suicidal. Either suicide by cop or suicide in a gang fight. Either way he would be killed.

She then thought she could have been killed at Viatect, and now she thought she was going to be killed on this trip. She knew she was going to have to learn from her mistakes. How many lives did she have left? She remembered thinking back to the mission at Viatect. Eric of Newport had told her after cutting the glass, he was leaving and would wait on her at the car. Both she and Eric had mics turned on for Mia, Wayne, and Little Jimmy to listen in the operation. The only reason she was alive was Eric did not leave. When she entered the master suite, Burnside was waiting on her. Someone had set her up. She cringed at the possibilities.

Chapter 12

Mia explained the long shot. Vicky had read the report from Max. Bill Duff and the Spanish assassin she had shot in the head at the hospital in Butler were thought to have killed two German physics professors at the Humboldt College in Berlin. Both had been tortured with toenails removed. Vicky thought there was a connection. She told Wayne what she suspected and her plan. He had a sudden flashback to Bill Duff and when he was tortured with his one nail being forceable removed with the needle nose pliers. He walked over to the window trying to hide the grimace on his face of the flashback.

***

Vicky had told everyone to meet her at the restaurant in Gallatin located in north Tennessee a few miles out of Nashville at 3:30 p.m. She remembered Little Jimmy eating a box of Chinese food and thought what a good way to relax while they discussed the plan.

***

Little Jimmy and Billy Ray had driven together in Little Jimmy's decked-out pickup. As they exited the truck, they noticed a baby blue with a white stripe Lamborghini with dark tinted windows pulling into the parking lot and parked next to them. Eric of Newport rolled down the driver side dark tinted window and asked, "What do you think?"

Little Jimmy smiled and Billy Ray said, "I thought you were supposed to go unnoticed, be inconspicuous. She is not going to like this."

Eric got out of the car and stood back with a proud smile. Little Jimmy asked, "How much and what year?"

"I got a good deal. The waiting list for a new model is a half year wait. This one is three years old."

Little Jimmy looked at Eric and tilted his sunglasses down. "How much?"

"I got a great deal. One-hundred-eighty-six thousand."

Billy Ray and Little Jimmy both shook their heads and laughed. They looked over at the nice restaurant in the next parking lot. They saw a man in a new model Camaro drive into the parking space and a very attractive brunette stepped out of the passenger side. The couple walked into the restaurant. Little Jimmy said, "Maybe you should have bought a Camaro. Look what comes with them, those legs go all the way up to her ass."

The two men bent down and looked in the window at the interior. They noticed an older model Toyota Tacoma with large tires and raised bumper and extended trailer hitch pull into the parking lot with a blonde driving. She glanced at the three men as she drove by. She turned the truck around and backed into the Camaro with the extended trailer hitch making an indention in the plastic Camaro bumper cover. She pulled away and Eric waved to her. She stopped and rolled her window down with a smile on her face. Eric could not help but tell she was a very pretty country girl. Eric said, "The owner of the Camaro just walked into the restaurant with a very pretty brunette lady. He had on a red shirt if you want to locate him in the restaurant and tell him you accidently hit his parked car."

The young lady asked, "Was she really pretty?"

All three men said "Yea, she was very nice looking" with Billy Ray saying she was "eye candy". The girl raised her sunglasses up onto her forehead and smiled again at them. She placed the truck into reverse and this time hit the Camaro really hard pushing it over the curb at the sidewalk. She pulled forward to the same spot. Eric could not help but laugh slightly. He then said, "If you really want to get back at your ex, let him see you having a drink with me over at Hicks Brewery Bar and Grill. That will make him mad."

Little Jimmy could tell Eric was attracted to this spunky little lady in the white tee shirt and the holey jeans. Little Jimmy shook his head, "This isn't going to end well."

Little Jimmy and Billy Ray walked into the restaurant and Eric of Newport waited on the young lady to park and walk to the door of the restaurant. They had a seat at the table near the bar.

Wayne had provided a ride for Mia. Vicky drove by herself, and Delores had been in Nashville going over the FBI's plan to locate the rogue NSA director.

Vicky recognized Little Jimmy's truck and parked next to the truck and then inspected the Lamborghini as she walked through the parking lot. She walked up to the table. Eric introduced his new friend, Casey, to Vicky. Mia walked over to the pool table where Wayne, Little Jimmy and Billy Ray were playing 9 ball. Mia mentioned Vicky has arrived.

Vicky smiled at Casey and said, "Hi. There must be someone in here doing well financially. There is a baby blue Lamborghini in the parking lot." She looked around inside the bar and then noticed Eric of Newport appearing nervous. Vicky asked, "Eric, who's Lamborghini is that in the parking lot?"

"That would be mine." As soon as he said it, the front door busted wide open and in walked a tall dark headed man in a red shirt and a lady following. He walked up to the table and said, "You God damn bitch. You hit my car." He looked at Eric and said, "I might not hit a bitch, but I am going to drag your sorry ass into the parking lot and beat the shit out of you."

Eric looked straight ahead and before he could say anything, Casey said, "Maybe you will think before you cheat on another woman."

Casey looked at the woman. "He will cheat on you after he gets you to make his car payments for him. He can't keep a job."

The brunette stared at her.

The man was now embarrassed, somewhat under the influence, and mad. He said, "Let's go outside God damn you. I'm going to stomp you a new one." Eric did not move. He sat still without any emotion.

Vicky now was starting to get angry. She said, "Please calm down, and please stop using our Lord's name in vain. He is not going to the parking lot with you. You need to leave."

The hostess, waitress, and cook came over to the bar area and were watching.

The man leaned over in Vicky's face and said, "Listen here, you bitch, I'm going to beat his God damn ass, and keep your opinions to your fucking self."

Vicky could smell his bad breath and without any hesitation Vicky placed her left hand on the back of the bar stool next to her and raised her body up off the bar stool and came down with her right fist on the bridge of his nose. They heard a loud pop, and he fell straight backward with blood running out his nose. He appeared to be startled. Casey said very loudly, "Holy Hell. I really like her."

The police had already been called. Eric could see them coming through the parking lot in two different cruisers. Wayne, Mia, Little Jimmy, and Billy Ray came over to the table and sat down. Eric looked at Casey and said, "You might want to slip out the back door."

Casey said, "They have my truck boxed in. Where would I go?"

Eric said, "Here is my address and the keys to the blue and white Lamborghini. Be careful with it."

She smiled and kissed him on the cheek and took the keys and went out the emergency rear door.

The female officer walked in with a younger male officer. The man was standing up with blood all over his red shirt. She looked at the table and then at the younger officer, "Take him out and secure his statement."

The man said, "The hell with you. Someone hit me when I was not looking. I am going to kick their ass."

He pushed the officer and walked toward the table. The officer responded by reaching and grabbing his arm trying to hold him in place. The man did not like being touched. The two started wrestling and fell to the floor. The man was getting ready to hit the officer when Little Jimmy grabbed his arm and pinned him to the floor with his weight. "You need to settle down."

The female officer noticed the pearl handled pistol in Little Jimmy's shoulder holster when he bent over as she stood back and watched her male partner stand.

She said, "Gun. Hold it right there." She placed her hand on her gun but did not pull her pistol.

Vicky said, "We all have a carry permit for our guns."

"Who else has a gun?"

Vicky's entire team acknowledged they all were carrying a gun except Billy Ray. "Okay, we all are going downtown and sort this out. Those permits do not make it okay to have a gun inside a bar where alcohol is being served." She looked at the officer and said, "David, cuff him and take him in your cruiser. The rest of you come outside with me."

When they got outside, she took everyone's gun except Wayne's, who had his federal license. Billy Ray was not carrying a gun, and the officer said, "You can leave. The rest of you will need to follow me downtown to get your guns and identification back. The sheriff will want to review this mess."

They walked into the Sumner County Sheriff's office, and the man was behind bars with blood all over his shirt and face. He was sitting down on a bench in an empty cell.

The lady officer said, "The sheriff is busy from a house fire last night where a lady died, but he will be right with you."

The team could see three men in an inner office with the blinds pulled open to the conference room. An officer was sitting at a table and talking to an older gentleman sitting across from him. The gentleman was almost in tears and appeared to be very upset. The third man had on a sheriff's uniform and was leaning against the wall watching the interview.

Another younger officer walked into the office without acknowledging anyone in the office except the female officer. He said to the female officer, "That was hers. It was in the gift box in the trunk of her car." He pointed to a long red nightgown lying on the desk.

He then said, "I just got the security film from the county where the elementary school is located across the street. The county personnel said the disc shows the fire." as he held up the disc. He walked over to the desk and laid the form on the file and then walked over to his desk and plugged in a floppy disc, turned on the computer, and watched the disc with the small home burning.

The female officer walked over and stood to the side and watched the video. He started watching the video a second time. Little Jimmy walked by the red nightgown lying in the tray and flipped the tag over and read the label while glancing at the full-length nightgown. Vicky walked over and opened the file on the detective's desk and looked at the top picture of a burned body with a fully intact skull with a hole in the back of the head. The rest of the skeleton was burned with no noticeable bones in the ashes. The foundation was the only part of the home left. She noticed the appliances and the water heater were all burned, but the metal could be noted in the fire debris. Mia and Eric kept watching the tape of the fire over the shoulder of the deputy.

The sheriff was the older man with grey hair standing to the side leaning against the block wall as the other two men were sitting at a table facing each other talking on the other side of the window in the conference room. The sheriff received the phone call and as he listened, he looked out the window of the office at Vicky standing at the desk of the detective who was conducting the interview with the older man. He noticed Eric and Mia watching the video from behind his deputies. He saw Little Jimmy placing the nightgown back into the tray. He walked out of the office over to the desk and said, "That is not something you should be reviewing. The lady died in the home fire last night." He closed the folder and took it and laid it on the young officer's desk and said, "File this." The officer watching the video was surprised that someone had walked over to the detective's desk and was looking at the file. He jumped up and took the file.

The sheriff looked at the group, "I just received a call from the United States Justice Department stating I need to give you your weapons back and allow you to leave. That was damn fast."

The sheriff looked at the group making eye contact with each of them. "Do you know how often the Justice Department has called this office in the past thirty-nine years. Never. They said they would have the State Attorney General call me in a few seconds. I guess you can have your weapons and ID's."

The group all got their weapons, and the three officers watched. Vicky finally said, "That is an interesting murder case you have."

"What murder case. She died in her sleep from the fire. You saw the photos in the file. She is burned to a crisp. We have her dental records, and they are a perfect match. We think she fell asleep while smoking."

Vicky said, "She was shot in the back of the head and the fluid leaked out of her skull. That is the only reason you were able to locate her skull fully intact. Otherwise, her skull would have exploded caused by the pressure from within her skull if the fluids in the skull had not leaked out prior to the fire. The only explanation for the hole in the back of the head is a small caliber bullet. You need to carefully sift through the debris and locate that bullet."

Little Jimmy, now leaning against the wall, said, "That nightgown is not a fake. That is a Schnell made in France with real silk. It cost seven-hundred dollars at Macy's. I heard your deputy say she was a maid. I am sorry, but someone with a lot of money purchased that for her."

Mia said, "The tape has been tampered with and spliced. There is close to five minutes missing on that tape. You can tell when the video is distorted in two places prior to the fire. Someone had access to the recording and altered it."

Eric of Newport said, "The person had to know something about the security system. The average person would not have the ability to use the mirror to divert the signal for the five minutes and then clean it up by splicing in the same feed in a loop. Someone with a certain skill set could only make that happen."

The sheriff and the two deputies looked at each person as the conversation was on going.

Vicky looked at the sheriff and said, "The older gentleman in the room being interviewed did not kill the woman."

The sheriff turned and glanced at his detective talking with the man behind the one-way glass in the interview room. "He loved her and purchased this very expensive gown for her, but he is not the killer." Vicky could see the pain of loss in his face. He was not faking. "Who had the most to gain from her death? Who would want to prevent her from marrying this man?"

The Sheriff looked at everyone in the room. He asked, "Who are you people?"

Vicky did not answer the question but asked, "How much money is the older gentleman worth, and who is the next of kin? Who would want her dead? Follow the money."

The young deputy holding the folder said, "He is loaded. He owns over a thousand acres with fifteen natural gas wells. The wells are all connected to one gas line which is connected to the national gas line system. His daughter's husband installs the security systems in the county."

The sheriff looked at the deputy and said, "Bring him in for questioning, and we need to go look for the bullet. He better have a good alibi, and a good explanation to splice that tape. He is going to be looking at murder one."

The sheriff then looked at the man in the red shirt with blood on his chin and shirt sitting in the jail area. He obviously had a broken nose. "What do I do with him?

What are the possible charges?" The sheriff turned and looked at the two deputies.

Vicky could tell the sheriff did not want to move forward with an arrest. She could tell he had a reservation about charges being filed against the young man. Vicky asked, "How do you know him?"

The sheriff hesitated a little and then said, "I go to church with his parents. The parents are good people."

Vicky said, "He got what he deserved with the broken nose. As far as I am concerned the worst charge is that he used our Lord's name in vain." They turned and walked out.

Chapter 13

Delores, Wayne, and Billy Ray pulled into the parking lot. They all got out of the three vehicles and walked over to the others. Delores looked at Vicky and said, "I understand you hit a man and broke his nose."

Eric said, "Yes, she did. He got what he deserved. He used our Lord's name in vain, and she nailed him coming down on the bridge of his nose with a right fist." The men all smiled.

Vicky, wanting to change the conversation, announced, "We are going to Germany. It is a long shot, but we need a certain man. He might not have what we need, but he is the great grandson and descendant of Professor Epstein. Professor Epstein was the Jewish German professor who completed in-depth research into the Vortex, but then disappeared. Mia has located letters written in an old Hebrew language, the old Jewish language which has been forgotten. The letters were to Albert Einstein in the late 1920's and the early 1930's before Epstein vanished.

Epstein told Einstein the power of the Vortex had more power than an atomic bomb. He tried to talk Einstein into switching his field of study from atomic power to the Vortex. Einstein's equation E=mc(2) contradicted this theory according to Einstein, but Epstein indicated there was missing data. He also noted an undercurrent of hatred for the Jewish people and was starting to get a little uneasy with the new regime taking over in Germany. He was Jewish, he wrote, and he needed to protect his family. Then, he just disappeared. Our mission is to locate his research. Mia was able to trace the only living relative to a professor at Humboldt College in Berlin. This person of interest was well hidden. Someone did not want him found.

We had Eric visit the library in Princeton and steal one of the envelopes sent to Einstein. We traced the DNA from where Epstein licked the envelope to seal the letter. The man is single and seems to have a very active social life. Social media has him out with several different coeds over the past few years. He teaches English at Humboldt University."

Delores spoke up. "I am going to be on the inside on this mission."

Vicky looked at her. "What would be your cover?"

Wayne knew Delores did not trust Vicky after the prior mission. He also sensed a slight ripple of some type between the two women. His boss in the State Department wanted to be involved even if the case was located outside the United States. The report of what happened at Viatect was that the CIA had not played ball with the FBI and the State Department and now the pressure was being applied to the CIA to be more forthcoming on this case. Every agent in the State Department, FBI and CIA wanted Burnside and the opportunity to unravel the identity of the Syndicate. This break could move any ambitious agent upward through the invisible glass ceilings in the said agencies. Max knew there had been too many agencies involved and now there were too many agents involved. Vicky had talked with Max and heard his complaints with him having to attend meeting after meeting in the White House and the other Federal Offices.

Wayne had tried to defend their actions at Viatect to his boss in the State Department, but he was told in the future to report to his boss first.

Wayne suggested, "She could go as a reporter for an American newspaper researching colleges abroad. She could interview American students in Germany and the

German faculty. It would appear to be an article that could provide the University good press in America."

Vicky was aware of the pressure being applied to Wayne from his boss. She also understood where Delores and the FBI stood with them being involved. She looked at Wayne and shook her head okay.

***

Eric on the ride back to his rental home in Butler, Tennessee with Little Jimmy and Billy Ray was concerned about giving his keys to Casey. He had just met her, and she freely mentioned she was a dancer at the Pink Poodle Strip Club in Nashville. She even said she enjoyed her job with no regrets. That was where she met the man in jail for resisting arrest. Eric had provided her his address and off she went in his one-hundred-eighty-six-thousand-dollar Lamborghini. He was now feeling a little apprehensive about her driving off in his car. After all, his prior career was stealing cars. He knew how easy it was and the temptation to steal a vehicle worth that much.

He was listening to Little Jimmy and Billy Ray talking about the new assignment and then football. Billy Ray had questioned him about what he was going to do if the car was gone or was wrecked. He and Little Jimmy laughed when Billy Ray mentioned how Casey seemed to like to back into other vehicles. They started betting on the number of dents in his car. He was sitting in the back seat hoping she was honest and a safe driver. He certainly liked her appearance in the distressed jeans, white tee shirt, cowboy boots, and most of all her bubbly personality and her beautiful crossbite smile.

When Little Jimmy pulled into the rental home driveway, Eric saw the rear of his car. He was certainly relieved as Little Jimmy pulled further into the driveway. The three men saw Casey washing his car wearing only a red bra and a red thong; he became excited.

Billy Ray said, "Let's park and watch her wash the car. She looks like the girl in the old Paul Newman movie where Paul was in prison working on a chain gang in Georgia. My old man would watch the episode repeatedly when I was little. The girl washed the car for one minute and thirty-seven seconds while the men in prison watched her from the ditch of the road in front of her home. The scene is known as one of the most seductive scenes in television history."

Little Jimmy said, "She acts like she does not know we are watching her, but she knows what she is doing."

Eric took a deep breath with relief and thought this might turn out better than he could have ever imagined. He looked at Casey with soap suds all over her bent over the top of the car reaching for the middle roof area and said as he opened the rear door, "Thanks for the history class on girls washing cars and the ride. Who the hell is Paul Newman?" He looked at his friends, smiled, closed the door, as he walked toward his car and Casey.

Chapter 14

The group met in a Villa near the campus of the Humboldt University in Berlin. The CIA had the Villa available, and the local agents had been assigned to provide backup and surveillance on Professor Patrick Roust. He lived with a student who was obtaining her master's degree in English.

Billy Ray said, "He seems to like living on college campus near the coeds. So far, all the videos of him show him talking to young pretty ladies."

Vicky and the group watched the video of him walking to his class and of him walking to his rental home.

Delores added, "He seems to always have that cane with him. Why would he have a walking cane?"

Wayne said, "I bet that is a hidden sword. Enlarge the photo of the cane and see if there is a switch or a seam where the handle could pull out."

Eric said, "He is too young to need assistance walking with no history in his medical reports of him being injured. I can guarantee you Patrick Roust has a sword hidden in the cane. I bet he has a history of fencing."

Mia enlarged the photo.

Wayne said, "Yes, that is a sword. See the seam which appears to be a decorated band near the handle."

Vicky said, "Maybe we need to look in his office without him knowing it. There might be some information he has hidden with regards to the Vortex. We are going to need to contact him at some point, but first, we need to know as much as possible about him. We need to know if he knows anything about the Vortex. We need him to trust us and be willing to work with us."

Wayne said, "I agree."

Mia pulled up the office building.

Wayne looked over her shoulder. "The building is old looking. We will need to go through the window on the third floor."

Eric said, "At least the buildings are getting shorter. The last two have been way higher than this."

Billy Ray said, "Your job is getting easier. We will need to cut your pay."

Little Jimmy said jokingly, "Don't cut his pay. He still has to pay for that car."

Eric smiled, "I have not been paid for the last job yet."

Little Jimmy said, "I will send in the invoice next week. By the way, where is the Lamborghini while you are here in Germany? I hope you have it locked up inside a garage somewhere."

Eric sat in silence. Billy Ray said, "Don't tell me. You let Casey drive it while you are gone."

Vicky turned her head around quickly and said, "You let her drive your Lamborghini, and you won't offer me an opportunity to drive it."

Mia asked, "What do you know about Casey anyway?"

Little Jimmy and Billy Ray laughed. Wayne said, "We all know what he likes about her."

Vicky and Dolores both rolled their eyes at him.

Eric said, "She seems to take care of it. She likes to wash it, and she says she lives with no regrets. Besides, her truck is getting the rear bumper repaired, and she needed some help with transportation."

***

Eric said, "This should be easy. The building was built in 1959 and has no window security. The latches can be flipped with a thin piece of metal. I won't need to cut any glass."

Wayne said, "You know what to look for. We need to know if he has information about the Vortex. Let's get this done."

***

Eric made certain the rope was tied off securely and latched to his harness. He backed over the wall and dropped down two floors to the window. Wayne looked over the wall and said, "There is a security man just turned the corner walking down the walkway."

Vicky came on the secure line in a rushed tone. "Billy Ray, you and Delores need to keep him looking at you. Make it look like you two are romantically involved. You need to keep his eyes looking down."

"Roger that."

Vicky smiled to herself thinking of those two together. Delores would hate the thought of her and Billy Ray together with him holding her tight. She thought of his redneck tattoo on Billy Ray's neck and smiled to herself.

The two had been able to keep their relationship private. They spent just about every night together in each other's arms. Billy Ray looked into Delores' eyes and smiled, and Delores returned the smile.

Eric came on the line and said, "I am hanging in the open up here. Billy Ray, you need to kiss her on the mouth to keep the guard looking at you."

Delores looked Billy Ray in the eyes and kept smiling. Billy Ray leaned in close and said, "He is coming this way." He kissed Delores on the neck. He kept inching up her neck. He came online again and said, "He is twenty-feet away and looking right at us."

Mia came online and said, "Delores you need to bend your leg and allow your shoe to fall off, so he will look at your foot as he passes."

Vicky looked over at Mia in surprise. Mia looked over and said, "If the guard is heterosexual, he will look at her foot as he passes them."

Vicky said, "Drop your shoe, Delores. Eric is in the open." The couple kissed with Dolores letting her shoe drop. When the guard was even, Billy Ray broke off the kiss and waved at the guard. The guard smiled and kept walking. Wayne was watching and noticed the officer turn the corner at the end of the block. He said, "You are clear."

Eric slid the thin sheet metal device through the crack in the old metal window and pushed the latch open. He entered and released the harness. He went to the desk and looked through every drawer securing photos of all items. He then went to the file cabinet and pulled the files and photographed all the contents. Half an hour later he announced, "I have secured photos of everything. I am now going to look around to see if there is a hidden nook." He looked at the ceiling with eight-inch crown molding. There was no sign it had been removed in years with over paint from the ceiling still showing. The walls and ceiling were old painted plaster. He looked in the air vent in the upper wall. Nothing. He looked around the walls behind the one picture. He looked through the books on the small bookshelf. He noticed the old baseboard had been reset near the wall heater. The paint over the nail heads was never refilled. He pried the baseboard off with his knife and located a folder hidden behind the baseboard in the cut out in the plaster. He secured the photos of the contents. He said, "I found a hidden folder with paper articles about two men being killed. There are photos of the two men. The article is written in German."

Vicky asked, "Do you see anything else in the wall cavity?"

Eric laid on the floor and shined his head lamp with the camera attached into the wall cavity. The camera was recording all virtually for Mia to review later. The entire feed was live with Mia and Vicky seeing everything Eric was seeing. Eric looked under the desk and two chairs, making certain the chairs still had the factory upholstery. He inspected the wall heater and the fan. Vicky said, "Okay, we got everything."

Eric walked over to the window. He could see Billy Ray and Delores still at their post. He smiled to himself. "I am leaving. I see the guard on the walkway. Billy Ray, you need to kiss Delores again and keep the guard's eyes looking down. I am in the open."

Eric continued smiling to himself as he started ascending back up the wall. Billy Ray pulled Delores into his arms and kissed her on the mouth.

Wayne walked over to the wall and looked up and down the street from his perch on the top of the building. "I do not see a guard on the street. Where is the guard?" Wayne looked at Billy Ray and Delores doing their part kissing on the street.

Eric said, "Maybe it was something in my eye."

Vicky started laughing and said, "You two can stop kissing. Let's close this up. I will see all of you at the villa."

Chapter 15

They reviewed all the contents of the folders. Most were class records and teaching literature for the past classes. There was also the updated roll. The professor seemed to rely on the automation system more than paper filings.

Vicky read the two articles to the group. Wayne said, "The only item we located that could be related to the Vortex and the Syndicate are the articles hidden behind the baseboard about the two professors who were killed and his letter to them asking them to review information pertaining to gravity and molecules. He must fear something. The murders took place close to two years ago. They were sending a message by leaving the bodies to be found, which were obviously tortured."

Mia had pulled additional articles from the German paper. Vicky read the newspaper reports and said, "The murders are unsolved. The professors were definitely tortured. A couple of the toenails were pulled off and the ends of the bones in the toes looked to be crushed. They were also cauterized."

Mia said, "What a horrible thing to do to someone."

Vicky announced, "The toes had the nails removed, and the toes have been squeezed by large pliers? It was the right big toenail on both men, and one professor had two additional nails removed, and the other one had one additional nail removed. All on the right foot of each man." Vicky then hesitated and looked mad and said, "Duff. Damn them."

Eric looked over at Vicky as Vicky was looking at Wayne. "Who is Duff?"

Wayne said, "He died in Butler Tennessee over a year ago. He had just started working officially for the Tennessee Highway Patrol but unofficially he worked for the late dead Senator Davis. He killed the young FBI agent working for Delores at the water tower in Butler, Tennessee. We will need to talk to Professor Roust. He is scared, and if these people are involved, he needs to be scared."

Chapter 16

With the new semester starting, Mia had placed Vicky in the freshman English class. She had accessed the database and built Vicky a profile. Dolores had approached the administration about interviewing some students and maybe an English-speaking professor. With her fake credentials, the administration very much was interested in free publicity in the United States. Colleges around the world had discovered the income stream from foreign students had become a lucrative proposition.

***

On the first day of class, Vicky wanted to look her part, which was a freshman from California with her long dark hair in a flowing perm with the ends highlighted in lite brown. She wore a tight-fitting short white sleeve shirt and a very short navy skirt with heels. She sat in the center seat in the front row of the class. She wanted Professor Patrick Roust to notice her and with her legs crossed and one leg sticking out from under her desk to the side, there was no way he would miss her. She allowed her shoe to slip off her heel and dangle on her toes. The room filled up and in walked the professor. He smiled at the class, set his cane down at the corner of his desk, and immediately noticed Vicky. He smiled at her. He introduced himself and explained what they should expect in the class.

Vicky was a little surprised with his high-pitched soft voice and his feminine gestures. He was witty and seemed friendly. He had a full head of hair and was about 5'8" tall. He went over additional ways to obtain extra credit and provided his phone number. He also provided a map to locate his office. He then explained if anyone was interested, he would be speaking to the poetry club in the main lobby of his office building tonight at 8 p.m. He stuck a brochure on the board for everyone to review. He spoke in German and in English to the class. He smiled and said, "The prerequisite for the class is you already must be able to speak English. This class does an in-depth study of American Literature."

He smiled again and said, "Learning English is by far the hardest language to learn to speak and write on planet earth. It is the only language that has so many inconsistencies."

He wrote on the black board as he was talking and said, "For example, farm is where you go and milk Susie the cow. Pharmacy is where you go to buy drugs after you have milked Susie the cow to soothe your aching back and wrist splints for your now hurting wrist."

He turned to the class and smiled for the effect. "You pronounce the beginning of the words the same. Beware there are hundreds of painful discrepancies dealing with the English language. This class focuses on the writing and punctuation that you will be providing in your written reports about certain American writers. I promise to make you a better writer, but I cannot promise you that I can help make you a master of the English language. No one ever masters the English language. Even English teachers and Professors in America do not agree."

The class had started laughing when he first mentioned Susie the cow and did not stop laughing until the class was over. Professor Patrick Roust was animated when he talked. He loved to be the center of attention and leading the class. He had a great deal of charm and for a young female student, he was adorable.

During the class, Vicky acted like she was absorbed in his lecture. She took notes and wrote his contact number on the outside of her folder in big red letters for him to notice. As soon as the bell rang, most of the students packed up their items and headed for the door. She, on the other hand, took her time and walked up to the board and took notes of his brochure and the advertised lecture tonight at his office building. All the other students had left, and he walked over and said, "I am speaking on American literature if you are interested."

Vicky smiled and placed her hand on his arm and asked in German with excitement, "You mean like Waldo Emerson?"

"Yes. He is one of my favorites. I try to make the speech more of an introduction into American literature than a lecture. If you're interested, please come. It starts at 8 p.m. There is always wine served."

When he said "wine", he raised his eyebrows and smiled at Vicky.

Vicky sat down in the chair next to the door and pulled the school street map out and acted like she needed further direction. The short white sleeve shirt was low cut and provided a full view of her cleavage. She provided him ample time and opportunity to view her. Just to make certain the professor might show her his office after the meeting, she allowed the shoe to slide partway off her foot and showed her white panties as she moved her leg and acted like she was putting up her school map in her backpack when her legs were uncrossed while she also adjusted her high heel shoe. He leaned back against his desk, holding his briefcase and cane. She noticed he had moved the briefcase in front of him to hide the fact he had become aroused.

They walked down the hall talking about Robert Frost and Ernest Hemingway. They said "goodbye," and Vicky knew when she wanted, she could look and sound seductive to a man. She smiled as she got into her car and thought that was easy.

Chapter 17

Vicky did not like Delores wanting to be part of the meeting. Matter of fact, she did not want Delores in the building. Vicky knew too well how prepared these men would be after dealing with Senator Davis and Bill Duff. She did not believe Dolores should be undercover since she had no history of working in that capacity. This was not a case to start an undercover career. She did not see Delores pulling the trigger and that is what they were faced with dealing with the Syndicate. She had seen the bodies where the Syndicate did not hesitate to kill someone, and she still was concerned about the prior mission at Viatect. Someone was leaking information. She had indicated she could handle the professor. He was a small man about 5'8" one hundred and sixty pounds. He reminded her of the actor from England named Dudley Moore.

Mia had been trying to obtain all the information she could on the two professors who had been tortured and killed. She discovered the local police had turned the investigation of the two murdered professors over to the Federal Police. She said, "Vicky, I was not able to obtain

copies of their investigative reports, but I discovered the detective for the Federal police was a man named Von Shultz. I cannot break into his reports, but there is a memo to him from the campus police outlining there appeared to be someone else who was following other professors including Professor Roust and Professor Nicoli. Their campus camera system had some people on campus who were not students or part of the campus employment."

Vicky said, "If there was someone else watching Professor Roust, then we need to identify them and also expedite our mission. We need to make contact with Professor Roust and get him the hell out of here. Delores you will not need to be involved. I can handle meeting Professor Roust tonight at his lecture. We can also assume they may have also made us. I will update Max."

Delores said, "No, I am going to be his contact on this mission."

Wayne supported Delores and said, "This would be her opportunity to play her role and act like a newspaper person conducting her interview."

Vicky shook her head no, but Dolores was not going to accept no. Billy Ray said, "I can be on the opposite roof looking down with my rifle. Eric can be on standby to enter and provide support on the inside. He can blend in with the other drunk students."

Wayne said, "Little Jimmy will be parked around the block monitoring the rear. I will be here with Mia listening and watching. Mia can review the network from the city-and school-owned cameras. We need his help, and he might be in danger. Everyone entering the building must walk through a metal detector. You won't be able to carry a gun."

Vicky said, "He is definitely in danger. These people are killers. I would rather work alone on this from the inside."

Eric looked at Vicky a little uneasy and said, "You might need help." She knew what Eric was referring to after the mission at Viatect.

Vicky hesitated and then asked, "Do we know where they are from?"

Mia responded, "The report from the school police to Von Shultz indicated the suspicious men on campus were never identified. There must be another team watching."

Vicky thought, "They know we are here." She looked at her team and said, "I have met Burnside. This is what he does. He sits back and plans and never does anything on impulse. Everything he does is premeditated. He is also ruthless." She looked around at the group with the realization they were being watched. "Burnside already knows we are here. He wants to know the players involved and wants us to lead him to Patrick Roust. He has been waiting for someone to show up for two years, and we just walked right into his trap. The only reason we are not dead is because he does not know who we are here to contact. We need to make contact and leave."

Everyone was quiet and then Vicky said, "I have a plan that might work."

Wayne liked the plan until Vicky explained she would be on her own. He liked the decoy part of the plan and the others thought they might could pull it off.

Delores finally said, "Vicky and I will make contact, and the rest of you will act as decoys and leave. By the time they figure out Professor Nicoli has no information, we will all be long gone. This is the only way I can see this working. My cover is airtight and if I show up tonight acting my role, no one will suspect anything." She looked at Vicky, "Do you think they made you today in class? Burnside knows what you look like."

Vicky thought, "I do not want to take any unnecessary chances, but once I convince Professor Roust his life is in danger, he will need to leave with me. I need Delores out of the picture."

Vicky did not want anyone to know her exit plan. Someone was leaking the intel. She had wished now that Eric of Newport had hidden a gun in the professor's office. Vicky said, "I do not believe they recognized me today. We will go with the best plan we have and get out of Germany as soon as possible. Let's get this done."

***

The team showed up at the restaurant where Professor Nicoli was eating. He was the Chemistry professor and had been somewhat acquainted with the now two dead physics professors. They tried to look like a surveillance team. They had walkie talkie type equipment and ear plugs which anyone could see. They were trying to make certain anyone following them would know who they were watching. Professor Nicoli was enjoying his meal with his wife and was unaware of the watching eyes. When the Professor left at 7:43 p.m. with his wife, the team followed in three different vehicles. The plan seemed to work.

Vicky and Mia noticed one and maybe two people following her team in two separate cars. The decoy plan had worked. Little Jimmy and Billy Ray had stood out walking around the exterior of the restaurant with walkie talkie equipment and ear plugs, and Wayne had opened the car door sitting near the sidewalk and exited the car while looking straight at the restaurant. When they all left following Professor Nicoli and his wife, Vicky was taken back by the other surveillance team and was concerned about her plan being leaked to Burnside. She did not tell anyone what her concerns were with the possible traitor.

Delores walked into the banquet hall at 7:45 p.m. She introduced herself and explained she had interviewed some students and a couple of professors. She explained to Patrick Roust she saw the flyer on the bulletin board in the student center. She thought this might be a great opportunity to meet professors in a social setting.

He seemed to be eager to be interviewed. He was on his second glass of wine before the impromptu meeting started. Right before his turn to address the audience he drank the third glass of wine. He even introduced Delores to the crowd as being an American writer. Delores stood and announced she was a newspaper writer not an author, and she acted tipsy. Everyone in the audience seemed to be tipsy. The meeting had just started, and there were already several empty wine bottles.

Vicky had waited and watched the outside of the building. The possible threats had left following her team. She pulled her cape over her head and walked across the street and through the door. The professor had everyone laughing and really liked being the center of attention and talking to the audience. Vicky walked toward the glasses of wine, pulled her hood back on her cape and waited. The professor saw her and came over to talk with her after his thirty-minute review of the several different American writers. He was promoting a field trip to Key West to see Hemingway's plantation. He also drank another glass of wine as soon as he walked over to the table with Vicky. The more he drank, the funnier he became. Vicky kept playing along, trying to get him to ask her to look at his office.

Delores kept watching Vicky and the professor. She finally said into her hidden mic, "I am going to see if I can move this upstairs." She walked over to them and introduced herself to Vicky and told her the professor agreed to be interviewed. The two American women acted like they had just met for the first time. Delores asked the professor if he had a copy of Hemingway's book, "Garden of Eden." She had recalled the book when

Eric had secured the interior photos of the office. He agreed to show the ladies his office.

Vicky and Delores were acting drunk, and Patrick Roust was drunk. He had his arms around both women as they walked up the stairs and down the hall to his office door. He had mentioned a threesome and understood in America it was a normal sexual encounter with two women and one man. He laughed when he said it. He dropped his keys and finally opened the locked door to his office on the third floor, and they walked inside. Vicky immediately locked the door and turned the lights off. Only the ambient light from the streetlights and the moon provided light through the window. Delores took the professor by his hand and led him to his desk. The professor was now understanding the two women were not drunk but very serious.

Vicky said, "Professor, we know about the two physics professors and if you do not co-operate with us, they will kill you next."

The professor was shocked. He seemed to sober up. He recalled the photos of the two men, and how they had been tortured. Vicky could see the frightened expression and the doubt on his face. She now knew he was in hiding. "Look, I am with the CIA, and she is with the

FBI. We both are American agents, and your life is in grave danger. You are being watched by men who will not hesitate to kill you. If you want to live, you need to help us."

He looked worried. "What do they want?"

Vicky said, "You know what they want. They want your grandfather, Dr. Epstein's research into the Vortex. The Syndicate has killed people all over the globe for this information. Where is it?"

He looked scared with the mention of his grandfather's name. "How did you find me and know I was related to Dr. Epstein? How did you know I have the research?"

"We located your grandfather's letters he wrote to Albert Einstein in the late 1920's. Princeton College kept all the letters and the envelopes for future historians. We stole one of the envelopes and had the DNA from where he licked the seal analyzed. We ran the DNA match through the system and located you. You are the sole survivor of your family. We are certain the Syndicate is after your grandfather's research."

"He was my great grandfather. My mother did not give birth until she was in her late forties. I was said to be a miracle baby. I never met my grandfather or my great grandfather. I was told my great grandfather was brilliant, but he also was Jewish living in Germany right before Hitler's terror. I was told they went to Poland and then they went to Sweden hiding out in the bottom of a boat as they crossed the Baltic Sea, which was the scariest part of the trip. If they had been discovered by the Germans, they would have been forced to walk the plank into the freezing waters. I have never been to Switzerland, but there is an old church where the research might be hidden. My great grandfather was never seen again once he left Sweden."

He looked up. "I just want this over. Do you know what it is like to live the last ten years of your life not knowing if you would be discovered and then tortured and killed? They tortured those professors. The news of their death was in the city newspaper. Everyone on campus was scared. I felt horrible. I asked those two physics professors if they could advise me. I was able to keep my true identity from them. I provided them just a small part of the research from my great grandfather which my grandmother had kept in some files. They seemed so interested in the theory behind the Vortex. When I mentioned the Vortex creates an energy force which someone can literally step through the door in space, they were intrigued. The basic theory is the object is held in place as the cosmos zooms right by. They provided a report on the research and the issues with testing the theories. Then the next thing I knew, they were tortured and killed. The case is unsolved even after two years."

He hesitated and appeared to be thinking. He looked at Delores and then Vicky, "My grandmother had told me the stories of how they got out of Germany and went to Poland. They did not know if they were going to make it across the border into Sweden. Every day, they had to face death. She told the story how they never knew who they could trust to help them. They had to trust non-Jewish people to hide them on their journey. She told me great granddad went back for his research, and they begged him not to go. He felt his research was too important to leave behind. He was afraid the research would be discovered by the wrong people or the wrong government. She said his research was his life's work. He loved his research. He felt he could travel the same route and trust the same people. Then, Russia and Germany both simultaneously attacked Poland when he was in Warsaw. She never heard from him again. My grandmother was a strong person. She never forgot she was Jewish, but she wanted her daughter, my mother, to be raised as a Christian and not exposed to the hatred that goes with being Jewish."

He paused and looked at both ladies and seemed to understand he had been discovered. He said, "She was contacted by a messenger from Poland who said great granddad had hidden out and finally died. I was told his research is hidden in an old church in Switzerland. He had waited for the Americans to get him out like so many other German scientists. I guess the family has waited now for ninety years and here we are. The Americans have finally arrived." He looked at Vicky and Delores when he made the comment.

The knock on the door startled all three of them. The man's voice in German was a deep harsh tone. He announced, "Professor, we need to talk with you. It is urgent." Vicky immediately grabbed Dolores blouse with both hands and pulled it apart causing the buttons to fly across the room exposing her pink bra. Delores looked confused, mad and said, "You bitch. This blouse cost two-hundred dollars."

The professor was talking to himself, and Vicky realized he sobered up to talk to them, but he was hysterically scared now with the voice from behind the locked door. He seemed more drunk than she first thought. She pulled the syringe out of her school backpack and stuck it in his neck. She turned him away from the door in his chair. The chair had a medium high back and was on wheels. She pulled the handle off the cane and held the sword. She looked at Delores and said, "You are now operational. You need to hike your skirt up and straddle him. You need to keep him between their guns and you. They will not shoot him. I need for them to be distracted."

The recognition of who was on the other side of the door had just registered with Delores. She looked scared but did as she was told. The professor was awake, but the drug made him appear to be drunk and left him without his ability to talk or move his limbs. He looked at Delores at first with a smile as she straddled him while he was sitting in his desk chair.

Vicky stood behind the door. She heard the lock being manipulated, and the same voice said, "We are with campus security. Professor you might be in danger. We want to check on you."

The door slowly opened. She could see the silencer and then the barrel. Delores held the professor's head into her chest as she sat facing him with her legs hanging out of the arms of the chair. When Delores saw the gun, she started to shrink down behind the professor, his chair, and the desk.

Vicky was not certain how many men there were, but she knew she had to take out the lead man and then use him as a shield. She held the sword pointing downward to her side and swung the small sword upward with great force cutting through the wrist bone and most of the flesh. He fired two bullets hitting the ceiling as the barrel tilted upward. Vicky reached and grabbed the barrel of the gun and turned the gun around pointing at the man while pushing the man back out the door. She pulled the gun loose from his grip and turned the gun and immediately shot the man to her right standing about two feet back from the door threshold. The first man looked like he was in shock as Vicky looked into his eyes as he kept trying to lift his arm while looking at his wrist and hand hanging by the skin and tendons swinging back and forth with blood running down his clothing and squirting with every pump of the heart. Vicky pushed him backward as the other two men tried to line her up with their aim. She reached around the man and shot the other two men, which were ten feet and twenty feet down the hallway. She then stepped back into the office and shot the stunned man in the heart twice. She turned and said, "We've got to get going."

Delores had dropped to her knees hiding behind the desk and in doing so the chair on wheels with the professor half turned to face the door. He watched the four men being shot. Delores stood up and looked down the hall and saw the four dead men and their guns.

Vicky said, "They will have additional men out front and on the main level. They now have figured out Professor Nicoli was a trick. We are cut off. She closed and locked the door. She pulled off her blood covered large cape and unrolled the rope she had hidden around her waist. She opened the window and tied the rope off on the gas line to the heater. She wrapped the rope around him under his armpits and tied the rope in front of Patrick Roust to hold him as he was going to be lowered.

She urgently directed, "Help me lower him to the bushes near the sidewalk."

The women lowered him three feet at a time. He was awake but could not talk or hardly move from the drug. He had a look of total horror on his face as he was being lifted over the window seal and lowered. When his feet hit the ground, he just fell over on his side. He immediately started upchucking on the grass next to the bushes.

Vicky said, "You need to follow me down the rope. I have a car waiting. They will kill you if you hesitate."

Vicky pulled her gloves out of her cape pocket and used them as she went down the rope quickly. She looked up and noticed Dolores wavered a little while she was trying to protect her bare hands from rope burns. She must have heard someone coming and slid down the rope. Vicky dragged the professor to the waiting car and pushed him into the back seat. She jumped in the driver's seat as Dolores opened the passenger door and sat down. She floored the gas pedal, causing the tires to squeal, and sped around several turns. She merged onto the congested major roadway and blended in with the traffic. Delores noticed Vicky kept looking into the mirror to see if anyone was following. Vicky turned off the main street and drove down a hill to the bank of the Spree River. She drove under a bridge and demanded that Delores get out of the car. They got out and Delores asked, "What is the plan?"

Vicky pulled the pistol from under the seat as she exited the driver's seat and aimed it at Delores, who was now standing in the darkness under the bridge behind the vehicle. She said, "Do not say another word." She then motioned, "Give me your phone and mic." Delores hesitated and looked at Vicky with surprise and concern. Delores laid the mic from her ear and then her cell phone on the ground. Vicky quickly picked them up and threw them in the river. She then threw her mic and phone in the river. She looked at Delores, who was surprised. Vicky said, "I believe it would be in your best interest for me to leave you here. You don't want to go where I am going.

She walked to the back seat and reached in the professor's pockets and located his phone and threw it in the river. She cut the rope around him. He was still under the influence of the drug and could not move or talk. He just watched her.

Delores looked at her and said, "I am going where he goes."

Vicky held the pistol to her side and said, "Get in and don't say I did not warn you. We are going off the grid."

They drove for about ten minutes to the shipyard, and Vicky turned off the lights to the car as she rolled slowly toward the chain link fence with three strands of razor wire at the top. The man walked out from behind a large metal container. Vicky rolled down her window and said, "We need out of here with no questions asked."

The man looked at Vicky and shined the flashlight into Delores and Professor Roust's face and said, "That will be the trick. Someone is pushing this as a kidnapping, and his face has been posted all over Europe. I thought there was only going to be two people, not three."

Vicky said, "The plan changed. There are three of us, and we need to get moving. The trail behind us is hot."

The man did not protest further. "This boat will provide you passage across the Pacific to where you can rendezvous in two days with another boat, which will take you to port. I was discreet like you requested, and they will meet you at the designated location. Be careful."

Vicky looked hard at the man. "Ivan, you know what will happen if you double cross me."

Ivan did not waver. "There is no double cross, but you have created a lot of noise. It is not safe in the open. You will need to stay below deck once you set sail. Every contact in Europe is on alert. Look at the news on my phone. His picture will be plastered on every newspaper in Europe with reward money offered in the morning."

Vicky noticed Patrick Roust looked uncomfortable and scared. She knew she had to get him on the ship before he freaked out. Ivan pointed to the other man and said, "This is the first mate, and this is a Belgium-owned ship. He will watch after you while you are on the ship. You will need to stay away from the other crew members. They might have seen his photo and alerted the authorities."

Vicky remembered the first time she met Ivan in his boss's mansion. At the end of the evening, she had killed five guards and Ivan's boss. She offered him a career or death, and he chose the career working indirectly for her and the CIA. He was a smart man, and Ivan would be aware if he double crossed Vicky, he was also a dead man.

The first mate said, "We need to hurry before the rest of the crew starts boarding." The three walked up the gangplank following the first mate. He showed them where to stay in an empty room with three bunks. He told them he would bring them food. He said the rest of the twenty-man crew was staying on the fourth floor. He hoped no one would come to the front of the boat where they were on the first floor. He figured two-and-half days until they met with the other boat. He was being paid to keep his mouth shut and deliver the three to the next boat in line. He knew the ten-thousand dollars for this job would be easy if no one else knew they were on the boat.

Chapter 18

Little Jimmy listened to Mia announce they had driven away with the professor. He turned his car around and headed the opposite way. Billy Ray and Eric were sitting near Professor Nicoli house watching the home, and they also quickly drove away. Wayne stayed at his post and noticed three men start running down the alley to get into their cars. Wayne knew the plan had worked with Professor Roust leaving out a window from the third floor. He counted four additional men leaving from the bar area. They had been watching Professor Nicoli. They must have realized they had been tricked. Wayne announced, "The plan appears to have worked. Everyone report in and let's head home."

Chapter 19

Delores looked at Patrick Roust sleeping and then glanced at her hands at the blisters from the rope burns. She turned and looked at Vicky. "What are you not telling me? I know you never intended to let me leave with you. I guess they would have killed me if I had stayed. I guess I should thank you for allowing me to come along."

Vicky looked around the room in thought and then said, "You should have stayed with Wayne. This is going to be a difficult journey. We are going to stay off the grid for a few days. That is the only way this is going to work. The Syndicate now knows who has the hidden material. They will conduct a massive search for our professor." She glanced at him as he was sleeping.

"Those four men you shot in the office building, who were they? They could not have been the syndicate people."

"They were Russian agents. I went to middle school and high school in Germany. My father was in the Airforce. I remember my German teacher explaining how difficult it is to teach someone from Russia how to correctly pronounce the ur letters. They over pronounce the ur sound. I knew they were Russian agents."

Delores looked perplexed and stared at Vicky with the now understanding there was more at stake. "How would the Russians know anything about this mission?"

"Vicky looked straight ahead, "Exactly. How would they?"

"Who do you not trust on your team? I know you did not tell them about going off the grid or leaving out the window. I know someone must be providing information to the other side. There is no way Burnside would have been expecting you unless someone told him you were coming for him that night."

"I was set up at Viatect. The only reason I am alive is because Eric of Newport did not do what he said he was going to do. He did not leave. Someone had to tell Burnside that I was closing in on him, and I walked right into the trap. He said he was waiting on me. He knew I was coming. He asked me how it felt to be betrayed? He intended to have me killed. I have no clue who helped him. As far as Burnside and the Syndicate, Max knew Burnside had one solid contact in the CIA. That person is no longer an employee. We believe the leak is coming from your team." She looked at Delores to check her reaction.

Delores paused and thought about someone inside the FBI who would be selling secrets. She then asked, "What is next? I know you have a plan."

Vicky glanced over at the professor slightly snoring. "I am going to deliver the professor to the CIA unit in the states and then they should be able to locate the missing research. Then, I am going to set a trap for Burnside and when he shows up, I am going to kill him. He will never give up the partners in the Syndicate. Besides, he has used kids as sacrificial lambs, and I have no tolerance for that sin. He did not try to deny it when I talked with him at Viatect. Although I like Max's other option, which is we torture him for information and whether he lives or not will be Max and the President's decision. This is going to get ugly." Vicky looked over at Delores. "This is not an appropriate mission for an FBI agent."

Delores shook her head in understanding and also understanding Vicky's commitment to kill someone who has a history of harming kids. Billy Ray would never talk about Vicky even when they were holding each other in bed. She remembered he did state that he would rather have Vicky next to him in an operation than any man he had ever been on assignment with during the time as a Green Beret or Special Forces.

"Do you really believe there is this great power that mankind had not considered until now, and this Vortex is this powerful unknown energy source?"

Vicky thought back to the notes on her husband's desk when he was deciding to obtain his Ph. D. in physics. His thesis was the study into the Vortex. His notes outlining Genesis 6:4 suggested space travel and how the friends of God came down and impregnated the women of earth, which led to the intelligent level of humans jumping forward ahead of all other animals. The mention of the Ark of the Covenant being a nuclear charged device left behind by the space travelers, which caused the sores on the tribe of people that captured the Ark from the Jewish people. The low levels of radiation caused the sores. The tribe gave the Ark back to the Jewish people because they were sick from being too close to it. They did not understand how to shield themselves from the radiation. The Ark could have caused the walls of Jericho to fall from nuclear waves aimed at the walls of the city. The only explanation is space travel through the Vortex. She thought the Vortex helped fill in the gaps and explain our history.

Vicky looked at Delores and then looked straight ahead. She thought the only time Matt really talked about his research was after their love making while in bed and while she acted like she was interested in his thesis. Matt had mentioned the gravitational pull on an object on earth being held in place was more than just the speed of the earth spinning. He had been perplexed about the math and was studying if the energy from the object in space spinning or rotating could be harvested, energy similar to a windmill. She had asked him if the Vortex was a hoax or was it real, and he had stared at the bedroom ceiling and not responded. She glanced over at Delores, "It does not matter what I believe. What matters is that someone out there believes the Vortex can open a window in space and hold the object still while the Milky Way flies on by. Or the zipper can be opened on earth and the person or ship can be held in place while the earth spins right by. There have been a lot of studies done on what nations were doing fighting for control of nuclear weapons in the 1940's. If one country has the technology, there will be war, but if two or more have the technology there will be peace. WW II was a blessing in that we and the allies took out Hitler. If Hitler had waited and gotten the atomic bomb before starting his war campaign, he would have destroyed the world. Hitler also made a terrible mistake invading Russia. History has shown he was not patient. Now we are dealing with the unknown Syndicate which appears to be patient. I am scared for the future of our country and the world as we know it. The Syndicate is real and has unlimited resources. They have spent millions trying to harness the power of the Vortex. This is what I know. If the Vortex is a hoax, why and by who was it created?" The two sat in quietness.

Vicky then looked at Delores and then the slight snoring professor. "I believe he is not telling us the truth. He knows the value of the research is worth billions. He was trying to figure this out by going through the now dead two professors. He wants to sell the research to the highest bidder. He will not give the research up for free. I believe he used the two professors to market the knowledge, and they did not have his contact information. They were tortured for information they did not have. The note Eric located with the papers had 9,505,700 Euro equals 10 million dollars." They both sat in quietness until both fell asleep.

Chapter 20

The first mate had done as he was told. He brought them food and blankets. He kept them updated on the journey. Now, they had pulled up to the speed boat. Delores walked out on the deck and felt the sea air for the first time in three days. The professor looked worried, but she could tell he was still hopeful. Vicky saw the first mate telling the men on the speedboat about them. He pointed at them. The captain of the speed boat did not like what was being said. The first mate was animated with his gestures. He motioned for them to come down the ladder. He had provided each of them with heavy raincoats.

Delores could tell these Spanish men were drug runners. The professor had no idea who these men were with the guns, speaking Spanish and tattoos all over their arms, backs, necks, and chest. They sat down in the bottom of the speedboat and headed east.

The four men on the speedboat watched them sit in quietness. There were two large tarps that had been over the cargo in the front and rear of the boat. The entire boat had been full of cargo and now with three additional passengers, the crew seemed relieved. One man mentioned in Spanish how he thought they should throw the man over the side and rape the women. The group laughed.

Delores kept trying to hold the raincoat over her and hold her blouse together with the missing buttons. Finally, one of the men approached her and said in Spanish they were ready to have some fun. She needed to pay him for the boat ride.

Vicky said in English, "Juan Canteno" and looked straight ahead. She did not want to make eye contact. The name Juan Canteno seemed to force the man to back down. The man turned and looked at his comrades and stepped backward with a look of indecisiveness. The men assumed they could not understand Spanish. The one man with the long hair kept talking about raping both Vicky and Delores. He started wanting to draw straws for who would be first.

The captain finally said, "No." He looked at Vicky when he said it.

One of the other men approached Delores and pulled her up on her feet and started rubbing his hands on her. The other guards started yelling and trying to egg the man on. Vicky stood and repeated Juan's name with a fierce look on her face. They all got quiet, and the captain got mad. He cursed the men and told them to leave the women alone. Finally, Vicky noticed land ahead, and she hoped the boat trip was coming to an end.

The professor had gotten seasick and upchucked several times. He had laid in the bottom of the boat in the fetal position. The guards wanted to throw him overboard, but the captain kept them away. The smell of the vomit was not pleasant. One of the men retrieved a bucket of water once the boat slowed and poured it on the professor to wash the boat and flush the vomit to the pump located in the bottom of the boat under the hatch.

Once on land, they were ushered to an old pickup truck and taken to an old warehouse. They were being guarded. The guards spoke in Spanish and kept talking about raping them and killing them. Then, a man in a suit walked into the room with another man. He yelled orders in Spanish. He looked at Vicky and noticed how dirty she was. He looked at Delores and asked in English if any of his men had pulled her shirt open. She was too shaken to respond and stared at the concrete floor. Although the guards had not spoken English, they had made it clear what they were wanting to do. Vicky could tell Delores was scared. The professor was now lying on the bench and looked sick. His clothing was all wrinkled, wet, and he was also very dirty. The air was hot and humid, and they had removed the heavy raincoats. The boat had not been cleaned, and they had not bathed in three days. Vicky looked straight ahead and said, "She is fine."

The man in the suit had a long scar on the side of his face and looked intimidating. He turned and looked at his men and asked in Spanish, "Where are her shoes?" while pointing at Vicky? The one guard with the long hair pointed at the sick man and answered that he threw up on them. They had thrown them overboard with the puke. The group of men laughed. The guard then said, "As soon as Juan is done with these two, I want to have my turn." The man in the suit smiled and looked at the three and back at his guards.

Vicky heard several vehicles drive up and several men get out. The guards seemed to relax and understood they were waiting on Juan. They had figured Juan would allow them to rape these women and kill all three. They had never met Juan but understood he had no tolerance for foreigners and trusted no one. Suddenly, the door busted open, and Juan with his most trusted guards walked into the room. He looked around. His men leveled their shotguns at the other guards. Vicky noticed surprise and fear in the guard's eyes, and the man in the suit seemed nervous. Juan looked around the room taking note of the men and walked over to Vicky and started apologizing for what had happened.

He got on his knee in front of Vicky and asked, "My Queen. What can I do to make this right?"

He bent down on one knee and bent over and kissed the top of her foot. He thought of his kids and how Vicky was their custodian and if anything happened to her, well he broke off the thought and was enraged. He then stood up with a mad expression on his face and walked over to Nicolas Santiago in the suit and slapped him. He grabbed him by the neck and gritted his teeth as he pushed him against the wall and yelled, "How dare you!"

Vicky stood up and said in Spanish, "We do not have time for this. We need to talk." She looked at the first guards. They knew who these men were with Juan. Juan's men all had several tattoos located on their forearms and necks with tear drops which signified the number of people they had killed. They had shotguns aimed at them and one had his hand on a long knife.

Nicolas now realized the significance of Juan's involvement with the three people after watching him kneel and kiss the top of Vicky's foot. He figured they were going to be tortured to death. He had never met

Juan's group of guards, although he had heard of them. He could hardly speak with the pressure being pushed in on his throat. He grunted out, "You can take all the money. I am sorry. We were not made aware of any of this." He was nervous and shaking. Juan released some of the pressure, and he then bent over and was trying to capture his breath. He said, "I was told an extra package was aboard. No one told me three people were going to be smuggled into my dock."

Nicolas's memories went back to when the deal with Juan had first been proposed. He had previously worked for the Mandazi Cartel until the United States Airforce dropped bombs on the cartel leader killing several dozen cartel men, and lieutenants a few months prior. Instead of fighting for the territory, Juan had decided to make a deal. He realized any deal would be better than nothing, and this territory had never been his. With the new markets opening in Russia, he set up Nicolas to run thirty-five percent of the white powder, and he supplied sixty-five percent. Nicolas had figured Juan was going to kill him as he was being held tied up in a small home north of the town where the bombing of his old boss had happened.

The other cartels in South America were all fighting for more territory and normally if deals were not made when a boss of a cartel died, the old employees were rounded up and killed.

He was surprised when Juan walked in and not only spared his life but had him untied and asked him personal questions and provided him food and water. He thought Juan sounded like an insurance salesman trying to sell him a homeowner policy.

Juan offered him a great deal to work with him in a partnership. Vicky's contact, Ivan Chevon, needed a supplier to build an empire. Vicky had explained to Juan she needed Ivan to help her inside Europe, and the money he made from the drug sales would give him power. The cartels measured the income in the number of eighteen wheelers full of cash and Ivan Chevon had become a power broker in less than a year in Europe.

Nicolas used his men to deliver the product to the designated point in the Pacific to meet the Russian merchant ship headed for port in Russia and make the trade, the money for the product. Juan had kept the contact with Ivan a secret, so Nicolas would not be tempted to double cross him.

Russia presented a huge opportunity to grow the drug business and the plan was simple and safe. Nicolas, as it turned out, did not have to be concerned about any authorities or offloading the product in Europe. He was also aware Juan did not need him as a partner. He could have set up arrangements and used his own men and product. He also knew Juan had no tolerance for failure, and he could easily be replaced. He actually thought he and his men were going to be killed, when Juan walked into the room with his personal guards then the barefooted woman who Juan had kissed the top of her foot and called her his queen.

Juan turned to him and said, "No. We have a deal. You can send my cut. The buyer wants twenty percent more product on the next shipment. Do not let him down. These three people will never be talked about again. You and your men are not to ever bring it up to anyone." Juan and Vicky walked out the door. Vicky explained that the three of them would need an opportunity to clean up and then they needed transportation to Mexico City. Juan nodded his head that he understood. Vicky knew once they made it to Mexico City, Max had a CIA jet waiting and only a handful of people would know about Professor Roust.

Chapter 21

Vicky had enjoyed the couple of days off work. She and Delores had delivered Professor Roust to the waiting CIA team in southern California. The mission was top secret and Vicky hoped the information Professor Roust possessed was worth all the dead bodies. She told Delores she was ready to focus on stopping the human slavery around the world. Max had not given her a new assignment in months. She was focused on the Vortex and now with that completed she wanted to move into Europe and Africa to stop the slave traders.

Delores had not understood the Spanish conversations between the men when they were being transported to South America and while in the warehouse. She suspected they were traveling with drug smugglers operated by one of the South America cartels. She was scared to make eye contact and noticed out of her peripheral vision when the large man walked into the warehouse bent down and kissed the top of Vicky's foot. She knew at that point Vicky was in charge. She realized she had underestimated her.

Vicky, while taking time off, had met with friends and taken a karate class with Betty Ogle, the retired Army instructor. She also went by the shooting range and met with Mark Smith, her old shooting instructor. Karate and shooting had always been a way for Vicky to relax and stay focused. She would practice both for hours at a time.

Matt was talking on the phone. Vicky walked up to him and said, "I am so sorry I have been gone so much." Matt hung up the phone. They embraced and kissed with Vicky leaning into her husband's chest and hugging him longer than he hugged her. Vicky was so happy to be home. She and Matt needed time alone.

Matt said, "I am the one who should apologize to you." She bent her head upward and arched her back to look into his eyes. "I was the sinner that introduced you to the sins of the flesh when we were in college. It was me who introduced you to those other men. I am so sorry for my behavior. I can only pray you forgive me."

"I love you more than you could imagine. That is the past. I want to be a good wife to you." He kissed her on the crown of her head as she hugged him tightly. She had talked him into going to the Smoky Mountains to hike to Mt. Leconte and stay in the cabins for two nights. She prayed she was justified in the Lord's eyes trying to stop the evil working with methods similar to the archangels. She lived with no regrets doing the Lord's work.

While sitting on the Cliff Top looking out over the view, she heard four men who had hiked the trail several times explaining the view to other hikers. They had pointed to Newfound Gap, Clingmans Dome, and the old Indian Trail that ran behind the Chimney Tops. After the other hikers had left, she stared at the view and realized the perfect scene and thought how if she was God, she would not change the view. She then realized that was how she felt about her loving husband. She knew she loved him with all her heart. She then came to terms with her actions and felt the Lord had protected her and her team. Her fight to protect the meek and especially the kids was not finished. She also had conceptualized who the one person was who betrayed her trust and almost caused her death had to be someone close to her. The thought of this person had been gut wrenching. She decided she had to confront the only person who could have betrayed her. She had thought about each person on her team for hours before she made her decision. She was stunned with the revelation of the identity of the guilty party. There could be no one else. She had prayed it was someone not in the unit, but there was no way anyone else could have known where she was going to be when she met Burnside.

She felt rejuvenated as she and Matt walked down the north face of the mountain on the Bull Head Trail and headed home. They had watched the moon rise, stars twinkle, and the sun set. They had spent extra time in the bed holding each other and deciding the next step in their relationship would be parenthood.

Matt had updated her on the two kids adopted by the Fosters. He had told Vicky that was what Bob and Sue Foster needed to move forward in their lives. "They both seem to be constantly smiling, and the two kids seem to be able to adapt to life in America. Both are playing soccer and have made friends in school and on the soccer teams."

Vicky had told no one they were the kids of one of the largest cartel leaders in South America. She had figured the kids would enjoy more freedom without having guards with guns constantly watching them. Bob Foster had taken Juan Jr. fishing with Jeff from church, and they caught a few more than their limit. They were joking about it in the men's group. Vicky was so relieved to hear the kids and the Foster's were doing much better. Bob and Sue Foster were committed Christians even after the loss of their son, Brian. Every time Vicky saw the couple at church, she said a prayer for them and thanked God for being gracious to show them how to love and forgive. Then, she would ask God to forgive her of her mortal sin of being selfish and seducing their only son and him dying trying to protect her identity. She would pray God understood her reckoning, and she understood her damnation.

Chapter 22

Vicky walked into Mia's computer shop and explained where Professor Roust was being held and protected. It had been two weeks and he finally gave up the location of the research. She explained to Mia where in Switzerland the research was being stored. That was the next mission, and they would leave for Ramstein Air Base located in Germany immediately. She would be needed to keep the live feeds open from satellite and manage the ground mission, which would take place in Switzerland.

***

Billy Ray and Little Jimmy were waiting at the north side of the graveyard well hidden behind a tombstone with a date 1903 carved into the stone. Eric reported movement. A man had entered from the south. Eric was stationed in the bell tower and watching from the church roof top on the other side of the graveyard. Wayne noted there was a car parked outside with two men watching. Wayne was in the alley of the old building. The seal team was ready and stationed at different intervals around the graveyard and were well hidden. Mia was trying to turn the channel. She kept repeating we have no audio. She seemed frustrated working on trying to obtain the audio signal. She would glance up at the visual display watching the silhouettes of men watching and men being watched, but the audio feed was a no go.

Delores had the FBI tech disconnect the sound from the operating live feed. They had monitored Mia's cell phone. Vicky, Delores, and Mia were watching from the office in Germany. The Seal unit outside the graveyard watched the two men in the car as they sat waiting in the driveway of the old graveyard.

The unit closed in and shot the two men as they went for their guns. Delores bent down and connected the wire to the router. They radioed the two men were dead. Wayne came on the secure line and acknowledged the two men were down. Billy Ray came on the line and said, "Roger that. We have one in the yard. When he enters the tomb, we will surround the tomb and take him. We are jamming his communication with his partners". The line went dead.

Vicky and Delores walked in behind Mia watching the trap work from the secure location in Ramstein Air Base located in Germany. Mia looked confused when she realized some of the men, she was watching were Billy Ray, Wayne and Little Jimmy. She said, "I thought Billy Ray and Little Jimmy were in California with Eric and Wayne watching out for Professor Roust."

Vicky said, "We moved this mission up twenty-four hours at the last minute. We had to set a trap to catch a traitor."

Delores pulled her gun and aimed it at Mia and said, "Mia you are under arrest for espionage."

Two FBI agents walked in the room and forced her to stand while they cuffed her.

Max walked in and asked, "Where is Burnside? We know you know how to get in touch with him. We saw your e-mail to him about this location. We were able to break your encrypted message."

Mia looked at Vicky and said, "No. Vicky please no."

Vicky said, "You were the only one who knew of this tomb and this location in Switzerland. You watched as we shot Burnside's men looking for this hoax. You told them we would not be arriving until tomorrow. The rest of the team and the seal team just arrived earlier today. They were not told why we were watching the graveyard. Now I will have to tell them. This was a trap to catch a traitor. You set me up at Viatect. Do you know what they were going to do to me before they killed me?"

Mia said, "I had no choice."

Vicky was direct and harsh, "Everyone has a choice, and you made yours. Everyone in this room wanted me to have you killed. I loved you like a sister, and you betrayed me. I saved you in the dungeon from a horrible death from the sicko killer, Ronald Mongold, and this is my thanks. Take her away."

Chapter 23

Wayne looked out the French doors in the loft and said, "I just could not believe Mia was the one who sold us out."

Little Jimmy said, "Hell no. I thought she was one of us."

Eric said, "She got what she deserved. I saw what they were going to do to Vicky at Viatect. How is Vicky taking the news?"

Wayne said, "She will not talk to anyone about it. She loved Mia like a sister, and Mia betrayed her. Mia will have a closed military trial, and the military judges normally are all very strict. She will get life in prison at best. She might get the death penalty. She has confessed which most likely will be seen as a gesture for mercy."

Chapter 24

Vicky did not like the thought of the visit. No one in her unit had been to see Mia. The group had not spoken Mia's name since they had returned to Tennessee. Mia's attorney had contacted Vicky outside her church after the Sunday service. He had walked up to her in the parking lot as she was headed toward her car. Vicky had not seen him in church and had not recognized him. She saw him approach. She placed her hand on her pistol in her purse as he closed the distance. He was very nice and courteous. He mentioned Mia wanted to apologize in person. He also mentioned he needed her help. "Mia will plead quilty for a life sentence but no death penalty. The sentence might be lessened if you could speak on her behalf at her trial, it would help her." Vicky did not like the thought of talking in the church parking lot with so many people around. She quickly took the information and told him she would call him. She did not hesitate to get in her car and drive off.

***

She hated walking into the federal military prison. Max had asked Vicky if she wanted him to attend with her. Vicky had said she would go alone.

Vicky sat down at the table and waited. Mia was ushered in by two large female officers and chained her lower legs to the floor in the chair and with her wrists being chained to the desktop. One of the officers said, "We will be at the door. Knock on the door or speak loudly when you are ready to leave."

Vicky looked at the guard and shook her head that she understood.

Vicky looked at Mia after she sat down across from her at the table. Mia had her head tilted forward and was sobbing. She did not show any signs of being able to stop crying and looked like she had not had any sleep. She had on no makeup and had dark rings under her eyes.

Vicky said, "Mia, the best I understand, you are going to be in this lovely place for life. I hope betraying me was worth it. As far as I am concerned, you deserve to grow old in this facility. Your attorney asked me to speak in court on your behalf. I am not certain my speaking at your trial would be in your best interest. You set me up to be raped and killed. Why would I help you?"

Mia looked up and stopped crying. She seemed surprised.

"I understand you asked for me to come and meet you. Is there something you want to tell me?"

Mia looked into Vicky's eyes and said, "I am sorry. Burnside was not meant to hurt you. I would never have given him notice you were coming for him if I thought he would have waited for you. He was supposed to have left, and you would have found nothing but an empty apartment at the top of the building. I am truly sorry."

"That is bullshit. The only reason I did not get raped and then cut into little pieces and flushed down the toilet was Eric of Newport did not do what he said he was going to do. You could have told us. Eric could have also been killed. Why in the hell would you ever trust Burnside?"

She looked up and wiped her tears. "They have my father. He is a nuclear engineer in Pakistan. I had to make a choice. The man who raised me or my friend was the choice. You know what Burnside is capable of doing, and what he is capable of doing to my family. I chose family, and I am sorry. I thought you and Eric would have been okay."

"Tell me now how to locate Burnside. Maybe I can help your father."

"Burnside has my family. He will kill all of them. You have seen what they do to people. After I provided him information about the location of the hidden research, he was going to release my father and the rest of my family. I know I made the wrong decision. Burnside will never be true to his word. He would always know where to find them."

"Well, I am leaving. I am also sorry. Maybe the next time you can decorate this place like you did your small computer shop next to Prestige Clothing in Butler Tennessee." Vicky pushed her chair back and started to walk over to the door.

Mia said, "Follow the porn."

Vicky stopped before reaching the door and turned and asked, "What does, 'follow the porn mean'?"

Mia said, "Everyone has their vices. Burnside is addicted to watching porn on the internet. He seems to like young petite blonds. That is how I tracked him. He would purchase the same porn web site. I tracked that signal. He must pay with a credit card. I was able to locate his credit card bills from five-to-ten years ago. I kept noticing a payment for nineteen dollars and ninety-nine cents. I tracked the company, Fast Tech Billing Company, located in Los Angeles. They produce porn and sell it daily on the internet. All you must do Vicky is set up a platform and create a web page with a young blonde and advertise it in front of the Fast Tech's website on the internet. The advertisements can be manipulated to target certain customers. Wait and see if he bites. Track the credit card payment back to his location."

Vicky knocked on the door and said, "Guards." She had to wipe the tears as she walked out of the prison. She remembered how she and Mia had spent extra time setting up her small office, their friendship had developed, and now she was in prison for life.

Chapter 25

Vicky set up the meeting with the video link. Max said he did not know if the plan would work.

Delores said, "The FBI has tracked a lot of criminals and terrorists using the porn industry. This is the best chance we have."

Eric said he would ask Casey if she would help the FBI. He looked at Vicky and Delores waiting for one of them to agree. "I could start a company and handle the automation and the business aspect of the job. Casey seems to like her job as a stripper and doing these virtually in front of a camera would be easier and more lucrative."

Wayne said, "With the FBI helping all this could be pushed to fruition in a couple of days. She would need to start a segment, so the FBI can start advertising her future segments."

Eric said, "The filming could take place in my new home. I just purchased the Judge's home at the lake for 1.2 million dollars."

Vicky looked at Wayne and said, "I did not know the home was for sale.

Wayne said, "The next of kin wanted the money and since there were two people who died in the home, they wanted it sold fast."

Dolores said, "It may be better if I as an FBI agent approach Casey about the job and her involvement. She will understand the importance of what she is doing. I can then mention Eric and Little Jimmy can set up a company to handle the administrative aspect. The business will have to be legal, and there is a lot involved in running a business like this. We can set up the platform on the internet and market the production in the best environment to locate Burnside. We need Burnside, and this could work. The FBI took out ninety-seven terrorists in the middle east in one day using the porn video to track them."

Chapter 26

Eric and Little Jimmy were surprised how much business was booming from Casey taking off her clothes and doing her thing in front of the camera. The segments were ten minutes long. They had been provided research from the FBI on what Burnside seemed to like. He liked to watch a high-class blonde young lady by herself but every now and then a male partner would be introduced. All the filming was completed in the large mansion Eric had purchased, and Casey was thrilled at the opportunity to move in and live with Eric. The FBI had set up the automation platform and could track all the purchases online simultaneously.

After the first week of sending two segments and the reruns to the web, they got their first suspicious purchase from a credit card in Denmark. The FBI tracked the card. They wanted additional purchases to verify the source and location was Burnside. So, they offered a new segment with Casey and waited.

Eric was surprised after one and half weeks of running the business to have a knock at his front door. He opened the door and a large man wanted to talk with Eric. He had a thick Russian accent, and Eric had to listen carefully to understand.

He said, "I understand you are Eric Reagan. We got your address off your business license. You owe the man I work for twenty-five percent of what you have been making on your porn business on the internet. If you do not pay up and start making payments to us weekly, we will shut you down. You can consider this a licensing franchise type fee for being in this business. Everyone must pay the fee."

Eric thought the man acted like this was normal. He was very polite and well dressed. When he spoke, his body language suggested a threat. Eric looked at the Russian and asked, "Who do you work for?"

He said while gesturing with his hands, "I work for Mr. Salkowski. We are located in Vegas and Los Angeles. This fee is for your license and the legal right to operate your business." He motioned with his large hand. "Otherwise, we will close your business, and you will not like it if we shut you down."

Eric said, "Before I kick your ass back to Russia, you better get the hell off my property and don't return, and please tell Mr. Salkowski to go fuck himself."

The Russian looked at Eric and waved his index finger back and forth, smiled, and said, "Mr. Salkowski will not like that answer. We will be back in touch and the percentage of our take will double." Eric pulled his shirt back showing his pistol. The Russian smiled and said, "We will be back in touch." Then he turned and left.

Casey walked in from the pool and asked, "Who was that who left so quickly?"

"Just someone wanting to go into business with us."

He looked at Casey who had opened the towel and then rewrapped it around her nude body. Her bronze body had been kissed from the early summer sun. She had spent thousands of dollars on her wardrobe. She was going weekly to Nashville for pedicures and manicures. She was paying for facials, private workout instructors, and even moisture treatments of some type for her feet. Eric could not believe how much the company was making.

He then felt responsible, and he had to protect her. He was the one who volunteered Casey for the assignment. He could only assume the Russians would come with muscle and blow right through them if he was not prepared.

Casey mentioned going out to dinner in Nashville. He wondered if Billy Ray might want to go and maybe Little Jimmy for extra protection. As he stood in the foyer, he glanced out the glass window in the formal dining room toward the road. He had a sudden feeling this situation might be ugly. The Russian mob would not provide him time to consider getting help and being prepared. He remembered listening to Vicky tell the story about John Brown, the abolitionist in 1859 and his men taking control over the national armory in Harpers Ferry, West Virginia prior to the civil war. Once General Lee had confirmed with John Brown he was not going to surrender, Lee's men attacked immediately, thus not providing Brown's men time to prepare for the all-out assault. Casey walked up stairs, and Eric punched in the number on his cell phone.

Vicky answered, "What's up?"

"We have an issue. I just got a visit from a west coast Russian thug who works for the Russian mob. He said he worked for someone named Salkowski, and they want twenty-five percent. I told him no and then he said they would be back and the next time they would get twice that amount. I got the feeling this was not the first time they had muscled in on someone."

"Watch yourself. They will be back. You need to call Little Jimmy to be on guard duty. I will make some phone calls and call you back."

Vicky called Max. Max said he knew Salkowski. "His nickname is The Mad Russian. He assisted the CIA about fifteen years ago with a couple of missions in Russia. We set him up on the west coast. He owned a nightclub, and somehow got involved in the porn industry where he has made millions."

Vicky was surprised with Max's response and said, "You set this maniac up? What were you thinking?"

"We figured he would stay small, and we would never hear from him again. We never thought he would be any more than a club owner. He is ruthless and has made a fortune in the porn industry."

"They threatened Eric and our operation. Eric is concerned about his employee being hurt. We will have to stop him. We also have not gotten another computer signal from Denmark. If we had Mia working on this, we would already have his location. The FBI people are not as good as Mia."

There was a pause. Max asked, "Do you trust her, because we can see if she will work for us while confined. Maybe we could have her relocated to a white-collar prison in exchange."

"I am not certain, but we need her. She really is the best at breaking into systems. The FBI employees follow too many rules. They will not do what is needed."

Max said, "I will go and see her. I will offer her a move to another location. She will have to be monitored when she is on the internet."

"She needs to be monitored by someone in the CIA and not the FBI. Some of what Mia has done to help us was illegal."

"I understand."

Chapter 27

Vicky had not told Max she had called Ivan Chezon, her Russian contact whom she had set up in the Russian underworld. He knew of the Mad Russian, Salkowski, who had started using women and kids in Russia in his porn industry. Ivan provided Vicky the web sites. Vicky demanded, "Why did you not tell me about this before now?"

"It is not illegal in Russia to film teenagers. But he might be forcing them to work for him. He is ruthless. He lives in your country. He does very little in Russia. I can check into him some more and call you."

Chapter 28

Casey started the segment talking about being frisky and hot. She was dressed in layers. She removed her cover and then her long night gown. The male partner walked into the scene completely naked. He started to rub her shoulders. She stepped away and told him to sit in the chair. She started taking off her layers of underwear.

The segment was about to be uploaded as Mia was ushered into a room by two large female guards. The room was empty except for a laptop sitting on the table and two chairs. There was an unopened bottle of water sitting next to her computer on the table. The man with thick lens glasses walked into the room and sat down across from Mia with another computer.

He announced, "The segment will start in one minute." He glanced at his watch. "My computer will be displaying everything you review. It will be a perfect mirror. You need to let me know if you think you see something remotely questionable, and I will call it in for the support team to clear it."

Mia reviewed the purchases of the segment and discarded batches of hundreds at a time. The man looked up from his computer at her with a questionable look. She stopped at the one purchase and looked at the purchase for a couple of seconds. The CIA employee sitting at the table watching and mirroring her activity noticed the purchase of the latest segment from Manila in the Philippines. She noticed it was routed from another site in South Korea. "This is him. He is in Seoul."

The computer tech was surprised and asked, "How do you know that is the target? Where is the proof? You went through hundreds at a time without even considering them." He thought to himself, "She has spent less than five minutes. The entire FBI team spent a day and half of the prior purchases and could not agree on the possible target."

Mia looked over at him and said, "That is the target. He is not going to ever be obvious unless he wants you to find him. You better call it in." The CIA man looked at Mia with doubt.

The CIA man picked up the cell phone and called Vicky. Mia had no idea who the CIA employee was talking with. "She located a possible person of interest in Seoul." Mia glanced over at the CIA person when he had said, "possible person of interest."

Vicky asked, "How certain are we that this is Burnside?"

The CIA man said, "I am not certain. There were over seventy-five thousand purchases made from all over the world within one hour of the segment being released. I have no clue how she spent less than five minutes reviewing thousands of purchases and picked this one. We are still having orders coming in buying the segment, and she still has forty thousand to review." He glanced at Mia with a doubtful expression as he was looking at his computer screen at the incoming data.

Vicky said, "Ask her how she narrowed the choice down to Seoul?"

Vicky could hear the question and then she heard Mia say, "Tell agent Donahue this was the only purchase which used a false site in the Philippines and the purchase of segment was purchased with an American issued credit card routed to a military outpost in South Korea near the North Korea line. You need to tell agent Donahue; Burnside will not stay in the same location. He will relocate somewhere in the South Korea region. She needs to upload another segment and be in South Korea ready to move on him."

Vicky smiled. The man started to repeat what Mia had said. Vicky cut him off and said, "Tell Mia thanks. I will try to help her family." She hung up.

She called Max and told him they needed to be headed to South Korea.

Chapter 29

Ivan said, "I have checked into the Mad Russian, Salkowski, like you asked." Vicky listened. "He is more than just ruthless. He is a maniac. He will enjoy personally killing the people that oppose him. He is worth millions. He works with the Almingo Cartel out of Chile to bring drugs into Southern California. He has connections set up all over America. He was a business partner with Val Vanwhik." He paused making certain Vicky remembered his prior employer's name. Vicky had shot him three times in his mansion and then killed five of his guards on a prior mission.

Vicky asked, "How do you know all of this?"

"There's more. I just found out he was the one who set up the hit on Canteno people, killing several of the Canteno Cartel members. I have a source, and I have been watching him since I took over in Russia. He will make a play on me at some point now that Val Vanwhik is dead. He used men working for the Almingo Cartel and tried to make it look like one of the other cartels. That is why the Canteno people cannot figure out who hit them. He and his partners want total control of the drug market in Europe. The leaders of the Almingo Cartel have complete anonymity. No one has been able to ID them, and I am still working on that. I have requested a meeting with them, but they will only send one of their managers."

"Are you certain about this intel?"

"Yes. I cannot prove anything, but you can trace the money and his involvement in the Almingo Cartel. They are the source of his drug empire." He hesitated. "He also deals in prostitution with underage girls in Europe and the west coast."

Vicky called Juan. She told him who killed his family members. She said, "They are on my list, but I am tied up with another mission. We will deal with the people in our country."

Juan looked at the man sitting in the chair with his hands tied behind him with blood all over him. He hung up the phone and said, "Untie him and let him go. He is telling the truth." His guards untied the man and gave him a ride to the medical clinic and dropped him off at the curb.

Chapter 30

Max had settled into his job as the Director of the CIA. He met two sometimes three days a week with President Grant. He tried to keep the briefing short and on point. He also met with his management team planning and discussing possible threats and the continuous flow of data. The CIA had people who would analysis the data all over the world. The possible threats would not be limited to high-risk nations but could be theoretically located inside any nation. President Grant had demanded to be kept updated on any possible threats and any new developments. When his secretary said Mike Davis, the Director of the DEA was in the lobby waiting to see him, Max knew this was not going to be a pleasant meeting. He knew how dedicated and frustrated the DEA was with the flow of the drugs coming into this country. They were fighting a losing battle. "Show him into the conference room on third floor. Max did not want him to see his plush office or talk to any of his managers. He knew how envious some agencies could become if they felt they were not receiving the same benefit as the CIA.

Max walked into the conference room and walked over to Mike Davis and his associate. The men introduced themselves. Max asked if they would like something to drink and if they would like to sit down. Max took a seat. Mike Davis walked around the table and sat down across from Max and his associate remained standing. Max held his hands out in a gesture to invite the two men and ask how can I assist?

Mike Davis had become frustrated with the lack of support from President Truman and now the newly elected President Grant. His people were reaching burn out and losing the battle against the influx of the drug smuggling into this country. He placed his index finger out and rammed it into the top of the table and said, "We at the DEA have requested your help and your agencies' help several times and yet you have refused. We know you know the identity of the Cartels in South America. We are fighting a losing battle. We want to talk to your lead agent over the unit with the nick name the Good Samaritans." He looked angerly at Max.

"That is not going to happen." Max could sense the anger and the frustration.

He waved his hand in a frivolous manner. "Do you know a man name Ozzie Lopez?"

Max could since a trap. "No. I do not believe I have heard the name of Ozzie Lopez."

"Let me tell who he was. He was a thirty-three-year-old agent of the DEA, father of four. He was apprehended by the police while working undercover for us in Bogota Colombia. By the time we could get the needed help to him, he was burned alive. One of the drug dealer dogs were shot and killed in the shootout. The dog was brought to the lab where we completed a DNA testing of what was in the dog's stomach and intestines. Do you know whose DNA we found?" He rammed his index finger into the tabletop. "Ozzie Lopez. So, while you and your agencies have done nothing to assist us, we are losing and yet we have now been told by two administrations the same damn thing. You know what we are up against, and you are not going to help us. You know the identity of the cartels." He stared at Max and poked his index finger in the tabletop. "Hell, do you know we cannot arrest a cartel leader or talk to them. They are all connected to the South American Governments and military. We just try to take out the middlemen, the mules, and intercept some of the money. All we can do at best is disrupt their organization just enough to temporarily slow them down."

Max looked into Mike Davis's eyes and could tell his conviction. He also knew how it felt to lose an agent. "I am sorry for your struggles. Is there anything else?"

Mike pushed his chair back and his face turned red with anger. He said, "You know where this is going. We know you have joint ventures with the FBI and the State Department. Don't be surprised that we end up working on the same joint venture. You are not going to be able to hide from this issue." He turned to leave.

"May I ask you one question?"

Mike Davis turned and looked at Max. "What?"

"Do you know a man named Von Salkowski?"

"Yes. Of course, I know that scum. He is thought to be over the mob on the west coast. He arranges for drugs to be brought into this country through several different methods. His right-hand man is called the executioner. His attorney is Ray Hodges. That scum attorney gets him out of all charges. Did you know I had an agent get so upset with the killing of agent Lopez, she marched into his office and while standing next to the executioner she spit on Von Salkowski. My agents have sacrificed. They have not got married because of this job. They live the job. We know he is dirty. His fucking attorney, Ray Hodges filed a harassment complaint against the DEA the next day with the Justice Department." He stared at Max and pointed his finger at Max. "Do you know what those cronies at the Justice Department told me after I tried to defend my agent? They told me it would have been better if she had gone into the office and shot Salkowski. Spiting on him looks bad in the press and is not acceptable." The two men stared at each other and then Mike turned to his associate and said, "Let's go."

Chapter 31

Vicky knew she needed to have more time watching and planning, but they had to relocate to South Korea. Vicky could feel the stress of the two separate missions. Dealing with the rogue NSA Director, Nathanial Burnside had become personal and now the kill order was given on Von Salkowski. She reached around and rubbed her neck. She could feel the stress. Max had told her about the visit with Mike Davis with the DEA. He had also mentioned the episode with the female DEA agent spitting on Von Salkowski and the attorney Ray Hodges fast action and filing the complaint which alleged his client was innocent. He would file a lawsuit if disciplined action against the agent and her manager were not enforced. Vicky knew those types of lawsuits filed against the DEA and other governmental agencies were used as free advertising for the lawyer when they broadcast in the free media web sites and newspapers. Max had his assistant to forward the information of the night club and the best time to strike. Max had told Vicky to have Wayne devise a plan of action.

Wayne at first had tried to talk her out of the assassination. She explained to Wayne the decision had already been made.

***

Wayne was on his third cup of coffee as he watched the surveillance tapes and reviewed the still photos of the large night club. He read the report from the analysis team from CIA headquarters. He said, "His security is set up for the night club and out of hand customers. He has eight bouncers that work the front door and the interior of the night club which is all routine with running a large nightclub in Los Angeles. He has a large office in the back of the club with an apartment. He has security at both entrances to the back-office area. This security consists of all men from Russia and is set up for his protection of his illegal activities. He is not worried about the FBI or local police. His attorney is Ray Hodges, who has a reputation for being a very good defense attorney, and very dirty. His personal bodyguard is nicknamed the executioner. The FBI has been watching Ray Hodges for years but never approached him. We really need more time." He slid the photos of the men mentioned over to

Vicky to study. He looked at Vicky knowing she was not going to wait.

***

Vicky walked into the upscale nightclub in Los Angeles and started walking up the rear steps to the office. It was three p.m., and the club was empty except for some staff placing stock behind the bar. One of the dancers was practicing using the pole to spin in circles while another lady watched her. The bouncers for the night club were not scheduled to work until six p.m. The large Russian guard cut her off and indicated she could not pass. She watched him as he rotated his weight to his left leg, and he stepped toward her. She also noticed he was Genu Valgum better known as knock-knees. He did not consider her a threat. She dropped and planted her left foot and extended her right foot into his left knee pushing the kneecap inverted. The large man did not recognize the fracture in his left kneecap until he was almost on the carpet. The other two guards ran toward her from the hallway leading to the back office when they saw the large guard fall. She pulled her pistol and shot each man in the chest approaching from down the hall. She shot the guard on the floor reaching for his knee twice in the head and spun quickly and shot the camera above the door. She listened in her earpiece as Little Jimmy explained where in the room the four people were standing. "Two in the middle of the room, one standing across from your entry point and one to the left." The satellite reveled the heat images on his monitor. She proceeded down the hall and opened the door. Mr. Salkowski was bent over playing pool taking a shot. He glanced up from his shot. Vicky recognized Ray Hodges and shot him in the center chest and the guard, the executioner who was standing further inside the room in the forehead as he reached for his gun. Mr. Salkowski dropped his pool cue and reached for his gun. She shot him in the shoulder and the middle of his back as he spun around and fell onto the plush carpet. She walked over and stood looking down at him. She shot him in the forehead. She turned to the young lady who was in the room to provide additional entertainment, "You need to get your clothes on and leave before the police arrive. You did not see anything." She stared at the young lady and said, "Remember Rochel you did not see anything." Rochel at first was in shock and moved slowly pulling her dress over her head and walked out the office door. Vicky unlocked the rear door by moving the large steel bar hanging from one door casing to the other and left through the back door. Wayne and Little Jimmy pulled up in the van. She hopped in the side door and said, "It is done." She removed her blond wig, the fake mole on her cheek, and her baggy pullover raincoat and said, "We need to head for Seoul, Korea. Tell Eric of Newport the threat has been eliminated."

Chapter 32

Mike picked up his cell phone. He was trying to relax while watching his granddaughter play tee ball. He noticed the caller ID and walked toward the outfield. "Hello".

His assistant said, "You need to turn the news on. You are not going to believe what is being reported in Los Angeles."

Mike said, "I am at a tee ball game watching my granddaughter. What is going on?"

The assistant looked at his note pad and said, "One female gunman at 3:55 p.m. west coast time walked into Von Salkowski's nightclub through the front door, and into the office located in the rear of the building and shot Salkowski three times. Once in the back, once in the shoulder and once through his open mouth. The bullet exited the rear of his head into the floor. He was executed. Three of his guards and the executioner have also been confirmed killed."

Mike smiled to himself and glanced out to the tee ball field when he heard the parents yelling for the child to throw the ball from the outfield to a teammate in the infield. "Is there any information who did this?"

"The information is all raw. One of the interior cameras was also shot. We are confused why since all the cameras were offline for twenty-four seconds. Our office in Los Angeles is just now arriving at the scene. There is one other person confirmed dead."

"Who else?"

"Ray Hodges was shot in the chest and was positively identified as one of the dead bodies. There was a witness that said the three men were being entertained by a young lady who was seen walking out the side door of the nightclub after the shooting. The local authorities are trying to locate her. This appears to be a professional hit. One female gunman entered the nightclub wearing gloves. The cameras on the inside of the building were somehow cut off and then restarted twenty-four seconds later except for the one camera that was shot. We have limited footage from the exterior cameras from the restaurant across the street and the redlight cameras. Do you think this had anything to do with our meeting which took place at Langley?"

Mike Davis smiled to himself. "Danny" He hesitated. "Danny, we were lied to while we were at Langley."

"You mean Max Doran lied to us?"

"Yes Danny. The director of the CIA, I can guarantee you knows the identity of our people who were killed in South America. He damn well knew who agent Ozzie Lopez was. He also was letting us know when he asked me if I knew who Von Salkowski was that the CIA was getting ready to take him out. This was not done by chance."

"So, you do think it was related to our meeting."

"What meeting? I would like a full report tomorrow. Maybe we can use the chaos this has started to our advantage to infiltrate the drug cartels. Thanks for the update."

Chapter 33

Eric was relieved to hear the news from Little Jimmy. He was watching Casey talk to her mother on the phone. Casey's mother had been in detox, and her brother was the cook making the meth. He was being released from jail next week. He had been able to perfect his technique of making crystal meth. He got caught with a couple of joints in a routine traffic stop. Casey had never known her father. He died when she was only one year old.

Eric now was feeling responsible for Casey. He was relieved to hear the Russians were not going to bother her. He had never mentioned them to her. He did not want to scare her. He had realized she was a nice girl, but she was always attracted to the wrong guys. He knew their relationship could not last. She enjoyed her job too much. The more men she met, the more addicted she became. She looked forward to getting her fix from different men weekly. She hung up the phone.

She looked at Eric as he walked into the family room. She said, "I am not going home anytime soon. Maybe we could go on a beach trip. I need a vacation. I need to stay away from my family. They will want me to give them my money."

Eric smiled at her, "A beach trip would be nice, but the FBI just called. They said your last segment worked. They have a lead. They need you to upload another segment as soon as possible similar to what you just performed." He paused and then added. "I have got to travel with the job, and I will be back in a few days. Maybe you could go stay with someone for a few days. I would worry about you if you stayed here."

"I will be okay by myself for two or three days. Who is going to bother me?"

Eric, more direct said, "No. You need to stay with someone and stay out of sight until I get back from the trip." He looked at Casey and could tell she was hurt. He added, "That man that came here the other day was from the Russian mob. He threatened me and you if I did not pay him twenty-five percent of what we make. So, I am concerned about your safety."

"Russian mob. Holy Hell, Eric. Do you not think you should have told me prior to now?"

"I read an article on the web about him. I was trying to figure out who he was. He was shot in his club in Los Angeles yesterday. He had a lot of enemies. He is dead, but other people might step in and take over the extortion business. I would feel better if I knew you were safe."

She looked at Eric and said, "The hell with you. You are trying to break up with me and don't have the balls. I will go stay with Joey. He seems to like me."

Eric knew Joey was the weightlifter and male model who performed with Casey in the last two segments. He looked like he was on steroids.

"No. I am not trying to break up with you. I am just worried about you." She started crying. Eric walked over and held her. He said, "I got to head out of town, so I need for you to go and stay with Joey. He can protect you. I will call you when I return. I packed your bags."

Casey pushed him away when she saw her suitcases in the doorway to the utility room and threw her glass down on the wood floor and said, "The hell with you. I know you are throwing me out." She picked up two of her suitcases and rolled the other one to the door. She turned at the door and said' "I was nothing to you. You used me."

She walked out the door slamming the door behind her. A few seconds later, Eric could hear the tires on the Toyota squealing as she spun out the driveway and around the corner of the driveway and the road. Eric thought to himself, "What just happened?"

Chapter 34

The military transport carrying the team landed, and they were driven to the motel in the downtown business district of Seoul. They had rented a villa and were waiting. Wayne was looking over the map of Seoul trying to become familiar with the roads. He and Little Jimmy had located the American air bases in the country of South Korea and the American Embassy in case of a need to retreat to safety.

Eric said, "Casey promised to send out a special segment," as Billy Ray was walking from window to window watching the surrounding area. Little Jimmy looked at Eric and could sense his downward turned mood. Little Jimmy had known his friend to be cheerful with a sarcastic personality. He always seemed to be in good frame of mind. He wondered what was bothering him.

Vicky was looking at her lap top screen. "Mia is now set up and waiting. Wayne, call Delores to have the segment released."

They waited patiently and said nothing. After forty minutes, Wayne said, "It might not work." Eric knew

Casey was upset and thought she might not have provided a good segue into the segment. The segue had to be good, or the segment would not be purchased. Eric pulled open his computer and walked out onto the balcony. He purchased the segment and waited. He watched Casey walk to the pool area holding hands with two completely naked men. She acted frisky as she removed her towel as she talked about performing with two large muscle-bound men. He turned the computer off before the segment was over and thought, "What have I done?"

The CIA person sitting with Mia came online and told them he was forwarding the address. Wayne wrote down the address and jumped up and looked at the map and then at the computer over Little Jimmy's shoulder who pulled the address up on the real estate website. "We are five miles away, and we have the satellite coming up now," said Little Jimmy.

Billy Ray had also looked over Little Jimmy's shoulder and said, "I cannot get a shot if he stays inside that compound. We will have to get inside the compound. There is a large stone fence around the entire complex with guards at the front and rear gates."

Vicky asked, "What is that place?" Vicky then watched Little Jimmy work the keyboard. She realized he was no way as fast and efficient as Mia working the keyboard. Mia also would anticipate the next request and have the information at her fingertips.

Little Jimmy punched on the keyboard and said, "It is a residence. It is one of many owned by Yuzhno, who is part owner of the coal supplier for the utility district. He has made a fortune selling coal to manufacture electricity for the people in South Korea. It is not like in America. He is the monopoly of the coal supply in South Korea. I bet Burnside is staying in that compound."

Little Jimmy then pulled up the live satellite feed from Washington. Billy Ray and Wayne stood behind him and looked at the compound. Billy Ray sat down in Vicky's chair once she stood. She kept watching Billy Ray stare at the compound photo security from the orbiting satellite with a live feed from the CIA desk in Washington. He was concentrating on the scene and printed a photo. He glanced up and asked Little Jimmy to zoom out twenty percent and print off another photo. He looked perplexed. Vicky asked, "What is bothering you, Billy Ray?"

Little Jimmy handed him the requested photo.

Billy Ray looked at the photo. "Burnside knows his stuff. There is no easy way to breach this complex without being in the open and once inside the complex our team would be sitting ducks. They have several firing points looking down at our advancement. An average shooter could take out several people in this area." He pointed at the map and the position. "With the razor wire around the top of the walls, we would have to take the time to cut the wire and be sitting ducks. The entire perimeter of the top of the wall is in the open with firing points looking down. This looks like we are walking into a possible trap. Even at night, if the power is cut to the property, there are those backup generators. There would be no way to knock out the lights and be in stealth mode. In addition, look at these points outside the compound." He pointed to eight different points located at the top of buildings stationed on all four exterior walls of the compound. "If they stationed shooters in these places, our men on the exterior will be exposed. Like shooting ducks on a pond. Do we know if there are underground tunnels leading into this compound?" He looked up from the printed map of the compound. He said, "During the Iraq War, we discovered hidden escape tunnels in some of the large compounds."

Vicky started rubbing the cross hanging around her neck. She knew something was not kosher. She said, "We do not have any additional intel on the compound, but this is a trap." She picked up her phone and hit the speed dial number. Max answered, "You need to put everything on hold."

Max asked in an urgent tone, "Why do we need to hold off?"

Vicky knew something was up. She could tell with his aggravated tone. "Something is not right. It is a hunch. I have met Burnside. He will be prepared for an assault."

"The South Korean Government wants to be part of the plan."

Vicky asked in a shocked voice, "How did the South Korean government find out about Burnside and this mission?"

Max rubbed his forehead while he hesitated. "I was asked by our newly elected President in my daily conference call two days ago what the status was. I wanted him to know we were making progress. I explained your unit had been tracking Burnside and located him in Seoul. He wanted to be kept up to date. I explained the most updated information when your team provided the address in South Korea. He told the South Korean President about the mission since they were talking about the summit with North Korea being in his country. I had no idea President Grant had mentioned any of this information to the South Korean President. When he mentioned it to me after he had already told the South Korean President, I yelled at him. I am surprised he did not fire me."

"Damn Max, I need to talk to Mia immediately and you need to make this happen as soon as possible. Get her on my line."

Vicky hung up. She rubbed her cross and felt angry and shocked that the new President could be so gullible. President Grant had never worked in foreign affairs. He didn't think about leaks in foreign governments.

She started pacing back and forth. Billy Ray started looking out the windows and asked Little Jimmy and Eric to keep a look out. Wayne walked in and was removing the battery from his phone and said, "There is a very good chance someone is looking for us. I am going to change phones."

About four minutes later, Vicky's phone buzzed. The operator said, "I have her on the line. The phone call will be recorded."

Vicky in an urgent voice asked, "How hard was it to locate the second signal?"

Mia did not hesitate and said, "Not hard. There were no hidden signals like before. It was like following the breadcrumbs in the open. It was obvious."

"Why the change? Why try to hide the purchase the first time, and not hide it the second time?"

Mia said, "He must have somehow found out about the fact he has been located. Burnside may have set a trap for your unit. However, he may not realize it has to do with the credit card. He seems to be hiding the purchase of the porn from his accounting firm. That is why the purchases bounce from place to place. He has contacts inside the South Korean government, and I am certain he is provided intel from a Korean contact. He worked for the United States Army and was stationed in that region for five years. After what he has done to me, I want you to take him out."

Vicky said, "Thanks Mia." She hung up. She looked at her unit, and before she could say anything, Wayne said, "We got to go. We have a meeting with the South Korean tactical squad. My boss just called me. The South Korean officials are upset that the United States has a unit in their country. The car is waiting for us downstairs."

Vicky looked at Billy Ray and said, "You are right. This is a trap. Burnside was told by someone inside the

South Korean Government we found him. He is going to have his men kill everyone that attacks that complex, and I bet he has already fled. I will tell Max to order the Seal team to remain on the base."

Chapter 35

Wayne and Vicky walked into the headquarters and saw the tactical soldiers being briefed on the mission. The commander walked up to them and said, "You were running a covert operation in our country and were getting ready to kill someone on our soil without contacting us. That is wrong."

Vicky could feel her anger heating up.

Wayne said, "We are here with your government's permission, and we were told you would do as we ask. This was a very fluid operation, and we just located the target. We had to verify if the information was accurate. We had no intention of leaving you out of the operation."

The commander said, "I doubt that. We have a plan to assault the compound. We do not need your help. Our men are the best in the world."

Vicky looked at the map hanging on the portable chalkboard. She could see the large picture of the compound. She looked at the commander and asked, "How many men are you going to use to assault the compound?"

He walked over to the chalkboard and pointed. "We have three squads of thirteen men. We will enter the front gate here and the rear gate here with two squads, and the third squad will be stationed here for support."

Vicky said, "Your men are walking into a trap. When the shooting stops, you will need thirty-nine body bags. Burnside will have them ambushed from here, here, and the squad in reserve will be in a crossfire from these three spots." She had pointed at the map. "You need to stand down and not enter that compound. All your men will be killed. He knows you are coming. He will be prepared with anti-tank rockets and several shooters."

In an aggravated tone he snapped, "My men are not your concern. We have live video. You can watch from my command center. I have my orders to take that compound. We have them surrounded, and they will not be expecting our assault. The city police will provide additional support if needed. There is no way they can escape. You do not know this is a trap. You are guessing, and we don't guess." He walked off.

Vicky looked at Wayne and asked, "Are they secure?"

Wayne said, "Little Jimmy sent me a message Eric, Billy Ray and himself are secure inside the confines of

Kunsan K8 airbase near Seoul. The seal team is standing down."

Vicky hit the speed dial number. Max immediately asked, "What did the commander say?"

"They are going to proceed. My team made it to the airbase. They are clear and cannot be blamed for this failure. Wayne will head to the Embassy. I will watch from the command center. Max, this is a trap, and all these men are going to die. You need to tell President Grant, so he will know before it happens. Grant needs to call the president here in South Korea and tell him to proceed with extreme caution. They need to check the surrounding building for snipers, and they need to assault this compound from the air. The mission starts in less than two minutes."

"I have told President Grant, and I could hear the Chief of Staff in the background telling President Grant we have no proof. I urged President Grant to call the president in South Korea. He just called him and told him we had some reservation about this being a trap but no facts. The mission is going to proceed."

Vicky could feel her gut turning. She knew what was about to happen. She looked at Wayne and said, "You need to get to the Embassy before this goes sideways. I have Diplomatic Immunity." Wayne looked concerned and walked quickly to the door.

His driver pulled up, and he said, "The American Embassy and don't spare the horses."

The commander was listening as the mission started with his first squad breaching the front gate with the explosion pushing the two gates wide open and the second squad simultaneously breaching the rear gate. She walked up next to the commander as the support staff and the commander watched the large screen video feed. Vicky said, "I hope you are correct, and this is not a trap." He glanced at her. She then said, "We will find out if there is a mole inside your government. If this is a trap, someone inside your government has sold your men out, and they all are going to die. My president should have never told your president, and you would not be about to watch your men be massacred. I am so sorry." He shifted his body weight and seemed uncomfortable.

"I have my orders. We are to take control of that compound."

As the time approached, Vicky knew there was nothing she could do for those men. It was like all battles as her father would explain as he studied WW II, the soldiers are only as good as the commanders. The first shot was from the balcony just as Billy Ray had predicted. The shooters were inside the rooms with the light intentionally creating a shadow to conceal themselves. The shooters were better than average. The front sniper took out five men before the unit realized they were being picked off. The unit leader was the first one to be shot and the bullet went through his goggles blowing out the back of his head. Then, the second shooter from the advantage perch on the other balcony shot three men at the rear entrance. The men did as Burnside had predicted and ran for cover against the wall. The bomb blast at the wall killed the eight men. Vicky watched as the signal went off the screen. The massacre was worse than she had thought. She yelled, "You need to abort and get the third unit out before they are killed."

The commander yelled, "We have wounded men penned down and need help. I cannot abandon them."

Vicky yelled, "That is by design. If you don't pull the third unit out now, they will also be killed. The first two units are already dead."

He turned and said to the unit leader, "Proceed."

Vicky turned and walked out the door and down the concrete stairs. She walked across the street down through the market. She dropped her jacket and picked up a scarf from the outdoor clothes rack. She walked through two alleys and saw a bike. She jumped on the bike leaning against the wall and peddled down the hill through the car tunnel. She jumped off the bike and opened the passenger door to the car and said, "Get me out of here." The driver drove her to the Kunsan K-8 Airforce Base, and her unit boarded the flight. She updated the unit on the massacre on the plane ride.

Chapter 36

Little Jimmy dropped Eric off at his front porch. They looked and saw Casey and Joey sitting in the old Toyota truck in the side driveway. Little Jimmy said, "I will see you tomorrow. We need to stay on alert. Vicky seemed to think Burnside would attack us because that is what she would do."

Eric looked over at Casey and Joey. He did not want to have to talk to them. He was tired and felt the jet lag. He remembered how Casey had cried and then decided they were breaking up. Eric had just wanted her to be in another location and safe. Yet here she was.

Eric got out and walked to the front door. Little Jimmy drove off. Eric heard Joey yell for him to wait. Eric turned around and watched the couple jog over toward him. Joey said, "You need to give Casey the four-thousand dollars you owe her." He looked mad and was trying to intimidate Eric.

Eric looked at Casey. He looked back at Joey and asked, "Joey what are you wanting to spend Casey's money on?"

Joey had not expected Eric to stand up to him being four inches taller and seventy-five pounds heavier. He said, "You need to give her the money, or I am going to take it out of your ass."

Eric was irritated and was not in the mood to be diplomatic. He dropped his bag. He said, "You piss me off."

He walked toward Joey. Joey was not certain what Eric was going to do. When Eric got within three feet, he spun and kicked Joey with the perfect karate kick to the chin. Joey's head flipped backward, and Eric landed balanced on both feet. He did not hesitate and followed up with a firm punch to the sternum driving his fist in between the rib cage. Joey lost his breath and fell over holding his mid-section. He laid on the driveway gasping for air.

Eric turned and walked back toward the front door. He turned and looked at Casey, "If you want to talk to me, Casey, you may come in my home, and we can talk. Joey you can go to hell. I do not ever want to see you on my property again."

He opened the front door, and Casey rushed toward him, "Hold on."

They walked into the foyer and then into the large family room. Eric went over to the bar and poured himself a stiff drink. Casey said, "Well hell, I did not know you knew karate."

"Tell Joey I am sorry. It has been a really long day." He reached behind his neck and rubbed his neck while taking a drink. He thought about the Korean men, which had walked into a trap and thirty-nine men were killed. The compound where Burnside was thought to be staying had a system of underground tunnels. All the bad guys got away. "We had to cancel our trip for the Children Around the World because of the conflict in the region. That is why I am home early and very pissed off." He took another drink. "What is Joey talking about when he mentioned I owe you four grand?"

Casey said, "I have worked hard doing those segments, and I figured I was owed five-hundred per segment. I want my money."

"What is Joey going to do with your money? Is he going to buy some more steroids or more coke?"

"That is none of your business."

He took another drink and poured himself another. "Okay Casey. You asked me to help you with saving your money. All those clothes you purchased and all your makeup and trips to the beauty shop for your cosmetic treatments, I expensed that cost through the company I created. I showed it all as an expense. I took your earned money after all your expenses and placed it in a savings account in your name. Do you remember when I met you? You had made car payments for that guy. You need to pick better guys. They are using you. Why did you think I owed you four-thousand dollars?"

Casey said, "I just thought I made four-thousand dollars, and I heard you tell the bank manager on the phone I had four grand. Joey said he made five hundred per segment, so I figured at five hundred per segment I was owed four thousand dollars."

"Casey. You have four-hundred thousand give or take a few thousand in your savings account. It is all yours. You asked me to help you with your finances, so I did. Your income is based on a percent of the purchases."

She placed her hand over her mouth in total surprise. "Why did you kick me out. I want to live here with you." She looked hopeful.

"I wanted you to be safe while I was out of town. The Russian Mob has a history of not playing fair. They try to muscle in on small companies like mine, which I was unaware of when I started my company."

"It sounds like you want me to move back into your home."

He took another drink and said, "Yes. I do."

"I will be right back." Casey ran out the door. Eric knew Joey would be upset as he watched Casey run by the living room windows on the sidewalk.

Chapter 37

Vicky hung up her phone. She looked at Wayne. "Professor Patrick Roust cannot remember the location of the research, or he is not telling. Max has had two different people interview him, and they were monitoring with a lie detector. They have nothing. Max indicated he has been moved to a white-collar prison to protect him. Max was concerned the Syndicate might have been able to locate him. The fewer people in the loop who know his location the better."

Wayne said, "He might not be telling the truth, and why would he tell us?" Delores walked into the bonus room above the Prestige Clothing store. She was wearing tight fitting jeans and boots. Her hair was blown back. Vicky was in deep thought. Little Jimmy asked, "Is Billy Ray washing his bike off?"

Delores nodded her head yes.

Vicky wondered why Delores would know if Billy Ray was washing his motorcycle. Vicky then said, "You know something? I never understood why Butler, Tennessee? Why Senator Davis? Why Judge David Larkin? Why the dentist, Eugene Baxter? Why the Germans who were headed to Butler and are still in jail arrested in Butler County for a bank robbery in Arkansas? Did the FBI agent that was killed at the tower in late May over a year ago by a rogue Army commando, Bill Duff, know something? What do we know about her? What is her background?"

Delores remembered her too well. She had recruited her to work undercover in Butler, Tennessee and then had to meet her parents and to tell them how she died. The parents wanted to see their daughter who had been cut into pieces with a machete. The mother passed out when the tech in the medical examiner's office pulled the sheet back to reveal the body. Delores said, "She was new to the job. She had just graduated from Quantico."

Vicky said, "I mean what did her family do for a living? What is her background? Wayne and I have looked over all her research records. We must have missed something."

Delores looked focused and recalled what she had remembered. "Her father owned and operated a cement plant in Florida near Dade County. The family was very successful in the concrete business. They had also owned a commercial construction company. She was working on a story on the history of Butler County." Delores started visualizing the papers found on her kitchen table after her death. Delores said, "She had reviewed different building projects when they started and when they ended. The old High School was built in 1929 with 50,000 cubic yards of concrete and then the replacement high school was built in 1963 with 300,000 cubic yards of concrete. The newest high school was finished in 1991 with 700,000 cubic yards of concrete. She had retrieved the copies of the invoices for concrete used in these projects from Dobbs Concrete Company and the county archives." Delores rubbed her forehead. She then said, "There was another invoice dated March 3, 1991, for 1,595,000 cubic yards of concrete. This was more than all the concrete in the three high schools combined."

Wayne said, "Do you mean 115,950 square feet? 115,950 cubic yards would fill a pro football stadium."

Delores said, "I am certain. She had circled the number on the invoice."

Vicky said, "That is what we missed. She would have worked summers in her family's business. She would have noticed something was not kosher with that much concrete on one job. Where did all that concrete go to be delivered?"

Delores said, "The name of the purchaser was Freedom Inc. It was taken to the address on Lake Moore Drive."

Wayne said, "Lake Moore is off Lake Shore. Lake Moore is the name of the short street where Senator Davis lived."

Chapter 38

Vicky had looked forward to the Sunday morning church service and seeing her church friends. She had been traveling and missed several Sunday morning services in the past six months. During the prayer service, Matt asked all who wanted to come to the front and have their own private prayer with God. Vicky bent down on her knees. She thanked God for giving her the courage to kill the wicked. She thanked God for protecting her and her team. She promised God if the Lord would allow her the time, she would complete her reckoning. She glanced to her side as she was standing and noticed she had been praying longer than anyone else. The folks who sat in the back of the church had already rotated through the prayer service.

Vicky had noticed the first service on this Sunday morning at the church was full to capacity. She was so proud of Matt. He had been the preacher at Middlebrook United Methodist Church for over a year and the church had more than tripled in size. He truly loved being the preacher and worked several hours each week preparing for the Sunday morning service. People were driving from the neighboring counties, Nashville, and southern

Kentucky to be part of the church. He had started by asking the congregation if they thought Jesus was ever afraid? Did they think he worried about diseases like cancer or other illnesses? Matt had paused and then answered his rhetorical questions. "There is no fear with true love. There is no fear when a person has nothing but love in their heart. There is no room for fear, gluttony, pride, anger, envy, sloth, or jealousy. Jesus taught us how to love. In the absence of the seven cardinal sins: fear, gluttony, pride, anger, envy, sloth and jealousy is love."

Vicky had tried to listen but kept thinking about being betrayed. She wondered if she could ever forgive Mia. She had remembered Jesus washing the feet of Judas at the last supper after the betrayal and before the crucifixion. She snapped out of her thoughts when she realized the sermon was over, and they were being asked to stand for the closing prayer.

Sunday afternoon, Vicky told Matt she would be back home the next day. She had to meet her boss. She had led Matt to believe she was going to meet Ethan Howard, the president of Children Around the World. She was in fact asked to visit the White House for the security meeting.

Before Max and Vicky were ushered into the oval office Max said, "Please do not say anything or suggest anything unless you are asked directly. It will come back and bite you. They will make you point on some mission to move their agenda forward. Take my word on this."

Vicky nodded that she understood. She never liked to visit the White House. All the prior visits had been unpredictable, and Vicky had decided she did not like unpredictable events. The general over the military stood and offered his hand along with the Vice President and a couple of Senators from each party. Stewart, the Chief of Staff, had walked over from the window and was standing off from the group. He had a frustrated look on his face. Vicky remembered she was there to listen and not speak unless she was asked something directly. She and Max did not say anything to Stewart, and Vicky noticed he was acting more unfriendly than usual.

The President walked in and said, "Thank you so much for coming." He had a worried look on his face. The general looked straight ahead, and the other people stopped talking and looked at the President. Stewart said, "You two certainly screwed up in South Korea. What were you thinking? We had Burnside trapped, and you pulled your men back. You don't pull your men back when you're in battle."

Vicky placed her hand on Max's forearm and cut Max off, "Burnside was not in that compound and my men were not going to walk into that trap and be slaughtered like cattle. Thirty-nine brave men were gunned down because Burnside was told we were coming. All the bad guys escaped through the hidden underground tunnels."

He turned toward Vicky, "They were not our men. Soldiers get killed in war, and your men could have made the difference." He then turned toward Max as he finished the statement with a disgusted look on his face.

Vicky walked up to him and hit him with a right fist in the sternum. Stewart immediately doubled over out of breath falling to the carpet floor and was coughing. She bent down and gritted her teeth in his ear, "There are thirty-nine men that will not be able to hold their kids and see their families because of you. Those men were ordered by unfit commanders who did not understand the landscape. You're a cold-blooded bastard."

Vickey stepped back and realized she had just leveled the Chief of Staff in the oval office in front of the President of the United States and a few top-ranking personnel. There was an awkward two second pause.

President Grant cleared his throat and said, "Stu. I believe you have met your match." He smiled at his friend lying on the carpet trying to get his breath with a red face. The Secret Service agents appeared from the side door. They had a look of intensity on their faces. The President said, "Everything is okay. You may leave." The President looked at all parties and smiled and said, "The President of South Korea has called me. They apprehended General Wando. He was arrested for espionage and shot and killed along with his eleven closest subordinates and Yuzhno the owner of the compound. They realized someone was crooked and killed everyone they thought was involved. The Koreans have little tolerance for that type of behavior. We are here to discuss the whereabouts of the former National Security Director, Nathanial Burnside."

Max said, "We have a lead on locating Burnside, but we would rather keep the lead to ourselves. We cannot afford to have our people killed in a trap."

He looked at Stu who was getting off the floor and sitting down in a chair.

The President said, "I can understand. I am new at this type of business. I will watch what I say in the future. I do not want him captured. That would be embarrassing to us since he was a general in our Army and the NSA director. We cannot explain that to the world. He needs to be taken out. I am giving you the order. This is a national security situation. We have no other choice."

Max glanced at the four other people present two from the republican party and two senators from the democratic party and said, "Please put that order in writing. We will get him. He cannot hide forever. Is there anything else?"

President Grant said, "I will put that in writing. He is a threat to our national security. I have talked to the Senators here from both parties, and they concur. I will keep the only copy of the order here at my desk." He looked at the General, the other guest, and then at Stu. He asked, "General, do you or Stu have any questions for our esteemed guests from the CIA?" Max thought about asking for a copy, but he knew he did not want to push the President.

The general indicated he was fine and had no questions. Stu looked at Vicky with an annoyed look on his face and then at Max. He finally said, "If you two can get him, I will try to forget about that sucker punch."

Max reached over and grabbed Vicky by the elbow and turned her to the door. He looked back and said, "We will not let you down, Sir."

Once they were outside walking toward the car, Max blew air out of his mouth and said, "That went great. I was worried you might say something and get yourself in trouble." He mocked a laugh. "I never dreamed in my wildest dreams you would kick that prick's ass in the oval office in front of the President of the United States." He smiled and then added, "Hell, I hope you never get mad at me."

Vicky did not answer and was trying to recall what Mia had said about Burnside not knowing about the trace on his credit card, which was through Viatect. She pulled out her phone and called Eric. Eric listened and said he understood.

Chapter 39

Wayne called Vicky and said, "We have been on sight for forty minutes. We have confirmed the concrete was used under Senator Davis's home to make some large concrete structure located beneath his basement and rear yard. Eric was able to locate the hidden door and stairs leading downward. The excess dirt was used to level the lake lot. The structure is over two stories deep. We located two vents cut at forty-five degrees leading to the surface and a hidden tunnel leading toward the lake with a hidden exit door. We have no idea what the purpose of this structure is. We cannot tell how thick the concrete walls and floors are. The ceiling appears to be three feet thick. We first thought it was a bomb shelter, but we just don't know. There were no supplies to support an extended stay."

Vicky listened and then asked, "Is it built like a pyramid? Is there a chamber in the middle connected to the two channels which are set at forty-five degrees which lead to the surface?"

"The chamber does have the vents connected. We will need to have an engineer look at this. We are confused."

"You have located the doorway to space travel. The concrete is to shield the atomic blast. We will need to keep this quiet, and I will tell Max. The President will need to be updated."

Chapter 40

Casey came down the stairs into the family room and announced, "Joey still was not happy, because I won't return his call." She walked up to Eric and said, "I am going to make you happy. I mean really happy." She placed her arms around him and started kissing Eric.

Eric pushed her backward and said, "Wait a minute. I was just talking to the FBI. They indicated they needed you to do a solo session as soon as possible. They believe the person of interest will order your session."

Casey licked her lips and said, "Well the soonest the video guy, Tony, can get here is in the morning about 10 a.m. So, now we have the rest of the day and all night to spend getting reacquainted. I missed you. The last few nights were fun, but day sex is the best."

Eric held her back and said, "Listen Casey. There was a movie in the 1960's where Paul Newman was in the chain gang. There was a scene where a young lady came out of the house and washed her car with the entire chain gang watching her. This is known as one of the most seductive scenes in all of television." Casey raised her eyebrows and looked mystified at Eric. "The director made the actress stay in a motel room by herself for two days prior to her session. It made a difference. She looked and acted frisky during the making of the scene."

"So, you are going to keep me locked up until 10:00 a.m. in the morning?"

"You need to be focused on your session. The FBI has indicated the results suggest the best case of success is for you to wear a lot of underwear and once removed, you need to use baby oil all over. Then, wash my car in the nude with nothing on but a thick layer of baby oil. I will sleep on the couch tonight."

"What are you going to do while I am performing my session? Are you going to watch and be my director?"

Eric said, "Tomorrow morning is Sunday, and I am going to attend church."

"I was wondering why not expand this business. Have more girls and more sessions. You could make a lot more money."

"I do not want to be in the porn industry. The FBI set this up on the network free of charge. They placed your session ahead of all others, and they ran hundreds of commercials advertising your segments. I am not certain how much the overhead would have cost us, but you are correct, we could make a lot more money." He turned and walked into the kitchen.

Chapter 41

Vicky walked into the prison. She did not dread it like she did the first visit. The halls were empty with metal-locked doors at the ends and several on both sides of the hall. The guards never smiled, and the inmates would not attempt eye contact. Vicky followed the large guard and was shown into one of the six small conference rooms. Mia walked into the room and smiled. She sat down across from Vicky, and this time she was not chained to the desk and chair. Vicky asked, "How are you holding up?"

"I am doing good." She broke eye contact with Vicky. "I am no longer in solitary confinement. They provided me opportunities to talk with the other inmates. I have better food and more time to exercise and watch tv. It is getting a little better. I am glad to hear you and the guys were not part of the massacre in South Korea."

"That is why I came to see you. We held Casey's last session up from being presented. We have her upcoming session advertised a great deal. We were hoping to try to figure out what continent Burnside is hiding. We are certain he left South Korea. We need to get him before he enters Russia or China. We need to be close, so we can get him before he slips past us again. His friends are dwindling. Where do you think he might go?"

"I would suggest you go to the continent of Australia. Just you, Wayne, Little Jimmy, Delores, Eric of Newport, Billy Ray Claiborne and myself." Vicky looked at Mia. Mia added, "Well I thought I would try to get a weekend pass."

"Why Australia?"

"People are like reptiles. They always go back to their habitat where they feel safe. Did you know snakes and turtles always go back to the same exact spot to lay their eggs and stay within a one-mile radius of that spot during the course of the year and their life? That is what Burnside will do. He has a daughter who lives in Australia. He has not seen her in ten years. He will want to see her and his grandkids before it is too late. He knows his time is limited. He cannot hide forever from the CIA."

Vicky said, "He is also desperate, and Max and I are concerned about the actions of a desperate man. He could have left South Korea and pulled his men out and those thirty-nine federal South Korean officers would not have been killed. He likes to kill and that is in his DNA. Vicky hesitated and smiled and said, "The team is ready. We just need to be close enough to him to catch him when he turns on his signal and pays for Casey's segment." Vicky broke the awkward couple of seconds of silence. "I have been having trouble getting in touch with Billy Ray. Wayne, Little Jimmy, and Eric are already packed and ready. Maybe I will see about getting you a weekend pass."

Mia said, "Call Delores's number. You can reach Billy Ray by calling Delores."

Vicky looked perplexed and asked, "Why would Delores know where Billy Ray Claiborne is located?"

She realized the "why" as she asked the question. She remembered the two walking into the bonus room above Prestige Clothing Store the other day with Delores wearing a pair of jeans and the look that her hair had been under a helmet. Vicky looked surprised and said, "You 've got to be kidding? There is no way."

Mia smiled. "They have been sleeping together for weeks. I believe they are in love."

Vicky looked surprised and thought out loud, "Sweet Mary mother of Jesus. Slap your grandmother. I would be hot damn. Choke the goose. That information would blow the screws out of the submarine. I did not see that happening. Yet you are in prison and know this." She looked at Mia with questionable look wondering how she had missed the two dating.

Mia started giggling. She loved to see Vicky wound up and surprised by the obvious. She repeated, "slap your grandmother and choke the goose" and kept laughing harder. She also was not accustomed to the metaphors and sayings used by Americans since she had grown up in Pakistan. Now that she had moved to middle Tennessee, she had heard several sayings only a southerner would use.

All the stress had built up over time with her being in prison. She started giggling and now could not stop laughing uncontrollably while watching Vicky act so serious trying to come to terms with the obvious.

Vicky keep talking, "The pretty black lady who graduated from Harvard Law with a photographic memory who attended all private schools, took ballet dance lessons for years as a child and a teenager, is always finished out perfectly with her attire, and the boy from south Texas that won the Webb County competition for catching the most rattle snakes in his teenage years, chews tobacco, never is clean shaven, drinks beer from a bottle like nobody's business, has tattoos on his oversized biceps and one on his neck that says redneck, are in love."

Mia looked at her and was still laughing out of control. Vicky had the look of bewilderment on her face and said, "I wonder what they talk about. I would love to hear them discuss politics."

Mia leaned back in her chair holding her side laughing. She loved to see her old friend so perplexed, wound-up, and upbeat.

Chapter 42

Mia was surprised to be sitting on the plane with her friends as they were about to land in Sydney, Australia. She was happy to be out of prison even if she was wearing her ankle bracelet providing her signal anywhere in the world, to the CIA team in Virginia. She looked over and saw Delores with her head lying back on Billy Ray's shoulder. Wayne was looking at maps and roads and trying to figure travel times. He looked up and said, "We need to catch Burnside when he is not expecting it." He looked back down at the maps, and no one answered him. She saw Eric and Little Jimmy leaning back in their seats with their eyes closed and headphones on listening to their music. She looked at Vicky who smiled at her.

***

Vicky said, "We got him. He paid with the credit card. He is staying at the Four Seasons Hotel 199 George Street. We need to stay back. He will have security watching out for him. The CIA team will follow up and find out how he entered the country. He would have been in disguise and using a phony passport."

***

Little Jimmy said, "He just left the Hotel walking down the street headed for the Museum."

Wayne came on the line, "He is taking a seat at the coffee shop out in the open. He is meeting his daughter and her family. He appears to be doing the grandfather thing. This could also be a trap. He will have guards posted. We need to proceed with caution."

Mia pulled up the video link from satellite showing the plaza live with Burnside sitting in the open. Wayne walked into the motel room. He said, "Little Jimmy has him in view. He is just sitting at the table drinking his drink. We got his ass this time."

Vicky asked, "Is this some type of trap? Where would he have a shooter stationed?"

Billy Ray said, "He would have a shooter in the shadows of one of those rooms." He pointed to the high-rise building. "He would also have assets close by, like that alley." He pointed to the alley. He might have other assets stationed at different places in the entrance area to the museum. There are a lot of people moving through the museum. Any number of them could be one of his assets. His fastest escape route would be back to the parking lot. Once he is in a vehicle, he would be hard to catch or follow unless we had a chopper."

Mia said, "His daughter and her two kids just arrived by taxi. They are walking toward him. That is why he is in the open. He is acting normal in front of his family and then he will disappear for good."

Vicky said, "We've got to move now. Billy Ray, take your position and let me know when you spot the sniper in the high-rise. Eric, you approach from the backside of the alley. Wayne, you watch the food market. Delores, you go and meet Little Jimmy and act like you two are together. You can cover the exit to the parking lot. I might need fast support. I am going to sit down across from Burnside and talk with him."

Wayne said, "That will be suicide. You know he has shooters all around him."

"He will not shoot with his grandkids close by. He won't take the chance of one of them being shot, and he would also not want them to see a dead body from a gunshot. I will tell him he is surrounded. We need him alive." The others looked at Vicky. They knew the kill order had been given by President Grant. No one said a word.

***

Vicky said, "Everyone check in."

Eric said, "I am in position, and I see someone at the other end of the alley who looks out of place."

Billy Ray was rotating from balcony to balcony with his binoculars and said, "I am in position but the view of the rooms on the building are all clear. I will keep watching for movement."

Wayne said, "I am in position."

Little Jimmy came online. "Delores and I are sitting at the table at the restaurant. We got you covered from this side. He is talking to his daughter. The two kids are being taken by the son-in-law to the bathroom, and his daughter is going to order food. We will cover the parking lot. That is the direction for him to leave quickly."

Vicky said, "I am going in." Vicky walked to the table as the daughter got up and went to order food. Burnside was startled as Vicky sat down across from him. He looked at Vicky with anger. Vicky said, "Don't think I won't shoot you in the gut in front of your grandkids. We can handle this in one of two ways. It is up to you."

He raised his hand up and placed his elbow on the table. Billy Ray came on the link. I got movement. I have a shooter.

Delores said, "Green light." Billy Ray saw the movement in the corner of the top floor balcony. The shooter was lying down on the patio and hid behind towels hanging over the rail. The shooter was very good. He had Vicky's face in the middle of the cross arrows. He smiled to himself, and he slowly pulled his index finger on the trigger.

Billy Ray picked up his rifle and located the shooter. He braced the gun on the tripod and gently tightened his index finger on the trigger. He fired his gun with the barrel aimed upward from the lower building across the plaza. The bullet hit the shooter in the front of the baseball cap piercing the top of his skull. "Target down."

Eric kept slowly walking toward the plaza down the alley. He saw the pistol machine gun being pulled out from under the man's shirt. The man was watching the table with Burnside and Vicky. He had not checked the alley from behind. Eric fired for the lower back hitting the man in the spine. The man fell against the wall, and before he could fall to the concrete, Eric ran to him placing his gun with the sound depressor in his waist band and carried him back down the alley with his feet dragging the asphalt floor of the alley. The man could not sit up, and Eric placed him against the dumpster and the fence. Eric removed his earpiece and mic and looked into the man's dying eyes. Eric glanced up and down the alley to make certain the alley was clear. He acted like he was helping the man who had fainted. The man could not move his extremities. He looked into the man's eyes a second time and saw fear. Eric said, "Target down."

Vicky could tell Burnside was trying to listen to his radio feed through the device in his ear. She said, "Why betray the United States? Why try to set off a Russian made nuclear bomb in Butler, Tennessee?"

Burnside kept his hand raised with his arm balanced on his elbow. He said, "I am a true American. I am trying to help America stay on top. Our country is sliding backwards, and America needs people like me to stand on the wall and fight our wars and keep everyone safe. Let me tell you something. No one would have gotten killed, and there would not have been any radiation from the blast. We are not ready to open the Vortex. You have no way to know what you have done. I am the only one who can control these people. We had an opportunity to steal three nuclear warheads, and we took it. Two were recovered by the Russians. We need the uranium from the bomb not the bomb. We were going to store the uranium and destroy the third bomb. It was part of the equation, but we still need the additional research."

Vicky said, while still watching his hand, "You don't have near enough information. A blast that large cannot be contained by two thousand cubic tons of concrete, which Senator Davis used to build this Vortex gateway. The concrete would not have been enough to contain that much energy." His eyebrows raised at the fact they had discovered the launch pad. "You do not know if the Vortex will work. You do not know how to control the power of the Vortex. You have no way to know where in the universe the Vortex will open the passage. There are just too many questions. What you were doing was taking an unacceptable risk not based on sound scientific proof." There was a pause. Vicky then said, "My sniper took out your sniper, and we have taken out your man in the alley. What will it be? Do you want to come with me? Or do I fulfill the kill order issued by our President and shoot you here in front of the only family you have left?" She paused and watched his eyes. She then added, "Unlike you and your men, we do not kill innocent people. Those thirty-nine men in Seoul did not deserve to die. I did not deserve to be killed in the suite at Viatect." Vicky glanced at his daughter, son in law and their two kids ordering their food.

He dropped his hand. Vicky saw his hand drop from her peripheral vison and immediately rolled out of her chair. The bullet hit her chair dead center. Burnside ran for the parking lot.

Wayne had noticed a lady acting like she was looking something up on her I-Phone and then glancing at a paper pamphlet while looking around her surroundings. She was by herself acting like a tourist. Wayne noticed how fit she was and thought why would someone in her early thirties go on vacation by herself. He walked up behind the lady trying to see an earpiece. Her hair was blocking the view. It was hot this time of year in Australia for her clothing. She was wearing long sweatpants and a matching jacket. He pulled the trigger on the stun gun and stuck it in her back in the crowded line near the cafeteria. She fell as she tried to pull her gun.

Billy Ray came online and said, "I took out the second target. He was on the roof behind the sign on the building located northwest of our location." He waited to hear if Vicky had been shot. He knew she was counting on him. Vicky had rolled on the concrete and then ran bent over into the crowd of people. "Check for additional snipers" Billy Ray was relieved to have heard her voice.

Burnside ran through the crowd and jumped in the first taxi. Little Jimmy asked, "Where to, sir?"

Burnside said, "Head for the interstate."

Little Jimmy paused and allowed another taxi to pull out in front of him. Burnside then yelled, "Hurry!" as he dropped a hundred-dollar bill over the front seat. Burnside noticed they were still not moving when the door on the other side of the taxi opened, and Delores sat down next to Burnside in the backseat with her gun pulled. "I am with the FBI, and you are under arrest."

Burnside hit her gun as she hesitated. He opened the rear door and exited the car.

Vicky, once she heard Billy Ray come online and announced the second target was down, ran for the parking lot staying low in the large crowd of people. She came around the taxi and held her gun even as Burnside started exiting the vehicle and said, "I will not hesitate to shoot you. Matter of fact, try me." She watched as Burnside took the bullet in the chest. She knew the shooter had to be high in a building from the opposite direction. She dove to the ground and rolled next to him. She hoped the taxi and the other vehicles provider her cover. He looked at her and said, "Beware of the B12. I am sorry. We are on the same team."

"Who shot you. Who is the mole inside the FBI leaking information to the Russian Government?"

He grunted out a whisper. "Do not let my family see me like this." He coughed up blood. He whispered and with his last breath he coughed out a name. Vicky tried to hear what he had said. The Russian's need me dead. She thought he said, Mike Brown. He leaned over and died with his eyes open. Vicky jumped into the back of the taxi and yelled "drive". Little Jimmy floored the car.

Vicky yelled into her mic, "Abort. We have another shooter. There must be a third team in the area. The target is down."

***

The CIA team all left on the CIA jet. She called Max and updated him. She could tell he was aggravated with the killing taken place in the open in a large metropolitan city. He had preferred a needle and a death by what appeared to be a heart attack. Vicky looked out the window of the jet and thought, "Our mission was to kill or capture Burnside. He is dead, but who killed him? Had someone else tracked him to the plaza or had he been shot by someone on his team." She looked around at her team and then reflected about what Burnside had said in the suite at Viatect about having the power of God and now he was dead. He also said beware of B12. She thought he pronounced the name of Mike Brown with the FBI as the mole with contacts in Russia. His voice was a whisper and that was his last breath he tried to mention a name. She wondered what was B12? She remembered asking Delores about Professor Roust. She concluded he was not telling what he knew about his great grandfather's research. The professor does not trust the people that are watching him. He is not safe, and he wants a huge payday. He also does not understand the research.

Her phone vibrated waking her from her deep thought. She answered the phone. To her surprise it was President Grant. She assumed he had called about Burnside. She knew the world news had by now reported the shootings with the dead body lying in the middle of the drive-up area to the large plaza. Once the identity of the former NSA director was discovered, the world media would create a feeding frenzy. This was not the way the CIA wanted to operate with dead bodies from gun shots out in the open. Mia had pulled up the national news channel in Australia. Mia had said, "The reports are stating the former United States Army General and NSA director was shot by an unknown female while on vacation. The female jumped into a taxi and fled the scene. They do not have footage of the shooting but are stating it appeared to be a professional hit. The authorities are trying to piece together what happened and are in the process of investigating the shooting." Vicky knew The CIA team cleaned up the other dead bodies before anyone located them. The three dead men working for Burnside were hauled away in a large garbage truck and the one female was thought to have passed out from a heat stroke. She was taken to the local hospital and has now disappeared. With Burnside being the only body found, she hoped this would minimize the fallout.

Vicky said, "Hello President Grant. He was shot by someone with a rifle. Whoever shot him did not want him to leave with us. We were going to take him alive to one of the offshore locations. We needed to know what he knows about the Syndicate. His cooperation could have been monumental. Sir, someone knows a lot more about the Vortex than Burnside, and they are getting close to testing their theory. I am not certain who can be trusted. There were very few people in the loop that knew where we were going. It was like we were followed and led the other party directly to him or the Syndicate took out one of their own. Burnside had a trap set for us. I doubt the professor is safe."

President Grant was a good listener. "We need to meet and discuss the Syndicate. Since Burnside has been neutralized, Max has indicated we will need to focus on locating the Syndicate. I have an important meeting concerning the Syndicate, and we might change our focus. Do not tell anyone about this upcoming meeting. I do not know who I can trust."

Vicky was surprised. She had assumed he would be calling her about the former NSA director being shot and killed in the middle of a large city with witnesses. She knew the political criticism by both the Republican and Democratic parties would be substantial with Congress wanting answers. With President Grant being an independent, he had no one he could count on or trust in the Senate or in the House of Representatives. The elected officials would try and make a name for themselves speaking out about the President and the CIA. He then said, "You and your unit did your job, and I am glad none of your people were injured."

"I will tell my unit you asked about them. They will be ready for the next mission."

The Last Revelations: The Beginning of the End

***

Vicky could tell the President was a lot more relaxed standing on the bank of the Potomac River and not in his office. The security detail was on alert and standing out of hearing range. One on one away from crowds and news personnel, he seemed to be an average type of guy.

"Yes. I needed a little time to find out some interesting facts." He smiled and looked around and seemed to relax. "You know I was not thought to be a threat to win the election. There was not a glimmer of hope. I guess you could say I snuck in the back door. History will show when the two parties split, I was left holding the bag with the most votes. The Syndicate did not want me to be the president. I believe Masengale, the republican nominee, is part of the Syndicate. He was a close friend with Senator Davis. I now know he was set up with that young Spanish girl, but without her, I would not have won. The American people turned on him when he lied, and the girl was interviewed live on CNN. The pictures of him with her were bad enough, but they had his love juice on her panties and were prepared to use that information against him. But, once he dropped so far in the polls, they withheld that information from the news. They did not want him to drop out of the race and give the Republican

Party an opportunity to replace him with a viable second choice. They knew he would not win, and the party would not know all the information until it was too late. He said he was drugged and then photos were taken with her on top of him. With the drug in his system, he might have been telling the truth about not remembering the details. They did a real number on him. The conservative voters could not bring themselves to vote for the liberal candidate, and her socialism scared the tax paying nation. I thought I could make a difference with jobs and the economy. I know how to run a business and create jobs. I am trying to force large companies to steer clear of the strategy to do more with less. I am planning on providing tax breaks for companies based on the number of employees they hire. To give companies incentives to hire additional workers. I discovered and believe the United States government does not want to solve the health insurance cost problem. The government has in the past used health insurance cost to control the citizens. They want people to work for large companies and pay taxes. The cost of health insurance has forced people to keep working for the large companies, which provide the health insurance benefits. Otherwise, our country would be flirting with bankruptcy like Greece where most of the population is self-employed, and no one pays their fair share of taxes. I was running literally to bring this out in the open while offering a national affordable health insurance plan, and I thought I could help the middle class and the poor if they are willing to work."

Vicky was surprised with his nostalgic conversation. She reached up and rubbed the cross around her neck. "President Grant, I thought you were elected because you ran on doing away with the speed limits on our interstate system." She smiled.

He smiled, "I was considering raising the limits to eighty-five miles per hour, passing laws to force the road construction to take place at nights, and forcing slow drivers to drive on the back roads and secondary roads. I do believe this would force the trucking companies to remove the slow driving mandates on their drivers and increase efficiencies. Plus, people going on vacations could be happier. I was also going to remove the states and the municipalities' abilities to issue speeding tickets by using the stationary cameras."

Vicky smiled at the now smiling President Grant knowing this was just a political ploy to get him noticed early in the election campaign.

He then said, "That position raised me from thirteen percent to thirty-three percent in the polls overnight. Americans truly hate speeding tickets administered by unmanned cameras."

"Sir. What do you know about the Syndicate?"

"There is a lot more. Your boss Max and the FBI director know more about the Syndicate than they have revealed. That is why I do not know who I can trust. There are some very rich people running the Syndicate. There is a very good chance I will be assassinated. As you know, I have very few friends in Washington. Since I am an independent, I have no one I can count on. I have learned to trust no one in Washington. The two parties are constantly fighting for power and control and planning for the next election. I just heard the Democratic Senator, Miran Fellowship from New York talked Supreme Court Judge Allen out of retiring until after the next election. They are hoping to win the next elections and to appoint the next Supreme Court Judge."

Vicky could not think of the best first question. She asked, "Sir. Why are you telling me this?"

He smirked, "We have friends in London. They have contacted me directly and provided proof, but this is not the type of proof that can be mentioned in a courtroom.

They were concerned with the most powerful nation on earth going rogue. They had me vetted. Now, I know where all that money came from for my campaign. I also know where all the dark rumors came from about the conservative and liberal nominees. They no doubt planted that underage girl. I truly had no knowledge about any of this until I met two days ago with the Englishman. He works for an English intelligence organization. I had to slip away from the Secret Service personnel to meet him. The meeting was set up without anyone's knowledge. The agent approached me through my son's school. They had been watching Senator Davis and trying to figure out what he was doing on the national level."

Vicky watched the President. He looked forward and rubbed his face with both hands. He seemed to be wanting help. "I have a plan, but I will need to go off the grid. I will contact you Mr. President when I find out something. I believe we can beat the Syndicate to their missing piece of the puzzle, which is the research. They have figured out how to open a zipper in space and hold an object still while space zooms right by. This creates the ultimate power in the universe. They understand the launch pad, which is built like the pyramids. We now suspect a race traveled to earth and built a pyramid type structure, so they could travel through space by using a vortex. Then, the human race was left with the structure and did not understand it. The Egyptians started building the pyramids without understanding the purpose and not being able to duplicate the original structure. We located the Syndicate's launch pad built underground in Butler, Tennessee. They can create the power to initiate the vortex with uranium from an atomic bomb, but what they cannot figure out is how to estimate distance, direction, and time with traveling through the zipper. They think Professor Epstein figured this part out in 1929 while in Germany."

President Grant listened to the plan. He agreed to meet her and do his part.

She looked sad now that she understood Max was mentioned as knowing more about the Syndicate than he had revealed. She really liked Max.

"He looked at Vicky standing in her pantsuit, dark sunglasses and hair in a wavy long perm with highlights hanging down her back. He said, "You are a remarkably beautiful sexy woman. You are also very smart and brave."

She glanced at him wondering where this conversation might lead. He held up his hands and said, "I am not flirting with you. I also understand your husband is a Methodist Preacher and is working on his Ph.D. in physics with his field of study being the Vortex. When we first met in the White House, I was surprised with your knowledge of the Vortex. No one else seems to have near the insight as you. Now I understand your husband is the foremost person with knowledge studying the Vortex. I was wondering if he could review the information on the Vortex and provide an opinion. We need his help. He is ahead of the other scientists who are now playing catch up. There is no one who has studied the Vortex."

"I do not want my husband involved. Everyone involved with the Vortex or Senator Davis ends up dead. There have been several hundred people around the world killed that we know of in the past year. I do not want my husband to be a target."

"I need you and your unit on this mission. Max hired your unit outside the normal channels within the CIA. I am not certain who I can trust. I am not part of either political party and nothing is getting accomplished. The democrats will not pass any bills and the republicans want to negotiate on every single piece of legislation." Vicky listened for the next ten minutes and was truly surprised at what the President told her.

Chapter 43

Vicky walked into the bonus room above the Prestige Clothing Store. She handed Billy Ray a black duffle bag full of money. She turned and handed Little Jimmy and Eric of Newport each a green and red duffle bag. She handed Wayne the fourth brown one. "This money is not traceable. You will need to open an account in a foreign bank outside the jurisdiction of the United States under an assumed name. You will need to have an alias set up and might need this money at some point to help you hide. Mia's father was found dead in Pakistan. We believe the Syndicate killed him. He was executed with two bullet holes in the back of his head. I had to tell her the bad news. The rest of her family had been released. She cried. Max had a team assigned the job of locating him, and his body was dumped in the middle of a highway in the middle of the night in north Pakistan."

Vicky held her thought for a moment and then said, "Delores and I are going on a mission. Eric you will need to assist us and then you will need to take a vacation. We will contact Wayne, Little Jimmy, and Billy Ray if we need you. Otherwise, you all need to hide. I believe we all are targets. I appreciate what you have done for me."

Billy Ray had unzipped and looked in the duffle bag full of hundred-dollar bills taped together. "How much are we getting paid?"

"Each one of you received ten million. Mia helped me empty the Russian mob Salkowski's bank accounts. Since he is no longer in need of all that money, I took it."

Chapter 44

Vicky and Delores walked into the detention facility. They signed the visitors check in list at the front gate and noticed men were jogging and walking the sidewalk around the inside of the fence located on the perimeter and some others were playing tennis. A few were shooting basketball and a few others were sitting around a table talking. Vicky and Delores glanced up and noticed the location of the two cameras mounted at each corner of the soffit of the building as they approached the front door. She had also noticed the two cameras at the front gate. Once they entered the gate, they did not see any guards as they walked up the sidewalk and stairs and then through the front door.

Professor Patrick Roust seemed happy to see them. Vicky did not introduce herself as an agent for the CIA and Delores as an FBI agent. They both knew the conversation was being recorded with a video recording them live. "It has been over three weeks Thomas since you have been in America. How do you like it so far?" Patrick was getting use to answering to his alias name Thomas.

Patrick Roust looked causally at both women with his smile dissipating. They could tell he had remembered them from his office and in Germany and the journey across the Pacific Ocean. "I like the American food and tv. I will be honest with you. I am ready to move out of this location."

They talked about the weather and general things. Delores walked back and forth next to the table and then stood directly in front of the camera installed in the other room behind the two-way mirror, blocking the view of the front of Vicky. Vicky said, "Thomas, I understand you are having trouble remembering certain information about some research." She held the card up for Professor Roust to read. (Don't say anything about his research. You are being recorded.) Vicky kept the card between herself, and the other camera located behind her in the upper corner of the room.

He read the card and blinked his eyes with a surprised expression. He looked at Vicky who had a matter-of-fact expression urging him to understand. Patrick Roust said, "That is correct. My memory is not as good as it once was." He tried to smile.

She held up the second card. He read the card and had a perplexed expression on his face. He then grimaced and shook his head slightly up and down.

Vicky placed the cards into her pocket and Delores walked back to the door. They said, "Goodbye Thomas."

The man running the camera was telling his partner to go interrupt the interview and ask Delores to move. He was beside himself that an officer stood in front of the camera in the two-way mirror. "She must be new to the job. What is she thinking?" The man stood and reached for the door as Dolores moved. Vicky had stood and the two women asked the guard to open the door. The man operating the camera and the other man standing outside the interrogation room watched in surprise as the two women exited the room quickly walked by them without noticing their presence in the hall headed for the exit. The man running the camera asked his partner, "What just happened?"

***

Vicky commented as they walked out of the prison watching the men still shooting basketball, "I cannot believe the security for these criminals is so relaxed. These men can walk right out the door anytime they want. The security appears to be set up to keep people out, not keep men in."

Delores said, "Why would they leave? They play cards, tennis, work out, read books, and shoot basketball. They are provided three meals a day, provided free medical and dental care and plenty of time to relax. If they were forced to leave, most would have to go back to nagging wives and face the humiliation they caused their families. That is why this prison is called a white-collar prison. Besides most have paid large fines and are in the final months of their sentence. They most likely will have been rehabilitated and the state and federal justice system will never hear from them again. I hope if we get caught for what we are getting ready to do, we end up in one of these prisons."

***

Vicky glanced at her watch. It was 8:53 p.m. She looked at Delores while waiting in the car parked next to the curb watching the gate of the prison and cleared her throat and said, "So, I understand you and Billy Ray Claiborne are in love. Please, do tell."

"There is nothing to tell. He grew up a poor white country boy, and I grew up a rich black girl. It is all normal."

Vicky could not help but smile. "I guess it is normal."

Delores glanced over at the smile on Vicky's face. "I heard what you said when you found out about me and Billy Ray. It was something like this, 'Sweet Mary mother of Jesus. Slap your grandmother. I will be hot damn. Choke the goose. That information would blow the screws out the side of the submarine. I did not see that happening.' So, I guess you were not in the know and a little surprised to find out about us."

Vicky looked straight ahead and said, "I guess I was not in the know. You can take the boy out of the country, but you can't take the country out of the boy. What do you two have in common?"

She turned and looked at Delores and asked, "What do you two talk about? Wait a minute. Do not answer that question. I really don't want to know. It is none of my business."

Delores looked out the front windshield, "Here he comes down the sidewalk along the fence row. He is still scared, or he otherwise would stay put. He knows he is not safe in the prison. I will push the button when he is within ten feet. Text Mia to kill the cameras."

"Roger that. Delores, you need to start the car."

Patrick Roust saw the car easing over toward the gate. The minimum-security facility in California was for low-risk and white-collar crimes. No one had ever escaped. There was no need. Professor Roust was being housed in the facility by the State Department. They had figured it would provide him a safe, comfortable place where they could keep an eye on him. The fear was the Syndicate had discovered his prior locations where the CIA had him initially housed. He was caught using a borrowed cell phone talking to his girlfriend in Germany, so Max had him temporarily moved. No one would think to look in a prison for him. He knew enough to be scared and want the help of the United States Government, but he also knew the research was a game changer. He had asked to see Vicky and Delores. He was surprised with the plan to bust him out of the secure location.

He heard the explosion and saw the white flash. The guard acted as predicted. He took several steps in the direction of the explosion, and Patrick Roust did not hesitate. He ran out the front gate, and Vicky opened the door to the rear passenger seat. He jumped in the car, and the car sped off. Vicky immediately reached over and unlocked the ankle bracelet and shoved it in the container of water. She screwed the lid on the container and then threw it out the window.

"Where are we going?" he asked.

Vicky looked at him and said, "We know you know the location of the research. Time is running out. There has been enough killing. You need to make up your mind right now, who are you going to trust. The men who killed the professors in Germany or us."

"How do I know you are not working for the people who killed the professors."

"You know we work for the FBI and CIA. We just walked into your prison. No one else would have been allowed to do that and besides we are not going to kill you if you don't cooperate with us, but they will. We will let you out at the airport, and you sir will be on your own."

He was becoming excited. He looked anxious. "Who are they? That is what I do not understand. Who are they?"

Vicky looked straight ahead sitting next to him in the back seat. Delores was driving in excess of seventy miles per hour as she noticed the sign, thirty-five miles per hour speed zone. Delores turned her head and looked at Professor Roust in the mirror. "All we know is they are an unidentified group called the Syndicate. We have tracked some of the members and watched them get killed before our very eyes before they could talk. The Syndicate will not hesitate to kill their members, and they will not hesitate to kill you. They now know your identity, and where you had been staying. You were not safe in the Federal prison. This facility was set up for men who are about to be released and are not a threat to run. The security is very relaxed. Once they have the information, you will be a liability. They will not want you to share the information with anyone else. The only way you are going to live is to come with us and cooperate with us. We now understand the Russian Government is involved. You only have one play."

"Why should I trust you or her? I want to go home."

Vicky said, "You won't ever be able to go home. They will kill you for the information. They will force you to talk. We can stop the car right now and let you out. These people have unlimited resources. You will not last one hour on the street by yourself. If you were dead, it might be easier for us. Then, we might beat them to the technology. We have some very smart people working on the science into the Vortex. If we can beat them to the final aspect of the pending link, we win. We now know where the launch pad is located, and we can have it duplicated. We understand the power it will take to start the Vortex and have the access to the source to initiate the Vortex. We work for the United States Government. We have access to uranium and boron. Boron is needed to absorb the neutrons after the uranium has been the trigger. The boron is used to shield the radiation when the Vortex has been activated. The power in a nuclear reaction is what is needed to open the Vortex. If you die and the research is never discovered, the playing surface becomes level. The research you're hiding is the missing piece of the puzzle."

Delores said, "When we were in Berlin, you indicated there was a church in Switzerland where the research might be hidden. Yet, your great grandfather went back to Poland from Sweden to retrieve the research and then Poland was attacked by Russia and Germany led armies in a simultaneous attack. He was trapped on the wrong side of the line. You also said you had never been to Switzerland. The research is not in Switzerland." Delores glanced in the rear-view mirror at Professor Roust. She turned into the small airport.

"Where are we going?"

Vicky said, "Moscow for starters. You and I are going off the grid. I am going to be honest with you. The Russian Government has a source inside the FBI. They either want you or want you dead before the Syndicate locates you. There are only three people who know about this mission. You are in a car with two of them and the President of the United States is the third person. After Moscow, then you are going to tell me where in Sweden the research is hidden. Sweden was one of the nine European countries which elected a neutrality policy during the World War ll. Early in the war, Sweden accepted Jews and other refugees from Germany. He made it out of Poland. He was not trapped in Poland. The dates you mentioned do not add up. The Russian and German armies did not attack Poland until eight months after he went back to Poland. He would have had enough time to escape Poland. We need for you to stop the lying and tell us where the research is hidden."

Chapter 45

The security guard was watching the street from his booth. He controlled the entrance gate, the sign in log, and he also would watch the prisoners out for late afternoon jogs or walks around the sidewalk located near the gate and perimeter fence. The curfew was set for 9:15 p.m. for all prisoners to be in their bunks. He saw the man walking his way slowly toward him on the sidewalk. He knew his name was Thomas and was new to the prison and had not been seen outside since he had arrived. He was going to ask him the common questions: how long will he be here, and where is he from? The loud explosion startled the guard, and he ran toward the explosion. He wanted to make certain no one was injured. He had his hand on his gun in case he needed it. He could feel his heartbeat with the tension in his body. He had volunteered for night shift hoping for an easy shift. He also wanted extra time to study for the bar exam. As the smoke was clearing, he glanced back at his post and noticed the man was gone. He engaged his mic and said, "Unknown person must have set off a small bomb north of the west gate. There is no one injured and no witnesses. The fence is damaged with a hole in the bottom. There is no fire just a lot of smoke."

The guard working the interior desk responded, "Roger that. No one injured and no one witnessed who threw the bomb against the fence. We will send two guards out to inspect and call for a city unit to investigate the exterior. You can return to your post."

As he walked back to the front gate, he became puzzled about the inmate who he saw walking. He was nowhere to be seen. He engaged his mic, "We need to have a head count. There was a prisoner walking toward the west gate when the bomb went off. I investigated the bomb and when I turned, the prisoner had vanished."

***

The manager said, "The numbers do not lie. We had one hundred and thirty-nine men incarcerated before the bomb, and we have one hundred and thirty-nine men after the bomb. All are in bed under lock and key. My understanding is the bomb did not blow a big enough hole in the fence for someone to escape. It created more smoke than damage. Must have been a couple of teenagers passing by and threw a M80 firecracker and a smoke bomb from the car window. Our cameras do not show anyone leaving."

The guard looked relieved but perplexed. He did not want someone escaping on his watch. "Are you certain all are accounted for? He just disappeared."

"Yes. We are certain we have all the prisoners. No one has ever escaped, and our record is still perfect." The guard at the interior desk ran the video back and forth and noticed the slight glitch in the tape prior to the blast but nothing else was noticed and nothing suspicious.

The guard retraced his steps and remembered he walked back to the front gate and as he returned from the inspection of the fence, he looked around the area trying to figure out how he missed seeing the man near the fence heading back into the building. There were several pole lights in the area with just a few shadows. He was truly perplexed. He walked back to the spot where he had stood when he turned around trying to visualize the time it took him to check out the explosion and then realized the man had disappeared. He recalled how slow the man's pace was as he was headed in his direction. Something just did not feel right.

Chapter 46

Vicky looked over at Patrick and said, "You know by helping me, you are doing the right thing. You seem a little nervous."

"I have never liked planes. How do I know I can trust you?"

Vicky looked at her watch. She pulled out her phone. "I want you to talk to someone."

She punched in the number and his face came online. She said, "Yes, Mr. President. He is here."

She handed Professor Roust the phone. Vicky could not hear President Grant, and Professor Roust listened. He finally said in his deepest authoritarian voice, "Yes sir."

He then handed the disconnected phone back to Vicky.

Vicky asked, "What will it be?"

"I guess I will help. Your President is very convincing. He said you are the only one he trusts. It is not going to be easy to locate the research. I was told when I walked into the graveyard at the church in Helsingborg, I would know which grave the research is hidden. With my grandmother, everything dealing with her father and his research was always in a riddle. I know I have been being watched, so I was scared I would be followed to Helsingborg. So, I have waited."

***

Vicky said, "You need to hold my hand. We are supposed to be on our sixth-year wedding anniversary. You need to smile and relax and stop looking around so much. You are acting like you are on the run or hiding out."

He reached over and took her hand. "We are hiding out and on the run. Why did we not fly into Sweden? Why fly into Moscow? There are probably one hundred agents from the KGB watching us right now."

Vicky could tell Professor Roust was still very nervous. She smiled and said, "The KGB is no longer in existence. Besides, we are part of this tour group from America. What we are doing is normal. Don't worry. The short hair, fake mustache, and fake beard hides your identity. The last place the Russian government will look for you is in Russia." Vicky looked around and then whispered. "We will check into the motel and leave early in the morning for Sweden. I need to meet a contact."

***

After eating at a Russian restaurant and returning to the motel room, now pacing the floor for more than two hours, Patrick Roust was sleepy. He walked around the small motel room in his light blue speedo type underwear almost completely naked suggesting they needed to act like they were married and on their six-year anniversary. Vicky had made him a bed on the floor while he was in the bathroom. She had gotten under the cover on the only bed and made it clear to him she would shoot him if he did not go to sleep. She had rolled over and laughed herself to sleep when he saw her pistol in bed with her. She had never seen a man lose an erection so fast.

He had asked where the pistol came from. "I know you did not have it on the plane." She did not answer and suggested he go to sleep. The CIA forward team had checked the room for electronic bugs and hidden the pistol. The CIA had between twenty and thirty agents hidden in Moscow at any given time. Checking motel rooms and planting guns were a routine assignment for them.

She drove the two hours, and Patrick talked the entire car ride. She met Ivan Chezon in Smolensk, Russia located near the border with Belarus. Ivan explained the small plane would go unnoticed. They had enough fuel for the trip to Helsingborg, Sweden. The pilot will file the flight plan once he crosses out of Russian airspace into Finland."

Chapter 47

Eric woke up in the prison cell and waited for the door to open. Once opened, he walked out the door to the cell and past another inmate who he met in the common area of the hallway in front of the rooms. The inmate asked, "Where is Thomas?"

Eric did not answer and kept walking down the hall and out the gate. He waved at the guard at the gate and said the night shift was very quiet. He got in the car and called Wayne on Facetime. Wayne smiled and said, "You look just like a prison guard in those clothes."

"I can't wait to get this uniform off. This might be my greatest hypocritical act of all time." Wayne smiled and hung up as Eric headed for the airport.

***

Eric walked into the kitchen, and Casey was bent over with nothing on but a short silk blue nightgown trying to locate a pot to boil her an egg. Eric noticed there were no suntan lines. He cleared his throat. She was startled but glad to see him. She came over and hugged him. He said,

"The FBI located the known terrorist. They are very appreciative of your help. You did very well."

She pulled him tighter with her arms around his neck and kissed him passionately in the mouth. "I really like my life, Eric. I am so happy living with you. I love my career."

Eric raised his eyebrow. "You know you were right. By you forcing me to stay in the bedroom by myself the night before the last segment, I was very frisky. It was my best film segment yet."

Eric said, "I bet the men watching did not even notice the $186,000 Lamborghini you were washing." He smiled and then said, "I bet they wish they were that car."

She smiled. "It sounds like you watched me wash your car. I have been doing nothing but working on these segments and now I am ready to spend time with you. I will wash you with my tongue." She started kissing him as she started removing his shirt, giving him hickeys on his chest. "I have been working out twice daily trying to keep my body in perfect shape, while eating boiled eggs and other healthy food that taste like cardboard. These toned leg muscles and sixpack stomach muscles come at a price. I want to have some fun. Let me take you upstairs and show you how I like to have fun."

She reached up with one hand and pulled his head towards her while kissing him on the mouth and at the same time pushing him backward toward the dining room table. She dropped her nightgown and turned to him as she sat on the table spreading her legs holding him tight kissing him.

Chapter 48

Vicky asked, "Does anything jump out at you? We have walked through the graveyard twice."

Patrick Roust said, "I have nothing. I figured the older section of tombs is where we should concentrate our search."

Vicky was wondering if he could be trusted or were they on a wild goose chase. "Maybe we need to go to a computer store and purchase a used computer to go online and complete research about the graveyard."

Vicky looked over to the west and noticed an elderly man walking into the graveyard. It was a pretty afternoon and a nice day to be outdoors. An early October cold front was going to turn for the worse later in the afternoon. The cold front was moving into Helsingborg with wind and heavy rain turning to ice and snow. The man walked straight to a grave and started paying his respects. Vicky was concerned about leaving Patrick who she did not trust. She was concerned he might walk off and leave her. She thought, "I need to take the chance." She walked over to the elderly man who had a tear on his cheek. The tomb read Ruth Ann Blackman 1904 to 1989.

Vicky thought that is an English name. She said, "Sir. I do not mean to bother you, but I need some help."

The man looked at Vicky and smiled and asked, "How can I help you?"

She thought, "Good, he speaks English."

Vicky turned and pointed to Patrick who was still looking at the older tombs. "My husband and I are trying to locate some very old relatives who might have run from the Germans in the late 1930's and settled here in Sweden. We were conducting some research of our ancestry while on vacation. Is there another graveyard where we might look in Helsingborg?"

"The man looked sincere and asked, "Are your relatives Jewish, because if they are, then you won't find them here. There is not one single Jewish grave in this graveyard. The Jewish people are all buried in the old graveyard behind the water tank down the private drive." He pointed south. Vicky could see a small drive. "In the late 1930's, the Swedish people could not be caught burying Jewish people or assisting the Jewish people. Sweden was neutral in the war but knew if they did not give Germany everything they asked, this country would end up like Poland or France. The Germans were at war with Jews, and they wanted to kill them all. The Swedish government had to hide something from the Germans and helping some Jewish people was one of the things they hid. So, they hid the Jewish graveyards from the Germans."

Vicky waved at Patrick and motioned for him to come over. She turned to the man and said, "Thank you very much. Are you visiting a family member?"

"Yes, I visit my wife's grave once a year. We met in New York City forty-two years ago. I volunteered to transfer with a company in the textile industry and never went back home. You know the Bible says the Jewish people are the chosen race of people. Chosen by God." He pointed at Vicky and then said, "They are the only race or tribe that is mentioned in the bible that are still around after all these years." He waved goodbye and walked back to the sidewalk and out the gate.

Patrick walked over, and Vicky explained what the man said about the hidden Jewish graveyard. She pointed to the private drive. "We need to hurry. It will be getting dark soon." She looked at the older man perplexed. She noticed the older man was walking a little faster on the sidewalk to an old model car then when he arrived. Something about the man just did not fit. She hoped he and Ruth Ann had enjoyed their life together while it lasted. She knew they needed to hurry and pushed him out of her head and reached for Patrick's hand pulling him in a hurry toward the car.

They stopped the car at the gate. The old graveyard was well maintained. Some of the oldest markers were nothing but slate rock with a name and a year scratched into the stone. Most were dated during the World War II time period. They looked around and started reading the names and kept hurrying down the rows. The sun was starting to set, and the cold air was blowing harder. The dates on the tombstones were random with some dating back to 1901 and a few in the late 1800's with some newer ones dated 1974. There was a very large number of young kids who had died within the first three years of their lives. They were starting to get cold. Neither one had on warm enough clothing to fight the wind chill. She could tell the cold wind was cutting through Patrick's small jacket. He had placed his hands in his pockets, and he would shiver from the bite of the coldness. They split up to cover more territory quicker. Patrick walked over to a tomb and stopped. Vicky noticed he was staring at one tombstone on the second row. She hurriedly walked toward him. She asked, "Did you find something?"

He looked over as she quickly approached. "Yes, I believe I did."

Vicky looked at the tombstone and read the name. She read the name a second time, "Patrick Roust 1901 to 1945". This must be the grave. She looked up and said, "Who is this man in this grave?"

"I believe we will find an empty grave with the hidden research." My grandmother had always told me to visit this graveyard when I was ready. She indicated the Americans are the only people on earth who could be trusted with the research. She did not want any of the European countries to have the research. She hated the Russians, but she hated the Germans more. She somehow knew the Russians killed the conquered people within the Soviet Union after the war with the mass killings orchestrated by the Russian government. The Russian government under dictator, Joseph Stalin, killed more people after the war than Hitler and his followers did during and prior to the war. The world has refused to acknowledge the mass killings inside Russia from the mid 1940's to the mid 1950's. Of course, we all knew what the Germans did during and prior to the war to the Jewish people and the Gypsies."

Vicky looked around and did not see anyone. She knew after listening to her father tell of the hidden graves inside Russia of over twenty million people killed by Stalin. She said, "The ground will be muddy after the rain. We will have to deal with the cold rain which might turn to snow. We will need to get some tools and prepare to dig." She looked at Professor Roust and wondered if he would be any help at digging.

Patrick kept staring at the tombstone. He said, "This tomb is the only tomb with a marble marker. Why is this the only marble tombstone? Did you just say the older gentlemen at the other graveyard said the Jewish people had to bury their relatives in hiding, so the German spies would not notice?"

Vicky looked at the tombstone closer. "Yes. He did say they hid the Jewish people and the graves."

"They would not have used marble for a tombstone in that time period. The entire world was in a depression and marble would cost a lot more. Besides, this tombstone is not as old as the other tombstones. The marker may have been set in the 1950's or maybe 1960's. How could that be possible?"

Vicky glanced around and saw a car slowly headed their way. She said, "We have company. We need to leave this grave and keep looking around. Come over here and hold my left hand. We need to act like we are a couple."

She placed her hand on the 9 mm Beretta under her jacket and flipped the strap off her holster. She pulled the gun and placed it in her right jacket pocket while chambering a bullet. She wanted the Beretta on this assignment with sixteen bullets in the clip. They started walking down the rows, and she would point in different directions at different tombstones. She noticed Patrick was very quiet. His hand was cold and sweaty. She said, "Just act normal. Are you okay?"

"What are the chances someone else would be visiting this old Jewish graveyard at the same time we are? Yes, I am concerned. If they have a rifle, we are dead. We are in the open and have no way to hide."

Vicky said, "They won't shoot us. They could not locate the research if they kill us. Remember the research is hidden. If they find the research, then they will try and kill us."

Vicky took his hand, and they walked across the graveyard, which provided her an opportunity to glance at the vehicle. The car pulled next to their car and stopped. The two men were just sitting in the vehicle watching.

Vicky whispered, "They have not gotten out of the vehicle. We will turn and walk back to our car, get in the car, and drive off. You need to smile and act like there is nothing wrong. If I pull my gun, you need to drop down and hide behind a tombstone."

As they approached the gate and started to exit the graveyard, the doors to the vehicle opened on both sides. Two older men exited the car. They had on large flannel coats, jeans and worn leather old boots. The passenger asked in English, "Can we help you?"

Vicky smiled and tried to look like a tourist and said, "We are visiting these old graves looking for old family members lost in the war. We are on vacation and doing genealogy research. Who are you?"

"We are the caretakers."

Vicky and Patrick walked next to their vehicle. Vicky had her hand on her pistol grip.

The men did not show any signs of being anything but caretakers. They were dressed in old work clothes and had wrinkles on their hands and faces from working in the outdoors. They looked like they had been accustomed to blue collar labor. "We noticed the one marble tombstone. Most of the other tombstones look to be made of slate. The one tombstone does not look as old as the other tombstones. Why is that?"

The man looked a little uneasy as he shifted his weight from left to right. He finally said, "The old tombstone had to be replaced. It was hit by a mower. The family wanted to go back with an upgrade."

"The person's name on the tomb is Patrick Roust." She pointed at Patrick who tried to smile. "He might be related to the deceased Patrick Roust. Who was Patrick Roust? We would like to talk to his family. Are they still in Helsingborg?"

The man looked at Patrick and then Vicky. He said, "You are standing next to the only Patrick Roust we know."

Chapter 49

President Grant asked Max to sit down. He was polite and well mannered. Max noticed there were a couple extra guards in the situation room in the White House. President Grant said, "Max, I need you to be honest with me." He looked at Max in the eyes and said, "Totally honest." Max could feel an uneasy feeling in the pit of his stomach. "What do you know about the Syndicate, and where it originated?"

Max said, "You have my daily briefs, and we have talked several times about this ongoing problem. Is there something else you want me to tell you?"

"I know you talked to Burnside two weeks prior to him being killed. Why have you not reported that to me?"

The guards took two steps closer and three additional Secret Service guards appeared. Max looked at the guards. He did not recognize any of the men. They had all been replaced with new personnel.

"Burnside called me. He was in a panic. He tried to warn me. I tried to talk him into coming in. He would not. He stressed he was forced to step into a leadership role with the Syndicate after Senator Davis died. He explained he could not control the other members. The Syndicate is departmentalized. Each department does a specific task. He would not go into the details, but it would appear the late Senator Davis from Tennessee was one of the main parts and was responsible for recruiting and setting up the network. He finally asked me to provide him a little more time, and he would work with us to expose the Syndicate. He asked me to pull back the hunt for himself. Throw the hunters off the trail so to speak. He needed time. He tricked me. He knew of the unit we had assigned to locate him. He mentioned Mia could locate him. He mentioned her name, and I assumed he somehow had been successful at infiltrating my newly formed unit, and they had been compromised. He in turn must have used the time to kidnap Mia's father in Pakistan and also try to take out the CIA unit, the Good Samaritans in the Philippines. He contacted Mia directly and used her for information. She was faced with a decision no one should ever have to make, family or duty." Max looked at the guards and then back at the President. The President did not say anything in the silent period. He sat patiently and waited.

"The CIA unit was in the process of taking him alive or at least giving him the option when some unknown party shot him. When the Syndicate was started, I have no clue. There were very few people who knew we had located Burnside. I believe the leak is coming from the FBI. I also suspect the Russian Government has ramped up their worldwide tricks after they lost the one nuclear missile. They are our number one suspect for killing Burnside. Burnside, we believe he knew the name of the leak within the FBI and the leak is the method the Russians have been updated on the Vortex."

He looked at President Grant the entire time he was talking to him and then said, "With or without your permission, the CIA needed to take out Burnside. We also knew we needed him alive, but we could not hesitate to take the shot. He could have been a liability, but the Russians needed him dead. He knew who the mole was inside the FBI. They had a team in Sydney. We were able to identify at least one Russian agent from the Federal Counterintelligence Service (FSK) from the surveillance cameras at the Sydney airport, and I believe they took the killing shot."

President Grant looked at Max and tried to determine if he was telling the truth. "I can tell you when and where the Syndicate was started. I have done my own research." Max looked at the President with a surprised look on his face. "The Syndicate was started in this very same room fourteen years ago."

Max was perplexed. "How do you know this?"

"The President at the time was President J. D. Washington. He is still living in Georgia. He is 92 years old. I went and talked to him. He laid the entire operation out. He said it was a matter of national security. When the first scientist had mentioned the Vortex and the huge possibilities no one listened. The man's name was Heath Bullen. He had come up with the theory after reading the Bible. He had mentioned some science behind his theory but no substantiated proof. His research was based only on theory. By him quoting a passage from Ezekiel and the flying craft as noted in the Bible, he lost the scientific community. So, no one believed him, and he was written off as a person trying to promote himself without any scientific evidence. According to President Washington, this all changed when another man named Christopher Reeves discovered gold in a very remote area in Greenland. We have all assumed the gold landed from outer space carried on meteorites before the dinosaurs over two hundred million years ago. We also know gold is costly to make and the heat required to make gold in large quantities must come from nuclear reactors.

Otherwise, gold is not indigenous to earth like other elements and metals on planet earth. It had to come from outer space to be found in Greenland. This is where it got really interesting. He carbon dated the gold and noted it was less than one-hundred years old. He made several trips back to the region looking for gold, but he also carbon dated the stone in the area. It was dated older than the planet earth. He dated the stone to be 20 billion years old. The earth is only 4.5 billion years old. This time this guy, Christopher Reeves, notified a friend who worked in the pentagon. President Washington said the next thing they were meeting about the Vortex and completed hidden expeditions to northern Greenland to verify the data. He had commissioned a small group to study the Vortex. The scientists who were hired were sworn to secrecy and came back with a startling revelation. The group ruled out every other option and what was left was the Vortex is real. There can be a zipper opened in space. It has been done by civilizations located on the other side of our universe and maybe billions of years older than we are. We suspect they left a small portable nuclear reactor, and they taught the Egyptians how to make gold. The gold had to come from somewhere. There was no evidence of that much gold in Egypt until after the time period of the pyramids and Egyptians. This is all theory with no proof."

Chapter 50

Patrick looked flush and dizzy. He was about to pass out. Vicky walked over and held his arm trying to support him. He laid down on the grass. He said, "I am not feeling good."

One of the men said, "Can you follow us to the office? We need to hurry. We are not safe in the open."

Vicky looked up at the two men while trying to make certain Patrick was not going to pass out. He looked stunned. "The storm is a few hours off."

The driver said, "We are not concerned about the storm. They are watching. They are always watching. I hope you did not talk to anyone."

She checked his pulse, "Before we agree to go anywhere with you, you two need to start talking. We need to know what is going on. You do not look surprised to see us."

The passenger said, "Patrick looks like his sugar has dropped. He needs something sweet, or he might pass out."

Vicky looked at him. "How do you know this? Are you a doctor?"

The passenger said, "No. I am not a doctor. He is just like his grandmother. She would pass out if she were fatigued and not eating properly. She told me the name of the disease, but I cannot remember. The disease had to do with her nervous system becoming fatigued. We need to take cover. There is a group that has been looking for the hidden one, and we have been waiting for Patrick for three decades."

They all got in the vehicles, and Vicky started following the other car. She looked over at Patrick. "Are you going to be alright?"

"Well, hell no. I am not going to be alright. They are going to kill me. Do you not see what is happening? They already have a grave with my name on it. All they need is my dead corpse."

Vicky smiled a little and looked over at Patrick in the passenger seat with his head resting against the window. He looked flushed. "If they were going to kill us, they would have killed us in the graveyard. They have been watching that grave for three decades. They knew who you were. They were expecting you. We need to find out who they fear, retrieve the information, and head back to America."

They followed the two men into an old farmhouse built in the 1940's with a detached garage. The home was a one story, stone home with a chimney next to the front door. They parked in the garage and the men closed the garage door. They walked across the yard to the side door and into the kitchen. The driver turned and said, "This is our converted office. You can stay here tonight, and, in the morning, we will assist Patrick with his task."

Patrick looked at the man and said, "My task. What do you know about my great grandfather, Epstein?"

"We never met him. We met your grandmother. She had quite a story. She paid us over the years, and we did as she asked. She had told us at some point the world would be ready for the research, and she would send her only grandson to retrieve it. We started noticing people coming around about ten years ago. They would walk through the graveyards just like you were doing. They were looking for a certain grave, but they had no clue the name. They were foreigners. They kept asking questions about any unusual people being buried. We knew they were looking for the hidden research. You Patrick are the only one who knows where the research is hidden."

Vicky blurted out, "Is the research not hidden in the ground under the marble tomb with his name?"

The driver said, "That is the only empty grave in the yard. The research is not in the ground under that tomb. We placed the marker at the request of your grandmother in 1963. We assume that is a clue for Patrick. There is no casket or anything in the ground at that tomb. We will be back to check on you two in the morning. You should be safe here tonight." They turned and walked out the door.

Patrick seemed to stare at the door where the men exited. He finally asked, "Do you trust them? I do not trust them. They seem to be odd old men."

Vicky could hear the car start up and drive off. She looked over at Patrick who had his hands covering his face. She said, "Patrick, you need to trust me. Those men are what they appear to be, which are Jewish men, and they work as caretakers."

"You do not understand. Adolf Hitler had plans to conquer the world. He knew the scientists were close with the nuclear bomb and understanding how to use nuclear warheads powered by rockets. What the world never knew was the Vortex was his ace in the hole. He thought he had this information and the research behind the Vortex was ahead of the nuclear research. Then, my great grandfather took the vital part of the research and disappeared prior to the war. Hitler and his army of agents looked everywhere. That was why Hitler teamed up with Russia to attack Poland. He needed to have his agents in Poland to locate the research. Hitler hated the Russians, but he needed their help to totally conquer Poland. The Russians had no clue. They were just being Russia and wanted to kill the Polish people and take their land. This was the best well-kept secret in the twentieth century." He looked at Vicky. "I still do not know if the world is ready. I do not want to be the one who starts World War III."

"The information will be figured out by someone in the near future. There are too many smart people on planet earth. You will ensure the right people will have a head start. Patrick, your grandmother must have told you something about the research and the hiding place."

"She never told me where it was hidden. She was afraid I would tell someone. I was only ten years old when she had a blood clot in the back of her brain. I found her in her bed the next day. She was rushed to the hospital. She was paralyzed in both arms and legs. She could not communicate. She seemed to be trying to tell me something, but she could not. I could see it in her eyes. She lasted a few weeks before she finally died. I found the data going through her items when I was a teenager. I provided the two physics professors a sample. I held that information in safe keeping for twenty-five years. She died twenty-five years ago. My parents had died when I was two. She raised me until her death. I never met my grandfather. He died years before my parents." Vicky thought he looked a little better. He had been eating crackers and cheese from the refrigerator.

Vicky said, "Your grandmother would not have left this for you unless she expected you to find it. You need to think. There must be some clues."

Patrick rubbed his hands over his face in frustration. "I cannot believe I am about to be tortured to death over some damn research which is close to eighty-to-hundred years old, and I truly have no clue where it is located."

Vicky walked to the refrigerator, opened the door and made a sandwich on the counter. She looked at Patrick and could tell he was pushing himself to remember something that would help. He asked, "How do we know we can trust those two men? How can we trust anyone?"

"We cannot trust anyone. I need you to think about what your grandmother told you about this research and let us get it and then get the hell out of Sweden. The tombstone is a clue. You heard the two caretakers tells us it was a clue." They heard a vehicle pull into the driveway. Vicky walked over to the window. She saw the elderly man from the graveyard earlier today get out of an old van and walk toward the front door. He had on a delivery coat carrying a package. She pulled her gun and said, "Be ready to leave." Patrick looked at Vicky with a bewildered expression.

He knocked on the door. Patrick nervously walked behind Vicky, not certain what to anticipate. When Vicky opened the door with one quick motion shot the man in the forehead. He fell dead in the yard next to the concrete sidewalk. She said, "Let's go."

Patrick froze in his spot. He looked terrified and could not comprehend what he had just witnessed.

Vicky reached behind her and grabbed Patrick by the front of the jacket and said, "Go get in his van. Now Patrick." He did not move. Vicky looked at him and pulled his arm. She said, "I need you to walk outside and get in the van. We need to go. They know we are here."

Patrick took one step at a time. He seemed to be mentally blank. He looked down as he stepped across the dead elderly man lying next to the sidewalk in the yard with his eyes frozen open and the bullet hole with a small amount of oozing drops of blood located in his center forehead. He saw the man had a pistol hidden behind the package. Vicky pulled his arm trying to get him to hurry. She opened the side cargo door and pushed him in the van. She ran around to the driver's side and started the van. She pulled the cell phone from her coat pocket and removed the battery in her phone in case someone was tracking her as she drove fast out the driveway. She kept looking in the rear-view mirror. She knew there would be someone chasing them, and she had to find a place to hide. She headed for the downtown area. She felt they could blend in with the locals. She heard Patrick mumbling about dead bodies. He was incoherent. She kept driving around the curves faster than normal. She hesitated when she heard Patrick yell about dead bodies a second time. She looked back at him, and he said, "The two caretakers are dead lying back here with me. My God what is happening?"

Vicky looked at the edge of the tarp and saw the dark brown worn boot with an ankle. She noticed the back of the flannel coat the driver was wearing. She pulled into a pub with a motel located above it. She drove toward the back of the parking lot and got out of the van. She made certain no one was close and opened the sliding side door which was facing away from the bar. She pulled Patrick out and lifted the plastic tarp. Vicky grabbed both dead men's caps lying near the bodies. There was blood running out from under the plastic toward the rear doors. She then quickly removed one of the caretaker's large flannel coats and put it on. Both men had been shot in the back of the heads with a small caliber gun. There was only the one bullet hole where the men had been executed. Patrick still appeared to be in a state of shock.

"We need to hide out and blend in with the other people. Let's go get you a drink and wear this hat to cover your face. There are cameras located on the street corners post and in the bars. Do not look up into the cameras. I am wearing this cap and this heavy coat to hide my identity. Now keep your head tilted down and the cap on. You need to do exactly as I say."

Patrick followed Vicky to a corner rear table that had just become available. Vicky took a seat watching the front door. Patrick had not made eye contact with anyone. He had his head tilted down and walked into another customer before reaching the table. He asked, "Can you tell me what is going on? Why did you shoot that old man?"

Vicky glanced around to see who was near and said, "Please keep your voice down."

The waitress walked over to their table and Vicky said, "Bring us two beers and two shots of Tennessee whisky."

The waitress seemed busy and walked quickly to the bar to place the order. Vicky said, "The old man said he had visited his wife every year once a year since she died. If they were the same age when they got married, he would have been close to 120 years old. The inconsistency did not register until I saw him walking toward the door. He executed the two caretakers." Vicky looked at Patrick. He was shaking his head no. Vicky had run out of patience with him.

The waitress set the drinks on the table, and Vicky smiled and paid her with a generous tip. Vicky looked at Patrick. "I need you to drink these drinks and calm down. I need for you to act like a man." She gritted her teeth, "You make me sick. You live on a college campus and teach English, which is simple. You take advantage of your looks and wit and sleep with all those coeds just to please yourself."

He reached over and drank one of the whisky drinks. He then drank some beer. Vicky pushed the other whisky drink over to him. He stared at it and then picked it up and drank it. He looked out the window and read the sign for the workout gym across the street. The sign had a picture of a muscle covered man and asked, "Do you want to be hard like granite?"

He said, "It is hard."

Vicky said, "The hell it is. You picked the easiest major with the most liberal students and take advantage of the eighteen-year-old girls who are wanting to experiment with sex. It is not hard. You make no commitments."

"No. Granite is hard."

Vicky looked into his eyes. "What are you talking about?"

He looked around to see if anyone was close enough to hear him. "What if the tombstone is made of granite and not marble." Vicky looked perplexed. "I mean what if we were wrong. The tombstone is granite and not marble."

"Okay. Let's say it is granite and not marble. What then?"

"My grandmother would tell me to stand strong as granite in the face of danger, and the answer would be inside me. She told me when I graduated from preschool and often during the course of a school year as I grew older. She would repeat the saying, and I remembered asking what that meant inside me. She said I would understand. What if the tombstone is hollow? The two caretakers indicated there was no grave below ground. What is the purpose to have a marker without a grave? What if the tomb has a hollow cavity in the bottom or where the horizontal piece and the vertical piece of granite are attached?"

Vicky was listening and watching the front entrance. She said while watching the front with an urgent expression, "We need to leave out the back door, and we need to leave now." She saw the two men. One middle aged and one in his late twenties walk into the bar. They did not fit in with the other bar customers who were dressed in the new wave attire. These two looked ex-military with short hair, no friendly smiles, and their eyes kept looking from person to person. They had on bulky jackets which could easily conceal a pistol. Vicky knew these two men were killers. "Keep your head down and follow me."

The bar was crowded with several people now looking for seats. Vicky opened the door and pulled Patrick's hand rushing him out the rear door. "Don't look back, but we need to walk very fast and around the corner."

They made it down the street a block and crossed the street. There were very few people in the area. There was nowhere for them to hide. The retail stores had closed. Vicky glanced behind her and saw the utility vehicle accelerating toward them. She pulled Patrick against her as she placed her back against the brick wall of the building. The sidewalk was approximately twelve feet wide with an eight-inch curb similar too most other city streets in a downtown location in America. She said, "You need to kiss me."

Patrick looked like he was in shock. He said, "We have men chasing us, trying to kill us after torturing me to death and you want me to kiss you? This is not the best time for your libido to start acting up."

Vicky pulled her gun and placed it in her pocket of her coat. She said, "They don't know for certain if we are the couple, they are hunting, and we will not have but a second to take advantage of the surprise. My libido is fine right where it is."

She reached up, gritted her teeth, and pulled him by his neck with her left hand and kissed him on the mouth. She kept him pulled tight against her body with her left hand on the back of his neck. She had extended her right hand in the flannel coat pocket pointing her pistol with silencer toward the street. She glanced over at Patrick, and too her surprised he had his eyes closed. She rotated her eyes to the approaching vehicle and the street. The utility vehicle had two men in the front and as the vehicle slowed the one man had extended his head out the passenger side window and said, "Excuse me."

The vehicle had stopped in the road. Vicky did not hesitate. She shot through the coat pocket hitting the passenger in the forehead and the driver in the temple. She broke off the kiss and pushed Patrick toward the vehicle. She opened the door and pulled the passenger out onto the sidewalk. The vehicle started rolling forward. Vicky jumped in the passenger seat and slid over opening the driver's door pushing the driver out the door as she simultaneously stepped on the brake. She told Patrick to get in the front. She looked both ways and did not see another car or any bystanders. Patrick took his time as he stepped over the dead man on the sidewalk. He looked confused as he sat down in the passenger seat. "You could have hurried a little faster."

Vicky drove off cutting left on a road and heading for the rural area. Patrick asked, "How do you know they were after us? They could have been totally innocent. You shot them like it was the normal thing to do."

"Do totally innocent men who are about twenty years difference in age stop and ask a couple kissing on the dark section of the street a question? They were carrying guns, and they were backing up the two men who walked in the bar. Our world is getting smaller. We need to keep moving."

"Where are we going? I want out. I do not want to be part of all this killing. I am a member of the English department at the college. I love words, poetry and American and English Literature. There is too much killing with you around." He looked like he was going to cry.

"We are headed to the graveyard. We are going to verify if the tomb is housing the hidden research. I will make it look like several areas in the graveyard were damaged by vandalism and not just the one tombstone. We need to retrieve the research and leave before we end up like the two caretakers. Do you remember the two caretakers?" Vicky turned the wipers on. The rain had started falling. The news on the radio had reported rain changing to snow with high winds.

Vicky glanced at the professor. He had a scared look on his face. The look of a man that had been pushed to his limit. She knew she needed to hurry, find the research, and exit the country. She also knew there would be reinforcements from the Syndicate headed to Sweden. She turned on the road where the graveyard was located. She did not see any vehicles in the parking lot. She accelerated and busted through the gate at the road. She glanced at the professor, and he did not move. He looked straight ahead. She came to the second gate at the Jewish cemetery and once again accelerated. This gate was made of one very old bar and a hidden lock in the metal box. The gate flew open, and Vicky did not slow down. She accelerated and started driving through the graveyard tearing down the small markers with the collision of the front bumper and the undercarriage of the vehicle. She hit the one big granite marker. She drove over it and hit a couple of additional old slate markers, then pulled the utility vehicle back to the side street and turned the front of the vehicle around sliding in the grass on the shoulder of the old road. She parked the vehicle with the headlights aimed at the granite tombstone and parked. She said, "Lets, see what we can find."

The professor looked confused and said, "You missed some of the tombstones. Are you certain you don't want to back up and desecrate some more?"

Vicky gritted her teeth and said, "I need for you to start acting like a man and not a baby."

She jumped out of the vehicle. She noticed the radiator was smoking and the grill was pushed inward from colliding with the tombstones. She knew the fluid was leaking out of the radiator. The professor slowly got out in the rain and walked over to the granite tombstone. Vicky bent down and pushed the leaning tombstone over into the grass. When the horizontal part of the stone fell over, she noticed the wooden plug in the bottom of the headstone that was now lying on the grass. She tried to pull the plug out, but it was stuck and would not budge. Vicky ran to the rear hatch and opened the tool pouch for the flat tire repair. She pulled the lug wrench out and ran back to the tomb. She shoved the sharp end of the wrench into the side and pushed the wrench over to the side. The sharp end lifted the plug a little. She rammed the sharp end again into the other side of the plug and again pushed the tool down, and the plug moved outward.

She glanced at Patrick who was standing watching and appeared not to be interested in helping with the manual task. The third time the tool did not slip, and the plug came out. She reached into the four-inch hollow cavity and pulled out several papers housed in an airtight plastic folder. She made certain there was nothing left in the tombstone cavity and placed the plug back into the hole and kicked it with the toe of her boot. She looked through the clear plastic and read the German words, "Door to space." She laid the plastic file down and pushed the tombstone further over so no one would at first notice the plug in the bottom. The wind and rain were picking up, and they both were soaked. Vicky still had on the large flannel coat she took from the dead caretaker. Professor Roust was shivering in his thin windbreaker and pants. She ordered, "Let's go."

She drove very fast leaving the cemetery. Instead of heading back into the city, she turned right and headed down the old country road. They had turned on several narrow roads. They had been driving by farmhouses and pastures. Vicky knew they needed to get as far from Helsingborg as possible and ditch the vehicle. The rain had turned to snow, and the wind had pushed the wind chill factor to below zero. Vicky also needed to find the direction to the airport. She knew she needed to check in with President Grant in the morning. She could smell smoke and noticed the vehicle was overheating. The needle was pointing to the H on the dash. Finally, Professor Roust said, "I smell smoke."

Vicky said, "The radiator is busted, and all the fluids have been leaking out since the graveyard. Do you know how to complete a temporary repair on the radiator?"

"I know nothing about cars."

"You are not much of a man. How could you not know anything about how to repair a vehicle?" She noticed a wide area on the shoulder of the street and a ditch leading down an embankment. She parked the vehicle and said, "Get out. We are walking."

Once he got clear, Vicky pushed the smoking vehicle out of park and allowed it to roll down the embankment.

"Where are we going to go?"

Vicky said, "I saw an old barn about two miles back down the road. We will try to find shelter and then find additional transportation in the morning."

"You say two miles like it is next door. I have never been so cold. I can't make it two miles."

"Listen Patrick. I have the research." She held it up in front of him in the plastic folder. "I am going to leave you here to die if you don't want to follow me. I intend to do the right thing and try to help you live. You need to jog with me to the barn, and we can warm up. Otherwise, you will die of hypothermia before those other people find you and torture you to death. What is it going to be?"

They started jogging with Vicky leading the way. He had to stop and rest four times and falling three times with Vicky waiting for him and pulling him along the road. The rain had soaked their clothing and now the sleet and snow with the wind had gotten more severe. They walked through a field to the barn. There was close to an inch of snow on the ground. They could see a couple of homes in the distance. One had a dim outside light and the other was dark. Vicky walked to the rear of the barn door and opened the door. She could hear horses in the stables. There was no light. She turned on the small flashlight she had pulled from the glove compartment of the vehicle and looked around. She opened the tack room door and pulled out a couple of heavy insulated wool horse blankets. Patrick had walked into the center of the room and was watching her.

Vicky could tell he was close to freezing to death. Her large coat she had taken from the caretaker had helped to keep her warm, and her boots had helped keep her feet somewhat dry. Her pants were soaking wet, and she could feel the wet material against her skin. Vicky knew the greatest source of heat loss was through the scalp and neither one had toboggans. Patrick had lost his ball cap, and Vicky's had fallen off when she shot the two men in the vehicle. Patrick was soaking wet and shivering and his shoes were not meant to repel water or provide warmth. She went to the side area of the barn where there were four rows of hay bales, three bales high. She then pulled out four additional bales of hay onto the floor. She quickly laid one of the horse blankets down on the hay between the stacked hay. She walked over to Patrick and said, "You need to get those wet clothes off and get under that other blanket. Our body heat will warm you up."

He kept shivering while Vicky removed his jacket and shirt. She removed his shoes and socks. He pulled his pants down and hesitated with his underwear. She said, "If they are wet, they need to come off."

Patrick removed his underwear and got on the one blanket and under the other blanket. He was shivering. Vicky removed her coat, shirts, and the rest of her clothes. She hung the clothing up on the wood shelves and hoped they would dry somewhat for the trip tomorrow. She walked over to the other hay bales and hid the research material between the bales of hay. She took down her ponytail and squeezed her hair allowing as much water to drip from her hair to the concrete floor in the barn as possible. She glanced over while her hair was dripping the rainwater and noticed Patrick was watching.

She said, "You need to breathe hot air under the blanket. You need to bury your head under that top blanket to warm yourself up."

"I have never been so cold. I am cold all the way to my bones."

Vicky could tell by his voice he was scared and frozen. She walked over and jumped under the blanket. She pushed him onto his side facing away from her. She made certain the top blanket was covering them lying between the hay bales. She placed her pistol above her head where she could reach it quickly if needed. She then started to rub his back and legs. She rubbed his feet and said, "Patrick. Keep blowing out hot air. You will warm up in a few minutes." He could feel her breast pushing up against his back as she held him tight. She kept rubbing his thighs and reached around and was rubbing his chest. He could feel her warm breath as she kept blowing out on his neck and upper back.

Fifteen minutes later, he finally started to warm up. He took her hand and rubbed it across his now hard penis. Vicky felt his erection and pulled her hand away. She rolled over and said "You will be okay. We need to get some sleep." He rolled over and placed his hand on her shoulder and pushed his penis against her butt and upper backside of her thighs. Vicky said firmly, "Patrick. You need to turn your body the other direction, don't crowd me, and go to sleep. This isn't going to happen. Remember I sleep with a pistol."

Patrick said, "You don't like me very much, do you?"

She felt Patrick pull away and turn over. She said, "I do not respect what you have done. Instead of helping the young female students and providing them with insightful helpful direction, you have taken advantage of them because they are easily persuaded and influenced by someone in your position. You have taken advantage of them for your own selfish enjoyment. You were left with this earth-shattering research, and you hid from your responsibilities that your grandmother placed on you. She had no one else she could trust. If you had revealed this information years ago, a lot of people would not now be dead. I am going to try do the right thing and get you to a safe place, so you won't be killed. In regard to dating you or sleeping with you, I have my standards. The men I choose to date, can lift me off the floor with me straddling their hard platform and hold my entire body suspended in the air for minutes at a time. Now go to sleep." She smiled to herself and closed her eyes.

He said, "Don't worry. You just mentioning 'the pistol', and I am scared. I will not ever forget 'the pistol' you sleep with. Since I have met you, you have fired 'the pistol' eight times and killed seven men with you shooting one poor bastard twice after you cut his wrist through with my sword. I don't doubt you would shoot me in a second. I actually thought if I could make love to you, I could prove to you my skill and value, and you would understand the need to extend my life and not shoot me. I figured that was the only hope I actually had to live."

Vicky giggled and said, "Patrick, don't let the bed bugs bite." She pushed her back up against his back and felt the warm skin. She knew he would still be cold. She then curled her legs up and placed her feet against the back of his legs to help keep them warm. She thought back to her college days and her friend would talk about running her hands through the curly headed boyfriend's hair when they made love. She also knew he was not the type of man to marry her friend as she yawned and fell asleep.

Chapter 51

Delores said, "Come on. I will go with you. I want to meet your father. Maybe we can help him with the home remodel. You can repair his roof while I help paint the interior."

"I have not seen him but twice in fourteen years. The last time was six years ago when mom died."

Eric of Newport and Little Jimmy walked in the bonus room above Prestige Cleaners. Little Jimmy asked, "Where are you planning on going?"

Dolores said, "I am trying to talk Billy Ray into going back to south Texas to visit his father. He mentioned he had some home repairs needed and money was tight. Where are you two headed?"

Eric said, "Casey and I were considering going someplace warm. We were thinking about renting a fifth wheel and hooking up too Little Jimmy's truck. We asked him if he wanted to come with us."

Little Jimmy said, "We could go to south Texas and help you two repair the home."

Billy Ray looked up, somewhat surprised. "My father never has been very sociable, but I guess Delores and I are going to be headed that way tomorrow, you three can come also. You can park the fifth wheel in the yard. We will fly and rent a truck at the airport."

***

Delores could tell Billy Ray was nervous. While on the plane, he kept twisting in the seat. She finally placed her hand on his hand and smiled and said, "Calm down. It will be okay."

Billy Ray said, "My father is not like most people. He is a hard man. A real hard man."

She smiled and said, "What is he going to do? What is the worst thing he can do to us? I love you. It will be okay."

He looked at Delores and his expression changed to serious. "I was ten years old, and I once saw him get mad at my older sister in the front yard. He was barefoot. He turned and kicked the side of a car door toe first without any shoes. It placed a large dent in the car door. I knew right then he was hard man."

Delores burst out laughing and had trouble stopping and controlling her laughter. She finally mumbled the words, "Dear God, it will be okay. We will rent a truck,

355

and if he wants to kick the rental, that will be fine." Billy Ray smiled at her continuous laughter.

When they pulled into the driveway, Billy Ray noticed the place had not been painted in years, and the tin roof was original to the home and had been patched with different colored metal. The yard and home looked smaller than he remembered. He parked the rental truck and went and knocked on the front door. The door slowly opened. Billy Ray said, "Hi Dad. It is me, Billy Ray. I wanted you to meet my girlfriend."

The man stepped out the front door. The screen door had been off the hinges years ago and only the screw holes could be seen in the jam. He was a big man in overalls and brown worn boots. Billy Ray said, "Dad, this is Delores Bailey. Delores this is Hulk Claiborne."

They stood out on the porch and talked for several minutes. Hulk was surprised to find out Delores was a Regional Manager for the FBI. Billy Ray finally said they were visiting for a week and were planning on helping with his remodel of the house. Hulk had explained the home was okay. Billy Ray pulled out ten thousand dollars and said, "This will get us started."

Hulk first thought this had to be drug money and then he remembered Delores was a manager with the FBI.

Billy Ray surprised his father when he announced he had been attending a Methodist Church in Tennessee and the Bible suggested kids needed to take care of their aging parents, and that was what he was going to do. He further explained there were three more friends on the way in a truck pulling a fifth wheel camper.

This was an old run-down one-story farm home, which had been originally built in 1956 with wood siding and a tin roof. Billy Ray had figured to tackle one major repair a day. Once the tin was removed and the new shingle roof was installed and the exterior of the home was painted with new shutters and new exterior doors and windows, they removed the flooring and replaced all of it.

Casey and Delores teamed up and painted the kitchen cabinets and the interior rooms. Each night they would sit in the backyard around a campfire and talk as friends. Little Jimmy could not help but notice how Eric of Newport and Casey seemed to be in love. Billy Ray seemed to talk openly with his father about growing up in Texas, and Hulk loved Delores.

Little Jimmy thought this might have been the best week they had spent as friends. He enjoyed sleeping in a hammock in the outdoors under the stars. They worked hard every day and came together and helped Billy Ray re-connect with his only living family. His older sister had died over eight years ago, and they had never been close.

The home looked nice when they were finished. They had also added some new furniture in the living room and appliances in the kitchen. Little Jimmy had been worried about Vicky. He had checked in with Wayne a couple of times and no new developments. Finally, his phone rang as they were saying goodbye to Hulk. Delores and Billy Ray were headed to the airport to catch the next flight back to Tennessee. Vicky was rushed and to the point. Little Jimmy listened and said he understood. Eric understood Little Jimmy could not talk about the next mission with Casey in the truck, but Eric could tell Little Jimmy was concerned about something. They drove the entire fourteen hours trip without stopping except to get gas.

Chapter 52

Little Jimmy drove through the neighborhood slowly. He kept looking for anything suspicious. He pulled in the driveway and knocked on the front door. Matt Donahue answered the door. He was holding a cup of coffee with a friendly smile. Matt said, "Good morning Little Jimmy. What brings you by my castle?"

Little Jimmy smiled and asked, "Can we talk in private for a second?"

Matt stepped to the side and said, "Certainly. Come on in. I heard you went to Texas for a few days."

He closed the front door, and Little Jimmy said, "Yes. I went down to Webb County to help a friend, Billy Ray Claiborne, with some home repairs." He held up his finger for Matt to be quiet as he pulled the signal detector out of his pocket while they walked into the living room. Matt looked surprised and took a drink of his coffee. Little Jimmy hurried and then turned on a signal sound blocking device and set it down on the coffee table. Little Jimmy then said, "This is urgent."

Matt raised his eyebrows and said, "Little Jimmy I hear confidential confessions all the time, and you can trust me. What you tell me will not be repeated. I do not record people."

Little Jimmy smiled and said, "I am not confessing, but you need to get on a change of clothes and grab your passport and license. We need to go to Paris, France." He could tell Matt was confused. "Vicky asked me to bring you to Paris, and I have a plane waiting for you at the Nashville airport. We need to leave right now."

Once on the road to the airport, Matt asked Little Jimmy several times about the trip. Little Jimmy said, "It is a surprise, and Vicky needs your help." Matt called Galon, the youth minster and explained he was going out of town, and he needed to lead the church tomorrow morning. He could tell Galon was hopeful and apprehensive all at the same time. He smiled to himself knowing this was his first time leading the church. Matt said, "Remember, Jesus was known to feed his audiences fish and bread and his first known miracle he turned water into wine. You, I believe Galon, will have that type of sermon."

He smiled and turned off his cell phone. He knew Galon struggled in front of large audiences. He then smiled and added, "I will pray for him and the church audience."

Little Jimmy sat down in the airplane seat and watched Matt sit in front of him. Eric, Wayne, and Mia were in the back of the small jet. They were acting like they were listening to music with headphones or reading a magazine, so Matt would not be suspicious. Matt seemed to take everything in stride and started reviewing something on his computer. He had no further questions. He seemed to act like everything was normal and accepted the situation in good faith.

Once they landed, they all got into a rental and drove around to verify that they were not being followed. They had arranged for Delores and Billy Ray to fly over a few hours prior and sit on the side street to watch if anyone was following. Delores watched the rental vehicle pass as she was sitting in a midsize car and reported all clear. Billy Ray watched the rental vehicle pass as he was sitting in a large van and reported the same. Billy Ray and Delores drove to the outskirts of Paris and watched the small home being rented by Vicky through her contact, Ivan Chezon.

The door opened and Vicky was truly happy to see Matt. They hugged and kissed for over a minute. Vicky then said, "I have something for you to review. It is written in German, and I have a German translator to assist."

Eric walked around the exterior looking for anything suspicious. Wayne walked in and checked the home and then the exterior for listening devices. Billy Ray and Delores kept driving around the area trying to become familiar with the neighbors and watching the roads. Vicky introduced Matt to Professor Patrick Roust. She then explained he was the great grandson of Professor Epstein, and he has some old documents dealing with the Vortex he discovered. Matt's eyes lit up. Vicky led him to the kitchen table and showed him the charts and formulas along with the other research. Professor Roust came over and read the description of the contents as outlined in the prologue. Matt was so surprised he had to sit down. He placed his hands on his cheeks in total surprise. He said, "This is the answer to my thesis."

Professor Roust translated the handwritten notes for Matt over the next six hours while sitting at the kitchen table. Vicky had never seen Matt so invested. He had four cups of coffee and was astonished at what he was reviewing. She could hear the professor read sentences and then Matt would note the theme of each sentence. The Professor had trouble discerning some of the shorthand symbols and written notes. The two would discuss what the research might have been saying.

Vicky kept asking for her unit to report in. Vicky had a feeling there had to be a leak somewhere. There were too many instances when the Syndicate happened to show up. She and Wayne had agreed after Burnside was shot, someone in Washington had to be working for the other side. Matt had no idea that Billy Ray and Delores were continuously driving around the area in two separate vehicles, and Eric of Newport was walking around the exterior. At one point, Eric climbed on the roof and watched the surroundings from the rooftop. Vicky walked into the kitchen and watched the two men. Both men were so intense reviewing the notes, they hardly noticed if someone walked into the kitchen. Matt finally glanced up and noticed Vicky watching them work. Vicky walked toward the table and mentioned she met Professor Roust through one of the programs sponsored by Children Around the World.

Matt seemed to accept the situation and went back to work. She heard him say the gravitational force is different depending on the distance from the planets and the stars. That is what that formula is addressing. Vicky thought he seemed to be like a kid in a candy store. When he concentrated so intensely, his forehead seemed to be more creased, a wrinkle more noticeable and his eyes never seemed to blink.

Little Jimmy kept watching the front driveway and had two assault rifles with a grenade launcher in the foyer closet. Wayne kept a watch on the rear of the home. He was sitting at the table with his back to the stone exterior wall of the home acting like he was reading a book. The home was a one-story ranch with stone exterior in a populated well-maintained community.

Delores came on the phone line, "There is a delivery truck approaching from the west." The line went dead. At that point, no one could hear each other. Vicky walked to the foyer and looked at Little Jimmy, "We need to leave."

Little Jimmy opened the door to the closet and grabbed the assault rifles. Vicky turned and walked into the kitchen. She looked at Matt and Professor Roust. "We need to be leaving." Professor Roust immediately jumped up from his chair. Matt seemed surprised. He was not finished. He looked perplexed. Mia came in from the office located in the back of the home and said, "Vicky, I need to have a word with you."

As the two ladies walked to the rear of the home, Wayne walked in holding one of the assault rifles, and

Little Jimmy was carrying a rifle with the grenade launcher. Little Jimmy said, "We need to head for the utility vehicle. Matt, you need to gather your notes and your computer."

Matt hesitated and looked to the hallway leading to the rear of the home for Vicky. Wayne walked over and picked up the items on the table keeping the research separate and handing Matt his computer and his notebook with his three ink pens. Wayne left the research on the table. Little Jimmy walked over and gently grabbed Matt's elbow and said, "Please come with me, Matt." Wayne motioned for Professor Roust to follow. Little Jimmy said, "Vicky will be out in a second."

Mia said, "All coms are down. Someone is jamming all signals. We are getting ready to get hit from all sides."

Vicky looked at Mia and said, "You need to leave with Little Jimmy, Wayne, Matt and Professor Roust, and you need to hurry."

As soon as Mia sat down in the back seat next to Professor Roust and closed the door, Wayne hit the locks on the doors and floored the vehicle. Matt asked, "What about Vicky? What is going on?"

Matt looked at Professor Roust and noticed he was quiet and appeared to be scared. He looked pale.

Matt turned his attention to the front of them when he heard Little Jimmy say, "Here we go."

Wayne accelerated directly toward another utility vehicle sitting stopped in the forks of the road. As he started to ask again what was going on, Matt saw a van come flying down the side road and hit the utility vehicle in the side and push it off the road. Wayne increased the speed to above seventy mph. Matt again looked over at Professor Roust and noticed he had his head tilted down. He heard him say, "I'm going to be sick."

Matt watched the professor upchuck in the floor of the utility vehicle between his feet. He looked up and had a tear running down the side of his face. The smell was hideous.

Billy Ray braced for impact when he was about ten feet away from the passenger side of the vehicle. The two men in the vehicle were killed by the impact, and the two men standing behind the vehicle with the assault rifles dove out of the way. He kept driving on the road looping around to the back of the home. He had hoped Delores was waiting on the others at her extraction point in the neighbor's driveway.

Steve Dwight Nichols

Eric said, "Come on Vicky. We have got to get over that wall and across the neighbor's backyard before the assault happens."

Vicky carried the research in her backpack and followed Eric as he ran up the ten-foot-high block wall. He jumped up and grabbed the top of the wall. He then pulled himself to the apex of the wall. He braced his legs to hold his position and reached down for Vicky's hand. Vicky did not hesitate. She ran up the wall and jumped upward. Eric grabbed her arm and pulled her to the top of the wall. They heard the gun fire and bullets hitting the top of the wall as they dropped to the ground. They ran across the neighbor's yard and while looking at Delores sitting in her car a hundred yards away. Billy Ray parked the damaged van and sat down in the passenger seat. They jumped in, and she sped away.

Vicky was angry and said, "Who are these people? How are they finding us? They are jamming our radio signals." No one said a word.

Delores headed for the American Embassy. Vicky said, "Change of plans. Delores, you need to head for this address after we drop Eric off." She gave Delores an address. Delores plugged it into her car's GPS. She

367

glanced in the rear-view mirror at Eric and then at Vicky in the passenger seat.

Chapter 53

Wayne pulled into the small private airport with the jet was sitting on the runway. He said, "We need to all get on that plane. He slammed the brakes and pushed the door locks. Mia and Professor Roust had not hesitated and immediately exited the backseat and climbed the stairs to the jet.

Little Jimmy opened Matt's door and said, "Preacher Donahue, please come with me."

Matt took his backpack off his lap and stepped out of the rear of the vehicle. He looked around and hesitated. He looked at Wayne and Little Jimmy holding the assault rifles and a grenade launcher. He said, "I want to know what is going on. I am not leaving my wife."

Wayne looked and said, "We've got company." Little Jimmy looked at the two approaching vehicles. He grabbed Matt by the left arm and walked him to the airplane at a quick pace.

"Who is coming? What is going on?"

Matt walked up the stairs to the airplane. Little Jimmy got down on one knee and thought about the instruction from Billy Ray about how to actually fire the grenade launcher. He pulled the safety, aimed at the front vehicle and pulled the trigger. The grenade hit the vehicle in the grille and the other vehicle collided with the rear of the vehicle. He looked at the grenade launcher and smiled and then said to himself, "Damn, I like this toy."

Professor Roust yelled, "He got it" as he was looking out the window at the two burning vehicles.

Little Jimmy bolted up the stairs pulling the ladder up behind him. He looked at Matt and said, "Please take a seat."

Wayne yelled at the pilots, "We must get out of French airspace as soon as possible. Get this plane in the air."

The pilots were retired Airforce pilots who worked for the CIA. They understood they were never to keep records of the trips. If Congress ever asked, they would be able to say they have full plausible deniability and recollection of any trip.

The pilot said into his mic as he looked out above the clouds, "The shortest distance is London.

Wayne said, "London will work. I will text you the airport location."

The Copilot said, "Not so fast. I am now picking up two aircraft on radar heading down the coastline on an intercept course. They are going to cut us off. What are our orders?"

The Copilot then added, "We cannot outrun the French Airforce. We are flying a Learjet 75 with top speed of 621 miles per hour. They most likely will be flying in the Rafale jet with top speed of 1128 miles per hour."

Wayne pulled his phone from his pocket and dialed a number. The man answered. Wayne explained the situation. The man said the pilot needs to change to another radio channel and change course. Wayne relayed the suggestion to the pilots. He could feel the plane change direction. The pilot said, "The French jets will be in sight in less than a minute. If they follow protocol, they will have a computer lock on us." Wayne looked at the passengers. He felt for Vicky. She had not wanted her husband involved. Matt looked upset and scared. He had no idea how much danger he was in. He looked at Professor Roust. He knew the danger and was having a very difficult time dealing with the stress of the mission. He was looking out the window trying to see if they were being followed. Mia had just lost her father and blamed herself for his death. The Syndicate was ruthless.

Wayne turned back to the front of the Learjet. He knew it was no match for experienced military trained pilots and the Rafale fighter jets. The pilot came on the mic, "One of the Rafale pilots has a computer lock on us from the rear. The second fighter jet has slowed and is flying alongside of us. He is motioning for us to land." The copilot was acting like they did not understand the request. After two minutes of the copilot acting like he did not understand and could not pick them up on the radio, the French pilot pulled away. Wayne could now see the Atlantic Ocean. The fighter jet behind them fired a missile which flew high and to the right by the plane.

The pilot came online, "That was a warning shot. The next one will take us out. He has computer lock on us. What are my orders?"

"You will not land this plane until we reach London." The pilots looked nervous. Professor Roust and the other passengers could hear the conversation. He upchucked in the floor. Matt was now praying. He looked up and yelled at Wayne, "The French Government does not send their fighters to shoot down innocent people, and Little Jimmy had just fired a grenade into a vehicle chasing us. What is going on?"

The pilot interrupted and repeated, "The fighter behind us still has a computer lock." The co-pilot looked back over his shoulder at Wayne standing in the doorway. Wayne looked at Matt and the others and then looked out the front windshield and then at the co-pilot. There was a very uneasy five seconds.

The French pilot started to flip the safety off the control to fire the missile. He suddenly noticed his warning lights. He jerked his head around and looked behind him. The other French pilot did the same. He engaged his mic. His voice was nervous. He said, "We are breaking off. Someone has a computer lock on us. They just appeared. We had no radar warning."

The order came back across the headset, "Do not break off. You need to shoot down the Learjet. Do you understand your orders?"

The pilot came back on. "There are two F35 United States Airforce Jets with a computer lock on us. If we twitch, we will be blown to Mars. Those jets have the ability to take out our rockets in midair. We are sitting ducks. We are breaking off."

The French pilots turned the jets back toward the airbase. The American F35 pilot pulled next to the plane and gave the thumbs up.

The co-pilot looked over at Wayne when he saw the F35 American jet fly next to them and said, "I was scared for about ten seconds. Which one of you passengers' shit in my pants?" He laughed in relief of the dire situation and looked at Wayne.

The other pilot stated, "There is always a bigger fish somewhere." He blew out a whistle sound. "Who was that you were talking with on your phone telling us to change course?"

Wayne smiled and said, "It might be better for you if you did not know."

Chapter 54

The Security Chief for the French Federal police turned and looked quizzingly at Senator Miran Fellowship. "F35 United States Airforce fighters dispatched from Germany no doubt." He stared at the Senator. "There is only one person who could give that order to fly those jets inside our country's airspace and that would be the President of the United States. I thought you said President Grant had put you in charge?"

Miran had been the Senator from New York for twenty-one years. He had been in tight situations in the past. He looked at the French Security Chief, pointed his finger, and said, "I will get to the bottom of all this. The Air Force will have access to the airbases in London, and they will arrest those people on that plane. I did not know if our Air Force would be summoned to help." He walked out of the French Security office with his security detail following him.

Chapter 55

Delores slammed on the brakes and tried to pull around the stalled traffic.

Vicky said, "Go Eric." He opened the rear door and started running down the sidewalk carrying the satchel. He jumped a baby stroller and slid across the hood of a stalled car. There were several police who started closing in from the sidewalks. They were blocking the entrance to the embassy.

Delores turned down a side street and headed away from the United States Embassy. She made several turns and then took a right into an underground parking garage. She circled through the garage and then parked next to an old looking red van. Vicky got out and said, "Tell Matt I am sorry. I am really sorry about all this. Tell him I love him. You two be careful. I will see you back in Tennessee in a week."

Chapter 56

Eric knew he could not run through the French police. They were equipped with pistols and tasers. He also knew what he was carrying was too important. He had to get the contents of the satchel inside the United State's Embassy even if he could not make it. He reversed and ran across traffic and down the street leading away from the front gate. He could see the officers running down the opposite sidewalk behind him. He crossed the street and jumped on the roof of a parked car. He slung the satchel by the strap over the brick wall with the electric fence mounted on top of the wall into the compound. He immediately turned and ran down the street and into the high-rise building. He went down the stairs two levels, opened the door to the parking lot, and jumped into the waiting van. The van exited on the opposite side of the building and drove to the international airport. He put on his disguise with the help of the CIA lady in the van and checked his passport. She asked him, "What is your name, and where are you from?"

He looked at his passport. I am Tom Horn from Kansas. My date of birth is June 1, 1985. I help my father grow grain."

"Take the one suitcase. The customs officer will be suspicious if you do not have at least one suitcase."

He got out of the van and walked into the international airport. He showed his passport to the officer at the window. The security man stared at him. "So, you have only the one bag?"

"Yes. Just the one suitcase." He was relieved once he boarded the plane headed for Chicago one hour later.

Chapter 57

Senator Miran Fellowship smiled to himself as he told the sergeant to hand him the satchel. Miran had left the French Security office and had his driver take him straight to the United States Embassy. He had never considered the research to be thrown over the wall inside the Embassy. The ambassador for the United States to France was out of town, and Miran had told the second in command he was in charge. He was on a diplomatic mission for the United States.

He looked at the black satchel and briefly opened it to note the documents looked old and the writing was in German. He patted the satchel and told the sergeant to have his jet ready to leave within the hour. He looked at the aide, "Tell the Ambassador to note in his report, I was never here, and you never saw this satchel. I thought my guy had failed and that is why I left the French Security Office early, but he was able to throw the satchel over the wall. I will take this to our President." He winked at the second in command and walked out the side door under the canopy into his waiting car.

***

Billy Ray and Delores knew neither one could speak French. They were both worried about the vehicle being tracked. Delores had memorized the roads from the street map in her preparation for the mission, but once she got off the grid, she had no way to communicate with anyone.

They pulled over and got out of the car. They walked into the small restaurant and acted like American tourists. Billy Ray sat watching the front door while Delores watched the street through the glass window.

They ordered drinks with the help of the waitress and about ten minutes had passed when the first man showed up looking at the car parked on the side of the street. Delores whispered under her breath, "There is our answer. The car is not safe. We need to leave out the back door. The man in the black shirt is looking through the driver side window. He has a walkie talkie and is talking to someone."

Billy Ray turned to his right and saw a second man walk over to the car and a third man was interviewing the merchant across the street. The merchant pointed at the restaurant where they were sitting. Billy Ray reach over and grab Delores's hand and pulled her to the rear door. He forced the door open, and they quickly turned down the alley on a slow run. They came out on a street and waved down a taxi. Billy Ray gave him one-hundred dollars and motioned for him to drive. Delores quietly said, "They will be watching the airport and still have the front entrance to the embassy blocked."

Billy Ray could tell Delores was nervous. Her eyes were full of fear and her bottom lip quivered when she stood still. Billy Ray said, "We need to head for the train station and head to the coast. We will catch the ferry to England."

He could tell Delores was stressed. He whispered, "Remember. We are on vacation. Our fake ID's will work. Just remember everything about your new self."

He looked at the taxi driver and made a train sound, and the taxi driver smiled and seemed to understand. Once in the train station, they were able to find assistance with an English-speaking employee who provided them the tickets and directions. Billy Ray paid with cash and tipped the lady for helping.

Delores seemed to finally relax once they were in their private train compartment. Billy Ray smiled as he remembered how she liked her entire body rubbed down with baby oil. He knew Delores had built up a lot of stress, and it needed to be released. He asked her if she trusted him.

She looked at him queasily and said, "Of course I trust you. I truly love you."

He held up his belt and baby oil. "Then you are going to enjoy being placed in bondage."

"You've got to be kidding. After what we have been through." He smiled and walked over behind her and started rubbing her shoulders and undressing her as he nibbled on her left ear.

"This is what spies do to release the stress of the day. Did you not ever watch a James Bond movie?"

She thought about his gentle smile and his humble personality. He could be very gentle when he wanted to be. She started to relax and accept her position as the one to be placed in bondage.

They enjoyed making love the entire four-hour ride, and Delores said she wanted to go back to Paris and do it all again.

Chapter 58

Vicky was told she would meet President Grant at Camp David. She walked into the great room following two Secret Service agents. The compound was well guarded. She had counted thirty-six agents since she entered the national park, and they all were wearing full tactical gear. She figured there were four times that number on alert. President Grant walked into the great room with a frustrated look on his face. She could hear in the background the Chief of Staff cursing in the other room about the incompetent employees. She handed President Grant the satchel. "This is the original. We have tracked the fake research that Senator Fellowship got at the American Embassy in France. We were able to locate a forger in Paris that could duplicate the old looking ink and print. He could not read the German language, so he completed the task without making copies. My husband has indicated the Vortex might work, but we need to move slowly with the technology. He is still trying to figure out the gravity forces involved. The human race is not ready to open the zipper, step through, and space travel. The tunnels or worm holes that the Vortex might create are only theories. In addition, the amount of power will have to be the perfect balance to stabilize the gravity, so the zipper will close. If the zipper remains open, that could create a single entity. What scientists refer to as a blackhole in space."

Vicky looked into the President's eyes. He looked very tired and asked, "Has anyone seen this research on the Vortex outside of your unit?"

"We have nothing yet to suggest there are copies. We do not know what Senator Fellowship has told the French. We will need to talk to Senator Fellowship and find out his involvement. He might be a key to locating the members of the Syndicate. My husband is the only person who has reviewed the data left by Dr. Epstein and can understand the science behind the Vortex. The German translator did not seem to understand what he was reading. The equations and theories behind the Vortex are complex. The rest of my team and myself were not listening. We were watching the surroundings and on guard duty during the time the research was being reviewed."

"So, your husband is the only one who has first-hand knowledge of the research?"

Vicky looked closely at the President trying to understand why he wanted to know who had read the data on the Vortex. "Yes. He is the only one who has inspected the data. I am going to talk to Senator Fellowship. We need to know what he knows about the Vortex and the Syndicate. Our hidden tracker still has not been located. The fake research has been moved to the company Viatect. Viatect has thousands of military personnel stationed around the globe. They are hired by the United States and other countries as independent contractors to provide security and reconnaissance for black ops. Plus, they take on some off the book operations for Army Intelligence. Whichever country has the most money can hire them. Burnside died with a lot of secrets. He was their number one supporter."

The President looked worried. He said "We believe the Syndicate has other launch sights below ground. The geologists are telling me if a Vortex is launched below the crest of earth the atomic aftershock could cause movement in the tectonic plates, not just in the continent where the Vortex is launched, but in the other continents. If the tectonic plate shifts, a chain reaction could ensue with the eruption of volcanoes and earthquakes. We wouldn't survive."

Vicky looked at the President and said, "Shifting of the tectonic plates is how the Rockies and the Appalachian Mountains were created. Florida could be under water along with other southern states if the ocean level rises." Vicky could tell by the President's expression; he had already been informed of these problems. She said, "You need to take out the Syndicate. I have gone from one mission to another without considering the ones around me and the risk. I have placed my team in harm's way too many times."

"I need you as a trusted friend and employee of the CIA. Max has said you are a natural at planning a mission and then carrying out the mission. I will tell Max to let you have some time off."

Chapter 59

Vicky was happy to be home. Matt had several questions. Vicky said, "Why don't we go on a walk and let me explain to you what I do for a living." After the five-mile walk, Vicky felt better about Matt knowing what she had been doing. The couple had made several decisions, and Vicky had explained she had one more mission and then she was submitting her resignation. She had talked to Max and President Grant.

***

Delores walked out of her office in Washington. She had been promoted to assistant director. She used her personal cell phone and called her friend. Vicky answered. "I wanted to let you know. We just discovered a dead Russian boy in the Washington D.C. landfill. He had been dead for twenty-four hours. He had been raped repeatedly and then strangled. There are no missing boys his age in the D.C. area or Maryland or any of the other states. We searched globally, and there is a missing boy with a similar description from Orel Russia, who went missing three weeks ago. We have no leads."

Vicky thought, "This must be the spy next work passing critical information by way of the slave traders." She hesitated, "We will investigate his death. Thanks for the heads up."

Vicky hung up the phone and reached up and rubbed the cross around her neck. She knew she had promised Matt she would retire after one more mission. She called Wayne and asked for any updates from the forward team. Wayne indicated they might have an angle. It would be risky. Vicky listened and then indicated she would call Max.

She knew Mia was in the secured CIA safe house located in D.C under watch by the CIA. She had plenty of time to spend on her task working for the CIA. She then called Mia and asked, "Mia can you investigate the slave trade network? Delores has just reported a boy from Orel, Russia located in the Washington D.C. landfill. I believe there must be a connection with the need of the Russian spy to send information to someone in Washington and using the kidnapped boy to transport the sensitive information." She knew Mia was very much aware of method. The dead NSA employee, Travis Borne, had told them that Senator Davis used the slave trade pipeline to transport the information. The spy was set up near the pedophile, so the child could be killed after the spy retrieved the information. Senator Davis was using the same network when dealing with the Asian countries. "We never located the network from Europe."

Mia could tell from Vicky's voice she wanted this moved to the top of the list. "Yes, I will see what I can find out."

Chapter 60

Senator Fellowship was a smart man. Once Viatect engineers had copied all the information in Dr. Epstein's research, he had taken the original report to the White House and presented it to the President. He had said this information was important and the National Security Agency should review it. He had acted like he was doing the right thing.

President Grant was gracious in the meeting with Senator Fellowship for bringing the research to him.

Now Vicky was reviewing the plan with her team in Washington. Senator Fellowship had a soft spot for young women. Over twenty years ago, he had made contacts in Washington. The contacts were discreet and tried to locate lovely young ladies from the colleges in the D.C. area. Coeds were always looking to supplement their income to pay for the cost of their expensive higher education. Mia had been able to locate one of the young females from Georgetown University. They had followed her and watched her. The forward team had documented her activities over forty-eight hours.

Wayne read the report. The young lady owes forty-six thousand in student loans, and she was still in undergraduate school. She has her major listed as pre-law.

Vicky said, "We will offer her some money, and I will take her place. We will give her no choice but to take the deal."

Wayne said, "The Senator might know who you are. His security detail will need to be distracted if you are going to slip past them. There is too big of a chance either the Senator or the security team will recognize you."

Vicky said, "It won't matter if he recognizes me or not. He is going to have to answer some questions, and I need to talk with him away from the media, his attorney, his aides, and other watching eyes. He knows we are aware he took the research in Paris." She looked at her team. They had all been good friends. She then said, "This is going to be my last mission. I have already told Max and President Grant. I was planning to stop the child slavery trail coming into this country. I wish I could have done more around the world. We have been blessed to have accomplished what we have accomplished. I have been totally consumed by this job, and I need to be the preacher's wife."

Wayne asked about the Russian boy and the investigation.

"Max has sent a couple of agents to the home of the Russian family. They are going to impersonate the local cops. We will see what they find out. Mia is also looking into the internet, and the man I shot in Tennessee, Ronald Mongold. His dark web links on his hard drive might lead us to the spy. Mia will work the problem until she finds the answer. I have never seen someone that can go without sleep like she can. Plus, her ability to hack into someone's account or a system is second to none. She is a world class hacker."

Chapter 61

Vicky looked into the mirror as she put on her lipstick. She knew there was no real sin with the Senator. His wife probably knew he saw young ladies when he traveled. He was sixty-five years old and looked like he was in his early fifties. He had been a lifelong government employee and a Democratic Senator representing New York. He had represented the liberal people in New York and provided for their needs. She pulled on her light blue dress that hung down to her mid-thigh. She placed the white belt on and walked out the door.

***

The Secret Service was expecting a young female. When Vicky walked up the stairs to the home; the Secret Service opened the door for her. One of the agents was female and the other agent was a younger male. Vicky took note, the female seemed to stare at her a little longer than the male agent. She followed the agents into the office where Senator Fellowship was reading papers sitting at his desk. The office had a large picture window located behind the desk and chair. There were bookshelves on both sides of the desk lining the two walls. There was a sofa and two chairs facing a tv mounted to the upper nine-foot-high wall. Over from the sofa was a table with two chairs and another doorway leading to a bathroom and a hallway. The plush office was trimmed in oak baseboards, oak window casing, oak crown molding to match the oak bookshelves.

He looked up and smiled. He stared at Vicky and his smile grew. While looking at Vicky, he sat back in his chair and removed his glasses. He then looked at the female agent and then the male agent and said, "I hoped you strip searched her." The agents both hesitated and looked surprised at the statement.

The senator smiled and finally said, "You never can tell."

Vicky walked over to the table and as she set her purse down. She set in the chair behind the table. As she sat down, she quickly placed her hand under the table and felt for the holster and gun where she had instructed Eric of Newport to place it with Velcro to the underside of the table. There was no gun or holster. She now knew she needed the agents to leave the room. She stood and looked at both agents standing near the door and reached behind her like this was a normal request and unzipped her dress. She allowed it to slide down her body until it fell on the floor. At that point, Vicky stepped out of her dress leaving it on the floor. "See I have nothing to hide." She turned a complete circle holding her arms out to her side. She smiled and said, "And at your request, I have shown up at exactly four p.m. I am really good at entertaining older gentlemen."

The Senator pushed back his chair and walked from behind his desk. He looked at Vicky standing with her arms held out from her sides in her white mesh thong panties, matching bra, stockings, white mesh gloves and pumps. He said, "My dear, you are here to discuss my re-election campaign. I was just joking about the strip search." He immediately looked at the two agents and said, "You are dismissed."

As they walked out the door, Vicky said, "Senator, I am sorry. The agents might suspect you are cheating on your wife of forty-two years."

Senator Fellowship had a condescending smile and held his hands out in front of him in a relaxed gesture. He said, "If she finds out, it won't be a big deal, but if the damn press finds out, she will have to act like she is mad at me and issue a statement to the press. She hates public speaking. In our party, we have this part of the plan down. Our wives are taught how to act mad and provide statements and guidance in dealing with the press. Hell, the Democratic Party chairperson writes the speeches for us."

Vicky sat down at the table and smiled at the Senator while reaching her hand under the table in front of the other chair. The Senator smiled. He said, "Mrs. Donahue, are you looking for this?"

He reached over and opened his desk drawer and held up the pistol with the silencer. He smiled. The two agents returned. He pointed the gun toward Vicky and said, "She is an agent working for the CIA and a very good one from what I understand. I assume there is a reason Max sent you here without following proper channels?"

Vicky did not move. She looked at the Senator and said, "The killing needs to stop. You are betraying your country, and we need to know who the contact is inside the Russian government." The female agent pulled her gun and aimed it at Vicky. Vicky said, "Do you two realize you are protecting one of the biggest traitors in American history? Vicky looked at the male agent and said, "Thomas, you need to pull your gun and aim it at your partner."

The Senator aimed Vicky's pistol and said, "I know nothing about me being a traitor. I am a United States Senator. I bleed red, white and blue."

Vicky could sense the standoff and looked at the young agent, Thomas who looked unsettled. Vicky said, "She has contacts with foreign governments, and I bet she will not arrest the Senator. Thomas, I work for President Grant and the CIA. You and I are on the same team. Senator Fellowship is correct. I have killed people who were trying to harm our country or were actively involved in the human slavery business. Now, I would suggest Thomas, you pull your gun and do not turn your back on your female partner."

Thomas turned and looked at the female agent as he was pulling his pistol. She turned her pistol and shot Thomas in the temple, and he fell dead. Vicky watched as the bullet from Billy Ray's rifle pierced the glass window and hit the lady agent in the forehead. She lunged backward falling on the carpet dead. Vicky did not hesitate and picked up agent Thomas's pistol and aimed it at the Senator. He looked surprised and off balance. Senator Fellowship had lowered the pistol by his side and looked perplexed at the two dead bodies. By the time he realized his protection detail was dead, Vicky had picked up the pistol from the dead agent and was aiming the gun at him. She said, "My sniper has the back of your head in the crosshairs of his scope You need to drop the pistol on the carpet and then we can talk about your reelection campaign. There is not going to be one." She pointed to the chair and demanded, "Sit down. You know who I am. You know I am going to kill you if you do not answer all my questions." He looked bewildered and dropped the gun on the carpet. He just realized his situation with a CIA agent holding a gun on him and his security team dead. He also understood the agent would not be in his office unless they considered killing him.

The Senator walked to the chair and sat down. He looked relieved. Vicky had figured he would have been scared, but he actually looked like a major load had been lifted. Vicky said, "I am here at the request of President Grant. Who in Russia have you been in contact with?"

"You don't understand." He looked like he didn't know how to explain something so complicated.

"It can't be that complicated. Who have you been talking with in Russia?"

He raised both arms with his palms upward in a gesture of compromise. "In Russia, no one. The Vortex all started about fourteen years ago. The Russians were our partners. I was the youngest Senator on the Armed Service Committee. I was one of the rookies. There were nine of us: four from each party and then the Senator from Virginia by the name of Marion Householder. He was chair and a republican. We all had to sign disclosure statements. There were four scientists hired, and they had to sign disclosure statements. Everyone signed the statements. The lead scientist was from Chicago University with a Ph. D in physics. Half the senators were up for re-election and were trying to campaign. Everyone was busy. We were nine months from the election and President Washington was in his second term. There were some very unique arguments within the committee. At first the scientist would report bi-weekly in our closed-door meetings. They were so excited. I remember Burnside attended a couple of the sessions. It was not that unusual to have someone from the military sitting in the audience. I was told President Washington needed our support. Our country needed us." He looked up into Vicky's eyes.

"They came up with this plan. The Russians were in some of the meetings. President Washington wanted the world to be a better world. He strongly felt sharing with the Russians the information, built unity. The then government felt the Russians could be trusted. We were told to talk with them about the Vortex, and what we were facing. They made it sound like a joint venture like the space shuttle and space station. I remembered arguing with Senator Davis and the chair Senator Householder. I know Burnside was in that meeting. He was a captain in the Army at that time, and he was sitting with the Army General. I believe they agreed with me, but they never were called to testify."

Vicky walked over in front of him. She was still aiming the pistol at his face. He looked up at the pistol and said, "The first senator to die was Senator Householder. He died of a heart attack two months prior to the election. He was older, overweight and never exercised. He did not look healthy and rumors were he was a functional alcoholic. No one was surprised. Senator Davis became the chair and the main person. The committee never added another person. Senator Davis ran all the operations, knew all the tests results, was in all the meetings and knew all the players. He somehow was in charge of ground zero for the science into the Vortex. At some point, maybe three months after President Washington's term was up, Senator Davis stopped sharing information with me. The oldest Democratic

Senator on the committee was the next to die before the end of the term. He died of an overdose of his insulin shots. He was my mentor. No one was suspicious of his death. He was found near his bottle which was low on insulin and a second empty shot was found on the shelf inside the refrigerator. The authorities ruled it an accidental death. There were no signs of anyone breaking into his home. He had security cameras and the best security system. Our numbers dropped to seven senators. After the election three senators on the committee were not reelected. I was moved to the Committee on Appropriations and worked on several sub-Appropriation committees, and I have stayed in that committee. We control the spending on the social programs and tell the Treasury Department where to spend all the revenue from taxes. This is the committee everyone wants to be on. The people of New York have benefited from me being on the committee.

I went to see Senator Davis a couple of times to discuss the Vortex after I had transferred to the other committee, and he blew me off. No one else who started out in the committee was on the committee by this time except Senator Davis. He always reminded me it was all top secret, and I better not ever bring it up. I took his comments as a threat.

There were always rumors about him. He knew people that could make someone go away permanently. We were in different parties and had different concerns and beliefs, but we never were on any of the same committees after my term was up on the Armed Service Committee."

He looked at Vicky standing in her underwear and pistol aimed at him. "There were several aides and senators on the original committee that ended up dead over the next few years. At first it did not register with me that someone could be killing them. Two died of an accidental overdose with their prescribed medications. Three died of heart failure.

I could not discuss the Vortex with members of the new committee. I found out years later through an associate, the new committee knew nothing of the Vortex. I knew then Senator Davis had kept the information secret, and I always thought Senator Davis was having not only the senators killed but the others. I figured I would be killed at some point. Why leave any loose ends? I hope you believe me."

"So far I am tracking what you are saying with resources that support your facts." Vicky looked irritated and asked, "Since you knew my identity, why the charade? These two agents would not have been shot, and I would not have removed my dress." Vicky walked over near the table while watching the Senator. She used the toe of her shoe to lift her dress from the floor grabbing it with her left hand. She laid the gun down and then pulled her dress on.

He watched. "I knew the people at Viatect were watching me very closely. I was not certain if one of these agents or both were on Viatect's payroll or even a foreign country's payroll. I also knew the NSA and maybe the CIA was watching me. I have no place to turn."

He held his hands out and palms up and said, "As far as watching you strip, your stomach muscles are very attractive. I believe they are called a six pack by the younger generation. The white mesh gloves add to the matching underwear. What can I say? I am a horny old man. I know I have sinned with my indiscretions."

He looked at Vicky holding the pistol. "Sleeping with my wife was like sleeping with a cold wet rag. We had a daughter and a good life. My wife was an attorney and enjoyed working long hours in her career. When I first became a senator, she loved the thought of being married to a senator. Early in my career, she would travel with me. We were pushing the social programs with after school day care for kids. The Republicans liked the program because more young married people could work and pay taxes. I liked the programs because I could help the people of New York. The government would subsidize the daycares.

My wife and I were meeting with some teachers and the school board in Buffalo. We were explaining the programs for after school and before school for the kids. My wife and a young very pretty teacher and I ended up for drinks at our hotel. The young teacher was frisky, and my wife just stood up and announced she had to fly back to our home in D.C., and I should stay for the follow up meetings with the other school board in the county. She made certain the pretty young teacher should show me to my room. She said it was not safe for me in public.

She left and the pretty teacher and I went upstairs to my room and screwed like racehorses. Afterwards she said my wife must really love me to allow her to service me."

He looked at Vicky. "My wife and I are friends. She likes to shop and travel. She also likes being married to a senator. Me on the other hand, I have fun with pretty young females. I am sorry I have sinned."

She shook her head at the comment as she picked the gun up and said, "Senator Fellowship that is the least of your worries. I will not judge you. I was not certain if your security team would recognize me or not, but when we realized this dead female agent was being paid under the table by a Russian agent, we assumed she would know who I was. We have been watching you since your return from Paris."

"Yet, you came in here anyway, knowing I might know who you were. Who would do something that crazy? Were you not scared?"

"I had backup. Remember the planted pistol was the first option, and the second option is that my sniper never misses. We were hoping your two agents would leave us alone, and they could have been spared. Thomas was innocent and a father of two. We were going to try to spare his life. The other agent knew she would be arrested."

"I heard nothing for over twelve years about the Vortex. I checked around a little with contacts in the Pentagon. I had to be very careful. I assumed it must have been a hoax. Then, Burnside had contacted me after

Senator Davis's death over one year ago. The science behind the Vortex was exciting when it was first mentioned. The scientists hired were all very charged with the possibilities. It actually provided the human race an opportunity to travel through space from one side of the Milky Way to the other. Can you only imagine how excited we all were? We all were so excited. Then, people like Senator Davis took over and then nothing.

I was surprised. According to Burnside, all the original scientists had died over a decade ago. Two were killed in a single car wreck and one burned up in an apartment fire. A fourth one was killed by a mugger with a knife. The police arrested some homeless person, and he is doing life in prison. I know the homeless person did not kill the scientist. I believe Burnside knew Senator Davis arranged for the hit and set up the drunk homeless person. Someone wanted all the people involved killed.

I had written down and hidden my reports. The reports were going to be sent to the Washington Post when I die. I thought someone needed to know.

Burnside remembered I was on the original committee, and he contacted me for the first time over one year ago. I swear I had not heard from anyone on the committee, any of the scientists or any of the aides until

Burnside called me. I remembered asking him, so the Vortex is still being studied? I could not believe my ears."

He looked at Vicky. "He gave me a warning and told me about all the original scientists being killed. He was slurring his words. He had given up, but more than that, he was scared. I tried to talk some sense into him. For God's sake, he had been a general in our Army and at that time the acting NSA director. He had indicated the players had gone rogue, and he was left holding the bag. He felt if we could test the Vortex, the other players would slow down. He felt he could show them he had the power and the research. He said I was the last living senator on the original committee. No one else in Congress has any knowledge of the Vortex. You do realize I was in France at the request of the contact inside Viatect."

Vicky acted neutral at the mention of the name Viatect.

Senator Fellowship paused and looked concerned. "Burnside then called me again two months ago and said there was nothing he could do. He was drunk when I met him at the second time at the Sundown Bar. It was late one afternoon, and we sat outside in the cold wind. He had just given up. He had just kept saying they are crazy, but it is not going to matter anyway because we all are going to be dead. Burnside said it is like being on a small boat looking up at a two-hundred-foot tidal wave."

He looked at Vicky and said, "I swear the use of the Vortex against our government, or any government was never part of the plan. In the beginning, it was the discovery sessions and the possibilities of space travel, which created such a lure. We were blinded by what those others like Senator Davis and his interior group were actually doing. I truly do not know who is behind the Vortex. Burnside would never mention to me the individuals he kept referring to as they. Besides, I took the research to our President. He and I are not in the same party. I tried to do the right thing."

Vicky said, "No one is in his party. He is an independent."

The Senator rubbed his face with his hands. He now looked like a man who was willing to accept his fate.

Vicky asked, "Did you know if the wrong amount of energy is used to open the zipper in the Vortex, it could be devastating? Not enough energy could cause a nuclear explosion with none of the energy being used to open the zipper and none of the power being produced from the blast would be transferred into outer space. There would be no shield. The blast would be like setting the bomb off next to us.

On the other hand, the uranium in the Bata nuclear bomb, my team intercepted in South America, would cause too much energy and the possibility of creating a single entity and turning our planet into a black hole when the zipper does not close. The entire planet would be destroyed."

"You are right. You need to go ahead and shoot me. I know I should have done more. I was too weak. I feared Senator Davis, and I kept my mouth shut. The science behind the Vortex was exciting when it was first mentioned. The scientists hired were all very charged with the possibilities. It actually provided the human race an opportunity to travel through space from one side of the Milky Way to the other. Can you only imagine how excited we all were? We all were so excited.

He looked at Vicky. "Burnside said the Republican candidate was the man they wanted in office. Once they had their man sitting in the White House, they would have total control. I asked him several times who are they. He never answered. He just sat in his chair drinking vodka.

Burnside had said he remembered me in the earlier meetings challenging Senator Davis on issues. Everyone feared Senator Davis. I was young and naïve and full of salt and vinegar. The older three senators in my party would never directly confront Senator Davis while on the committee floor. We four would meet, and they would tell me what to question during the sessions. I did not understand until later, they were scared. Hell, I believe Senator Davis actually respected me for standing up to him. I especially challenged him on the issue of allowing the Russians to be part of our research, and we needed to hire additional scientists. I finally backed down. Everyone backed down dealing with Senator Davis." He looked at Vicky with a sad expression.

"In France, you got the research. Where did you take it?"

"I took it to our president. I hand delivered it to him in the White House."

Vicky looked at him knowing he had somewhat told the truth. He left out the part about taking the research to Viatect first and then the White House. "You know I am going to shoot you in your right kneecap if you lie to me." He looked scared. Where else did you take the research?"

He looked uneasy and glanced at the two dead agents. He rubbed his hair back and thought for a second. "I took it to the Viatect lab in Indianapolis. They also have another office in Annapolis and one in Texas and California. They copied it and then I was told to take it to the White House. I did not know who else to take the research to. After dealing with Senator Davis, I did not know who in our government I could trust. Besides, just because someone is a private citizen does not mean they are not a good American. Viatect has several contracts with the Pentagon. I had to trust someone, and they had indicated I was working for someone in the White House."

"Why Viatect? They are a security company who has a lot of x-military people working on their payroll located all around the world. Who owns Viatect?"

"They have been vetted by other committees in Congress and have several contracts worth billions of dollars with the Pentagon. They are owned by foreign investors from Russia, China, South Korea, and Saudi Arabia. They have soldiers from all over the globe. However, the majority ownership are people like Senator Davis and other rich Americans.

Burnside provided me a name inside Viatect, Bob Scarborough. He named him as a trusted American. In return, Bob asked me to assist with providing intel on the Vortex. Burnside had contacted Bob after Senator Davis died. He said he had just discovered information about the Vortex, and he needed help. Bob provided me with information about your unit, and said they needed me to work with the French Government to obtain the research. He indicated the Russian Government could not be trusted.

Nothing about the Vortex is illegal. No one person or one country owns the Vortex. Bob was trying to beat these other people to the research just like what you were trying to do."

Vicky was stunned to hear that people in Viatect knew the identity of her unit. "How did he know about me and my unit?"

"Someone in the White House must be leaking the information to Viatect. They told me to go to France and intercede for them. I was never told who in the White House is the source. You and your unit have been compromised. I truly do not know who these other people are. Bob Scarborough did not know who they were either. At first when I met Burnside at the bar, he was asking me questions about the people now involved in the Vortex. He thought I knew. When I convinced him, I had not heard any information about the Vortex in over twelve years, he got very upset and kept drinking. He was nervous and gave me the contact inside Viatect. He said if anything happened to him for me to call the contact.

I was happy to hear of Senator Davis's heart attack. I never trusted that man. He had the eyes of a coldblooded killer."

"He was a cruel man and a killer. I watched him die, and he never asked our Lord for forgiveness. He will burn in hell for eternity."

She looked at the Senator. He glanced at the two dead bodies and then back at Vicky with the now understanding that the CIA took out Senator Davis. Vicky could tell he now was concerned that he might be killed.

"Why did Viatect not kill you? What use to them are you? You know too much."

"Viatect needs all the friends they can obtain in the United States Senate. Viatect is trying to sell soldiers for hire around the globe with the blessing of the Pentagon. They want to be a country's first best choice to fight guerilla type battles.

They have access to jets, ships, and other top-rated equipment. Countries will pay millions for their services. There would be no need for the cost of funding an Army. There would be no Prisoners of War. Every country in the Middle East wants to hire Viatect. They can deploy trained soldiers anywhere in the world within hours. They are a force to be dealt with inside our government. The FBI has not investigated Viatect because our government won't allow it. Like I said, they have billions of dollars in contracts with the Pentagon.

At this point, we cannot stop paying them. If we stop paying them, they could easily go to another country to get paid and believe me there are several hundred countries wanting to hire them. They give to my campaign, and in return, I leave them alone. That is why I am not dead. Besides whom would I call? I couldn't call the NSA or the CIA." Vicky looked at him, understanding his dilemma.

He then said, "In the beginning, I tried to fight Viatect years ago. Then I realized it is better to be one of the sheep. You remember the reporter from the Washington Post seven years ago who was writing articles on Viatect. He was exposing the nation to Viatect and the perils of having a private company run the defense of our country and simultaneously other countries. Viatect target markets were the small countries. They would sign multi-million-dollar contracts with the dictators of the small countries and provide them an army to defend the dictatorship.

The reporter was found tortured to death. His toenails had been ripped out and then his toes had been crushed on the end. His feet had been beaten with a hammer. That was my guy. He did not know who I was. I fed him privileged information about the Pentagon spending habits with Viatect and suggested the power was being shifted away from the watchful eyes of Congress. After Watergate every reporter in Washington wants a deep throat. I was his insider, and I am sure he thought he had hit the honey hole right up until Senator Davis's men showed up."

Vicky asked, "Who is the mole inside our government selling our secrets on the Vortex? There have been too many situations where people inside the Syndicate have been killed when my unit was getting too close. There is no way that is by chance."

"I understand Mike Brown with the FBI has complete access to the Vortex information, and he might be your guy with contacts with the Russian Government. I truly do not know how Viatect is obtaining their information about your unit, but it must be someone in the White House. Years ago, we were told to share information with the Russian Government. I believe there is more than one person talking with the Russians, and I have no clue who else. Burnside would have known. He somehow was aware of Mike Brown. I guess Brown was reporting to Burnside also."

Vicky said, "You need to come with me while we still have time."

"You can't protect me. I do not know who is part of the Syndicate. I do not know if Viatect is part of the Syndicate. Viatect's people understood my predicament with the research, and they suggested I deliver the research to the White House. Why would they do that if they were part of the syndicate?"

She shook her head understanding. Vicky was perplexed. "No, I cannot protect you, but what choice do you have? You might be arrested depending on the President, but either way if you tell the truth, I will not kill you."

Chapter 62

Vicky walked in the back entrance to the gay biker night club in the Washington D.C. area. She could hear Little Jimmy breathing hard behind her as she walked up the stairs by the ticket counter. The building was a rundown brick facility built in the 1940's. The night club was on the second floor and the entrance was located in the rear of the building with an iron rail staircase. Billy Ray punched the bouncer in the face as he tried to stop Vicky and question Little Jimmy. At 2 p.m. the place was dead with very few customers. Little Jimmy followed Vicky to the office door. Mia had been able to hack into the City Metropolitan Planning Commission's office and review the architect's plan when the bar was finished out. Vicky knew exactly the layout of the business and stepped to the side. With one big kick by Little Jimmy, the door was knocked off the hinges. The three customers saw the bouncer lying on his back knocked out and the manager's door being kicked down by the large black man, and they ran for the exit. The manager was sitting at his desk trying to view the images on his security cameras to load on his computer.

He thought the internet connection had failed due to the land line becoming ajar. He had not realized Mia had installed the virus and had been watching his usage. The system was running a mirror program, and Mia had complete control of his system. She had spotted the dark web and the child porn site. She had noticed the link with the contact in Russia. Mia went back and reviewed the information from the pedophile killer, Ronald Mongold. He was the maniac killer Senator Davis had turned girls over to be disposed of. Mia had assumed the FBI would have completed a comprehensive inspection of his internet usage. The FBI had not been able to obtain access to the most private section of Ronald's hard drive. On the black web, Mia was able to trace the computer to the one in Washington D.C. owned by Vitoly Cronkite.

The man was bent over his computer trying to reconnect his cable for the internet. Vicky walked over to Vitoly Cronkite, who was in a sleeveless tee shirt and had a piercing in his tongue. He had gauges in both ear lobes, bleached blond hair and a suntan. He was a fit man about five foot-eight. He looked healthy with clear skin and just one tattoo on his arm. He was a pretty man with feminine features. She noticed the dress, heels, and women's underwear hanging on the clothes rack. She placed her barrel with the sound depressor against his temple. "I am going to ask you one time who the person was who brought you this Russian boy two weeks ago."

She showed him the picture of the Russian kid. He shook his head no. She lowered the gun and shot him in the leg between the joint in the middle of the knee cap. He fell to the floor in piercing pain. Billy Ray rushed and tied a gag in his mouth, and Little Jimmy picked the man up and yanked one of the gauges out of his ear. Billy Ray shoved a cloth laundry bag over his head and down to his waist and pulled the string tight. Vitoly was moaning in pain holding his knee. Little Jimmy carried him out to the fire escape located on the side of the building facing the alley and down the stairs to the waiting van.

Mia was sitting at the offsite location in D.C. in a home owned by the CIA and waited an extra minute before she turned the cameras back on. She erased the video of Billy Ray, Little Jimmy, and Vicky entering the nightclub. She leaned back in the chair and waited for a call from Vicky for the next assignment. She looked at the man in the room with her. The CIA man watching her closed his computer.

Wayne pulled the van into the old warehouse in the old district in Washington. Billy Ray yanked the sliding van door open, and Little Jimmy pushed the man out the van door. Wayne reached down and pulled the laundry bag off of his head and removed the gag from his mouth. The man was covered in sweat. He looked to be nauseated. He glanced around his surrounding and noticed the dilapidated building and the four people standing in a circle around him. Vicky said, "I am going to ask you one more time. Who brought this boy for you to rape and then kill? We know you were friends with Ronald Mongold. We know both of you were in the mental hospital in New York together and released by Judge David Larkin. I shot and killed your friend Ronald Mongold. I watched as Judge David Larkin died like a coward. So, if you think for one second, I will not shoot to kill then you are mistaken."

The man shook his head no. He said he wanted an attorney. Vicky said, "That is not going to happen. I just shot you in the kneecap. Do you really think we are going to arrest you? This is going to be very bad for you if you do not talk."

"I have nothing to say. I know some people. You will be sorry." With his wrist tied, he reached for his knee. She shot him in the left hand. Wayne placed the gag back in his mouth.

They stood around and waited for five minutes watching the surroundings in the old factory The pain was unbearable. With each heartbeat, the nerves in the hand and knee would produce piercing pain. She knew he would talk at some point. He was tied up and was continuously moaning. Vicky said, "I have morphine, and I can stop the pain with these shots of Lidocaine. She held up the shots. You are going to have to provide me with some plausible intel. Do you understand?" The man shook his head yes. Vicky thought he must have a high tolerance for pain. He was handling it better than she expected. Wayne reached down and removed the gag and the zip ties around his wrist.

The man was moaning, sweating and looked pale, "Give me the morphine and the shots."

Vicky watched the man lean over and hold his knee and cried pulling his hand into his midsection. His ear had stopped bleeding and that pain had subsided. He kept moaning and crying while holding his knee. She waited for him to look up at her. He glanced up in a hopeful voice and said, "Please."

Vicky knew she needed to provide him hope and a way out, or he might take the information to the grave with him. She was concern he might go into shock from the acute pain. She asked, "Do you want to live? Do you want the morphine? You need to tell me who delivered this boy to you. We know you killed him. We found a piece of your hair on his body. The DNA does not lie. There is not going to be a court or a trial. I am here to provide you both justice and mercy."

"Mischa Fedorov and her people. Now please give me the morphine. I told you."

"Who is Mischa Fedorov?"

He was struggling to be coherent. Vicky could tell the pain was at the point of him passing out. "She is the Ambassador from Russia. She brought me here from Russia fourteen years ago. I was arrested and then Judge Larkin let me out. I am certain Mischa Fedorov was involved in getting me out of that horrible hospital. Ronald was the only friend I had. After I got out, Mischa came to see me and explained what I had to do. She funded my night club. They used me to have affairs with certain men in Washington. You need to believe me. I am not a killer, but I had no choice. I did not kill the kid. One of her guards killed him."

"You raped that boy. Give him a shot and load him back up. We will need to turn him over to the interrogation squad in Asia."

"No! Not Asia. I will tell you anything. Please."

"We do not have time. You are not an American Citizen. You are a sick man, and you deserve nothing better."

Chapter 63

Max said, "The Ambassador to Russia is too well-guarded. She has not been out of the embassy in months. She has diplomatic immunity. We cannot arrest her." Max knew he did not have the authority to kill a foreign diplomat without President Grant's approval. He also knew he needed to plant the seed in Vicky's mind. He knew if Vicky had the proof confirmed that the Ambassador was involved in the abduction of the child, she would want to take lethal action.

Vicky with a stern look on her face, said, "I also have diplomatic immunity." She turned and stared into Max's eyes. "She has crossed the line. She has summoned this child from her country who was brutally raped and killed. She thinks she has gotten away with this sin." She hesitated and looked out the window. "Besides, this is my last mission. We know the mole is the Deputy Director of the FBI, Mike Brown. I had Mia check into him. He is from Maryland. He lives in a $900,000 home in Washington D.C. He was in Washington when the boy was brought into our country. His kids all go to the best private schools and his expenses are a lot more than he makes on his salary. His wife does not work. She was an attorney for a firm that specialized in real estate named Dunn and Fitzgerald. She stopped working two years ago. There are no other sources of income. His mortgage, car payments, and tuition are over $300,000 a year. We know the Syndicate was using the slave network to transport information. Remember that is what we discovered from Travis Borne, the agent for NSA. Max, you will need to take out the Syndicate members. Both the Ambassador and Agent Brown need to be taken out. My unit will do it and then I am done." Max looked at Vicky understanding she had no tolerance for the people killing innocent kids. He was surprised with her intel into the Russian Ambassador. He knew she had already made up her mind. She had done more than he had ever thought possible. He had hired her to develop contacts in certain third world countries. He had known in fighting for human rights and discovering the human slave network, she would have to meet and work with certain unsavory people or people who wanted to be unknown. She had turned out to be the perfect CIA agent. He knew he could not replace her. No one could do what she had done. He shook his head in understanding.

Chapter 64

The jet took off from Dulles International Airport near D.C. The pilot first flew out over the Atlantic and then turned northwest to fly through Canadian airspace on the way to Moscow. Delores and Vicky took turns providing the Ambassador and her three crew members their drinks and snacks. They acted like the perfect stewards. Vicky surprised the passengers when she spoke in Russia to the Ambassador telling her how pretty her first name was, and she understood the name Mischa meant to be Godlike. The Ambassador looked suspiciously at Vicky and demanded to know where she learned the Russian language. The other three passengers looked at Vicky with questionable expressions. Vicky said, "Ambassador Fedorov, I grew up in Germany and studied the Russian language for two years while in school. I love to travel." She smiled and walked to the rear of the jet.

Delores whispered to Vicky, "When the pilot announced we were out of American airspace, the folks seemed to relax."

Vicky said, "Yes I heard them clap and the Ambassador smiled."

Billy Ray unbuckled his seat belt and stood from his seat in the co-pilot's position, He was wearing the pilot's uniform, and walked to the back of the Learjet 75. Delores hesitated and then she walked to the back of the plane. Billy Ray could tell Delores was nervous. Billy Ray said, "Don't worry. Just remember your fifteen-minute training class on how to parachute from a jet at one-hundred-thirty-five miles per hour. I will be right next to you. I love you."

She rolled her eyes and frowned as she thought about the jump. Billy Ray carried the bag to the front of the plane. The passengers were enjoying the Russian Vodka and laughing. Vicky could tell they were happy to be going home and out of America. President Grant had issued a law which was passed by the emergency session of Congress for all non-Americans citizens to be expelled from the United States. He had sent out a warning for all Americans abroad to return home.

Once in the pilot's cabin, Billy Ray opened the large bag and handed the pilot his parachute and helmet. The pilot placed the jet on auto pilot and removed his shirt and pants. He had on a thermal Under Armor-style jumpsuit made for sky diving in cold weather under his uniform. Billy Ray had done the same. Vicky had walked to the back of the jet and Delores handed her the parachute and said, "You need to hurry."

Delores took a deep breath and blew out. Vicky smiled and said, "Delores, take another deep breath and remember the fifteen-minute class."

Delores looked at her while she was double checking her harness. "You are very calm for someone who is about to jump from a jet for the first time, and there is a lot more to skydiving than a fifteen-minute class."

Vicky smiled and said, "When I was in high school, the joke when someone looked surprised was you look like the man who forgot his parachute. Now, I finally got the joke and think that saying is funny. Can you check my harness?"

Delores laughed.

Vicky looked serious, "Are you okay with this mission? There will be four dead bodies after we are done."

"I believe the Russians turned Mike Brown without giving him an option. He used to be a good man. I worked with him years ago when I first started with the FBI. They blackmailed him, and I have seen the evidence on the boy. They are all killers in my book. Yes. I am okay with this mission. She has diplomatic immunity.

This is the only way to provide justice. I will see you on the ground. Good luck."

Billy Ray walked out of the cockpit with his helmet on suited up. He was carrying a dart pistol. Vicky walked out of the rear with her helmet on suited up carrying two dart pistols. The passengers got very quiet as Billy Ray appeared. He shot the passenger next to the ambassador in the middle chest. The man arched his back as he tried to stand. He fell back into his seat. The two passengers on the right started to jump up, and Vicky shot both in the back. The Russian Ambassador looked around and saw her countrymen passing out with the darts sticking in their chest and back and said, "What is the meaning of this? I am the Russian Ambassador and have been granted privileges"

The pilot walked from the cockpit to the exit door and opened the door. The cold air blew through the jet. The pilot did not hesitate. He jumped out. Vicky stepped to the side and allowed Delores to pass and walk to the exit door. She waited. Billy Ray quickly reached and placed a handcuff with a four-foot nylon strap to the Ambassador's wrist and then locked it to the metal leg of the seat across the aisle. He made certain the nylon hand cuff was very snug on her wrist as he latched the small lock. He then retrieved the three darts from the sleeping passengers. He turned and walked behind Delores, and they both jumped simultaneously out the door. Vicky walked by the Ambassador and said, "Ambassador Fedorov, you do have certain privileges, and that privilege is to crash and burn. I will show you the same mercy you showed a child when he was turned over to that monster, Vitoly Cronkite." Vicky paused as she noticed the Ambassador's expression changed at the mention of Vitoly's name. "I am going to jump out the door. The pilot has already jumped. I know you know how to fly a small jet. You grew up as a privileged Russian in a family who never had to ask for anything. Your father was a general in the Russian Army and your mother's family was influential in the finance department in the Russian Government. You could have helped the poor family and instead you took their son. Now, do you want the privilege to fly the jet, be Godlike, and save your three friends? If you do, you will need to ask the one true God to provide you with a miracle and forgive you of your sins."

"You have no right. What child?" Vicky took a step toward the exit door. Vicky could tell the cold air was bothering the Ambassador. The cold wind was blowing her hair out of place. She was not dressed for the sudden cold wind inside the jet. She glanced over at her employees who were passed out.

Vicky said, "Let me tell you what your country has done. They have produced Gamma Nuclear Bombs which are against the standing treaty with my country. The Russian government has tried to steal the information on the Vortex. You used the human trafficking network with an innocent boy being raped and killed. He was tagged with the orders for you to assign the task to your spy network and steal the latest information on the Vortex which we obtained in Sweden. I have no tolerance for that sin of killing an innocent child." The Ambassador shook her head no. Vicky said, "Now we are forced to use our Nuclear War machine to defend ourselves. So, while you and your friends are crashing, I want you to think about what you and your country have started."

"You are wrong. You can't prove any of this."

Vicky pulled out the picture of the boy. "Do you recognize this child?

The ambassador studied the photo and shook her head no.

"He was from Orel, Russia. He was innocent. Your government had to get the secret intel to you about the contact within my country. He was the sacrificial lamb. You allowed your own people to kill an innocent child. The monster you gave the child to, Vitoly Cronkite, has told us everything. We know you set him up and funded his nightclub and arranged for him to meet certain men in Washington and capture the encounters on video. You would then blackmail the men. We already know Deputy Director Mike Brown with the FBI is our last mole. The beginning of the end has started."

The Ambassador looked at Vicky and said, "You need to release me. This is all a mistake. You have no proof. We work with your country through the proper channels." She seemed to understand what was going to happen.

Vicky looked at the Ambassador and said, "Mischa, we have tracked the boy to your country, the city, his address and his parents. We have the proof. We sent an agent to their home with his photo taken in the Washington D.C. crime lab and confirmed his identity. We compared his DNA from the hairbrush from his home. He was from a poor family who was struggling. Instead of your Government helping the family, they took their son. The information on the Vortex that Mike Brown provided you was fake."

Mischa looked like she understood she was out of bargaining chips. "We had never considered using the human trade industry to smuggle secrets until we turned your FBI agent Mike Brown. He explained how safe the network was and in Asia it had worked for decades. As far as setting up Vitoly Cronkite, we used him to meet men in Washington. That is how we met Mike Brown, and there were a lot of others. Your country is morally sick."

"You need to be like God and stop this jet from crashing if you want to live. You should not have killed the innocent kid and for that sin, I am going to condemn you to eternal hell. My God has granted me the privilege and fortitude to act as an avenging angel and strike down those who have committed this sin against this child." Vicky held the key to the lock on the chain and threw the key out the door opening. She pulled her gun and shot the ambassador in the left shin with the bullet entering the front of the leg and exiting the rear. She then turned and walked to the exit door and did not hesitate. She jumped out the door.

The ambassador bent over her knee reaching for her shin. The pain was piercing. She looked up and saw Vicky exit the door. She cringed with pain and knew

433

what she had to do. She pulled at the nylon strap and then hurriedly tried to wake her passengers. She frantically smacked the aide sitting next to her while yelling at him. She tried to stand and limped to the other two passengers and did the same. She pulled as hard as she could against the nylon strap and the chair. Her left leg was bleeding, and the pain was crippling. She looked out the window and could see Mount Logan in north Canada. She could tell the jet was getting lower and lower. She could hear the automated voice box repeating, "Alert. Alert, pull up. Alert. Alert, pull up."

***

Vicky spread her arms and looked down toward the ground. She could see the spotlight. She knew she should have jumped sooner. She tucked her body and tried to drift toward the light. She looked at the moon covered ground and thought how beautiful it was. She checked her watch for the distance and reached over and pulled the chute. She felt the sudden pull on her harness as the chute opened. She knew the GPS on her wrist would send the signal to assist the land crew to locate her. She said, "God is great." She really loved looking out over the beautiful snow-covered land with the moon light providing a view as she watched the ground getting closer. She reached and pulled her flare from her pants side pocket and dropped it toward the ground and looked back over her shoulder as the jet was heading nose first into the large mountain. Vicky pushed the remote button on her wrist and watched the brilliant light in the sky as the Learjet exploded. "I will be your huckleberry. Thank you, Lord. I want to serve only you."

Chapter 65

Mike Brown waited in the elevator until the security guard pushed the button for the garage. He smiled to himself thinking of the last payment he received as he descended watching the buttons light up one floor at a time. He walked out of the elevator before he noticed how quiet the garage was. He had taken six fast steps and paused. This was not normal this time of day. There were always people in the garage. The sound of cars starting up or turning curves with the tires squealing. He looked around, and the elevator door had closed. Vicky stepped out from behind the concrete pillar. Mike jumped backward. Vicky could tell he was embarrassed that he jumped. He looked at Vicky and then he stared at her. He had a nauseating feeling when he recognized her. He started looking around and reaching for his pistol. Wayne opened the passenger door, and Little Jimmy opened the cargo door to the van with both men jumping out. Wayne said while pointing his pistol at Mike Brown, "I would not do that if I were you."

Little Jimmy held a short barrel shotgun, and he motioned for Mike to raise his hands. Mike demanded, "Wait a minute. What is the meaning of this?"

Billy Ray opened the metal door near the elevator and walked from the stairs. He walked up to Mike and pulled his pistol out of the holster. He stepped back. Vicky looked at Mike and asked, "Do you know who we are?"

He turned and looked at Vicky. He was nervous and looked at the cameras mounted on the concrete ceiling near the stairs and elevator, and noticed they were off and flashing red. He glanced around for help or at least a witness. He said, "No. I have never met you. I am very busy, and I do not have time to talk with you."

Little Jimmy chambered a shell while aiming the gun barrel at his chest. He now looked very scared.

Vicky said, "We are the CIA unit called the Good Samaritans. We were sent here by President Grant and FBI Director Bass to meet you, and there will be only one outcome. Notice all the cameras are off, and there is no one else in the garage. This is all by design. Ambassador Fedorov did not deny the use of a kid to transport secrets. Matter of fact she indicated you recommended the use of an innocent child."

He interrupted, "I have no knowledge of who you are talking about. This is all wrong." He turned to walk away, and Billy Ray stepped in front of him blocking his path.

"Did you know an innocent boy was killed, so the Russians could provide you your last payment for our country's insight into the Vortex? And by the way the intel was fake which was given to Viatect." Mike grimaced realizing the CIA knew Viatect had the research, and it was fake. The flash went through his mind about retaliation from the Russians. Failure was not acceptable, and he had guaranteed the research was worth millions. "After the Russians lost the one nuclear bomb and almost lost two others, they turned you, so they could steal our secrets. We have talked with Ambassador Fedorov and her assassin. They did not deny the boy was used as a pack mule and then killed. The Russian Ambassador implicated you before she died. You were her contact."

"You cannot prove any of this. I will have my attorney call you."

"If I must shoot you, the truth will come out that you were the spy, and you sold your country out. You almost had me and my team killed several times with the secrets you sold. We watched as the information you sold to the Russians were used to kill Burnside and Professor Ho from China. It is really hard to hide that much cash. We know about the cost of the private schools and the property you purchased in Boston and New Jersey under your wife's father's name." She paused and looked him directly in the eyes. "This would be very embarrassing even earth shattering to your four kids, wife, other family members and friends. We also know about Vitoly Cronkite and your affair with him." She saw the expression on his face change when his secret lover's name was mentioned. "The second option we are offering you is to take this injection and die like a man. It will be pain-free for everyone." He looked at Vicky with a pleading expression. He had read about the plane exploding in Canada with the four Russian bodies confirmed dead, one being Ambassador Fedorov. The DNA test results had confirmed the identities of the four dead bodies. The report had listed mechanical failure as the cause of the crash. The report had indicated the search for the additional bodies would be re-scheduled for the spring of the year. The winter was no time to be launching a ground rescue in northern Canada. A large snowstorm had blanketed the crash site the next day and any attempt to locate survivors would have been futile.

Vicky pulled the syringe from her jacket pocket and laid it on the hood of the car sitting next to her. He asked, "Why? I never meant to harm anyone. You don't understand. The Russians had photos of me and that man. I was drugged, and it looked like I was enjoying the sex. I swear. I have no knowledge of a boy being killed."

"You are a liar. Your affair lasted for two months with Vitoly. You have the reports where the Syndicate had learned and developed the human traffic industry as a safe method of transporting secrets from one spy to another. We also know you have read the reports outlining what happens to the slaves who are used as pack mules and then sold. You know they are raped and killed. You will sin no more." She looked at him and then looked at the syringe. He paused and looked at Vicky and realized he was not going to receive sympathy. He had remembered the rumors which mentioned the people her unit had been credited with killing over the past few months. He knew she would not hesitate to kill him. He realized the decision had already been made with only one outcome. He hesitated and then walked over and shoved the needle into his forearm and pushed the syringe inward. He looked into the eyes of Vicky and then Billy Ray. He gradually fell to his knees and hands and then laid down on the concrete floor and closed his eyes. Vicky waited thirty seconds and then checked his pulse.

She picked up the syringe, and they all got in the van and drove off.

Chapter 66

Vicky was so happy to be going home. She knew she had type A personality. As long as she worked, she would live and breathe the job twenty-four hours a day, seven days a week. She just could not turn the switch off. Max had told her President Grant would not accept her resignation. Max had also explained if she needed to take off work a month that would be okay. He mentioned the CIA would move forward with taking out the Syndicate, and the entire network. The kill order had been made. Most of Congress had stood together and voted for war against the Syndicate, and the job was to kill the fifty-six people on the list. The list was received by the CIA and FBI from Burnside after his death.

Burnside had written a letter with the names of the Syndicate members and documented proof. He compared himself to George Washington. After President Washington's four-year term was over, he did not try to be a king. He wanted democracy to win. President Washington stepped to the side to allow voters the opportunity to decide the country's future and the next President. Burnside then noted he was sorry.

She walked out the door of the airport in Nashville truly feeling happy and relieved. She had prayed and asked God to forgive her of her sins and assist her with her struggles. She had finally reached a happy place in her life. She felt exonerated for her sins and being able to help the innocent kids in the slave industry. She saw Matt waiting for her standing next to his truck in the traffic line next to the sidewalk in a row of taxis and other vehicles in front of the busy airport. She could hardly wait to hold him and tell him she was finished working. She was ready to hold babies and would love to be a homemaker, a member of the PTA, and drive a minivan. She could not help but smile as she approached. She started to drop her carry-on bag and rushed to reach for her husband's outstretched arms. She saw his expression change from a smile to a frown. He was looking at something or someone behind her. As she turned, Matt reached her and pulled her behind him pushing her down to the asphalt road between the taxi and his truck while standing in front of her. As she was falling to the roadway, she heard someone yell "gun" and heard footsteps.

Vicky fell between the taxi and Matt's truck and heard the unmistakable sound of a gun with a sound depressor firing multiple bullets. She had fired too many guns not to recognize the small puff of the sound.

The entire area sounded like a chaotic scene. She could hear the walkie talkie of a police officer running down the sidewalk as she looked out around the back of the truck on the roadside. She could see a man running in a blue and white jacket, in blue jeans and a green baseball hat into the large parking garage and sprint through to the far side and jump the three-foot high brick knee wall and run into the much larger outdoor parking lot. He disappeared running bent over behind the parked vehicles.

Vicky slowly turned on all fours to check on Matt when she saw his shoes and the bottom of his pant legs as she crawled closer to the curb. She stood and noticed him lying on the sidewalk. She ran from behind the taxi and his truck to the sidewalk and noticed Matt was bleeding from three bullet holes, two from his chest and one from his head. She glanced past Matt's body and saw there were two other people lying on the sidewalk bleeding and one was a police officer who had been stationed at the doorway to the airport. She reached for Matt with his eyes frozen open, kissing him on the head, holding him covered in blood and screamed for help as she cried. She knew there was no heartbeat. The bullets had done the damage. Her husband was dead.

ACKNOWLEDGMENTS

***

To my editor Carolyn Pegram for all the hard work.
To Chesnie Nichols for the book cover and formatting the book.
To big sister, Sherrie Rutherford, for all the loving help in writing book four.